It seemed to be all the invitation he needed. Before she could react, he'd wrapped an arm around her, drawn her up flush against his body, and begun a slow, seductive plundering of her mouth, his tongue enticing her lips to part.

He tasted wicked, of something darker than the wine she'd drunk earlier. Her body hummed, erupting with pleasure, like little bubbles in champagne, cascading through her, popping along her nerve ends.

She clung to Westcliffe, because to do otherwise would see her on the floor in a pool of muslin.

It was the most marvelous thing she'd ever experienced.

"Heath steals your heart, then takes you on a journey that will leave you torn between tears and joy."
Christina Dodd

"Lorraine Heath's deftly skilled storytelling entrances and enthralls from the first page to last."
Karen Hawkins

By Lorraine Heath

PASSIONS OF A WICKED EARL
MIDNIGHT PLEASURES WITH A SCOUNDREL
SURRENDER TO THE DEVIL
BETWEEN THE DEVIL AND DESIRE
IN BED WITH THE DEVIL
JUST WICKED ENOUGH
A DUKE OF HER OWN
PROMISE ME FOREVER
A MATTER OF TEMPTATION
AS AN EARL DESIRES
AN INVITATION TO SEDUCTION
LOVE WITH A SCANDALOUS LORD
TO MARRY AN HEIRESS
THE OUTLAW AND THE LADY
NEVER MARRY A COWBOY
NEVER LOVE A COWBOY
A ROGUE IN TEXAS

Coming Soon

PLEASURES OF A NOTORIOUS GENTLEMAN

LORRAINE HEATH

PASSIONS OF A WICKED EARL

A V O N

An Imprint of HarperCollinsPublishers

This is a work of fiction. Names, characters, places, and incidents are products of the author's imagination or are used fictitiously and are not to be construed as real. Any resemblance to actual events, locales, organizations, or persons, living or dead, is entirely coincidental.

AVON BOOKS
An Imprint of HarperCollinsPublishers
10 East 53rd Street
New York, New York 10022-5299

Copyright © 2010 by Jan Nowasky
Excerpt from *Pleasures of a Notorious Gentleman* copyright © 2010
by Jan Nowasky
ISBN 978-0-06-192296-1
www.avonromance.com

First Avon Books paperback printing: November 2010

Avon Trademark Reg. U.S. Pat. Off. and in Other Countries, Marca Registrada, Hecho en U.S.A.
HarperCollins® is a registered trademark of HarperCollins Publishers.

Printed in the U.S.A.

10 9 8 7 6 5 4 3 2 1

For the amazing May Chen,
who understood my vision for this story
better than I did.
Thanks, May—*for everything*.

PASSIONS
OF A
WICKED EARL

Chapter 1

London
1853

Morgan Lyons, the eighth Earl of Westcliffe, unhurriedly trailed his fingers over the slender bare back—the appearance of which always delighted him. A light touch, barely there, as soft as a cloud drifting across the late-afternoon sky. He'd discovered that Anne responded best to only the hint of sensation, as though the torment of being denied more pressure heightened her pleasure.

She was such a wonderfully carnal creature, willing to explore passion and pleasure in all its forms. It was the very reason he sought her company.

She was soundly asleep, not reacting to his subtle gestures, but she would be miffed if he took his leave without giving her a proper farewell. Gathering up her hair, with its hints of red that often made it seem as though it might ignite at any moment, he draped it over one shoulder, exposing the nape of her slender neck. Shifting his body so she was cradled beneath him, he pressed his hot, moist mouth to the ridge of her spine and began to leisurely travel downward.

Moaning low, she stretched languorously, like a feline lazing in the sun. "Mmm, I do so enjoy the way you awaken me."

Her voice, lazy, raspy, sultry, caused him to harden swiftly and painfully. With his knees, he spread her thighs, opening her to him, and slid into her velvety haven. It was only here, when he could become lost in wicked sensations, that he was master, that the world and all its disappointments receded.

Welcoming him with a groan of satisfaction, she lifted her hips slightly, and he delved deeper. Now he was the one to groan, a growl really, low and throaty. This was what he needed, what he always needed. Hands gliding, fingers teasing, mouths devouring.

Theirs was an ancient ritual of writhing bodies, escalating sighs, and intense sensations. With a triumphant laugh, she bucked him off, straddled him, claimed him. Even as he took her again, even as he caused her to cry out his name, he felt nothing beyond the searing press of flesh. Why the bloody hell couldn't he feel more—true enjoyment, immense satisfaction, contentment—instead of this bloody wasteland of lackluster emotion?

The room echoed with their grunts, their shouts,

their cries. He knew how to touch, how to stroke, how to please, how to bring her the ultimate in pleasure.

Even when she collapsed over him, he fought his own cataclysm, staved it off as long as possible, until it consumed him, came crashing around him.

Replete, exhausted, breathing heavily, he lay beneath her. As always it was never enough. His legendary prowess mocked him, leaving him dissatisfied. Ah, the physical release was grand, but afterward, he always experienced a keen sense of bereavement, of something amiss, something that he could wrap neither his head nor his heart around.

He was always left wanting more, but for the life of him, he couldn't define exactly what the more should be.

He knew only that for all her exquisite beauty, she didn't provide it. But he also knew the fault resided with him, not her. He lacked something essential. It was the reason no woman had ever loved him.

As gently as possible, he eased her off him. Her green eyes lethargic, she gifted him with a contented curl of her lips, a cat that had lapped up the last of the cream. He pressed a kiss to her forehead before rolling out of bed.

He gathered up his clothes from where they'd landed on the floor when she'd first divested him of them hours earlier. It wasn't until he'd sat in the purple velveteen chair to pull on his boots that she scooted to the foot of the bed and said, "Tell me what's troubling you."

He peered over at her, now wrapped modestly in the red satin sheet. She swung her legs off the end of the bed and grabbed one post. She gave the appearance of someone sitting on a swing, and he was reminded of a golden-haired girl he'd long ago seen in that exact pose. If he were capable of flowery emotions, he might have thought he'd begun to fall in love with Claire that day. *Silly thought.*

"You've grown bored with me," Anne said succinctly, before he could answer. Not that he would have. He was not in the habit of sharing anything that resided within him. He allowed only the outer shell to be available for her amusement.

Haughtily, making a great show of securing the sheet more tightly around herself, she walked to the window. "They say no woman can hold on to you. I thought to prove them all wrong."

After tugging on his boots, he crossed the room and wound his arms around her waist, inhaling her fading scent mixed with the musky fragrance of passion he'd unleashed earlier. "I've not grown bored with you."

"Then stay the night. For once, stay the night."

He tucked his finger beneath her chin, tilted her head around, and took her mouth as though he owned it. Only when she turned and sagged against him, did he lift her into his arms and carry her to the bed. Setting her down gently, he drew the covers over her. "Not tonight."

As he was striding toward the door, she called out, "I hate you!"

Her words gave him no pause. He'd heard them before, from others. The first time he was five-and-twenty. The words had pained him then, but never since. Why did women not understand that hate could not hurt if there was no semblance of love? She didn't love him. He knew that, accepted it.

She was as frosty as he. It was the reason they were well suited, the reason he'd not yet grown bored with her.

"Westcliffe?"

Striving to come up with a way to communicate that he wasn't upset with her, he glanced back and merely said, "Tomorrow."

"I expect to receive a very nice bauble."

He gave her a grin and a wink. "Something to match the green of your eyes, I should think."

She blew him a kiss. She was so easily mollified. He was weary of growing bored, but ennui hovered nearby, waiting impatiently—

He would not succumb. Not this time. She deserved better.

He hurried down the stairs and out the front door into the lightly falling rain, where his carriage waited, illuminated by the distant gas streetlamps. The footman leaped forward and opened the door.

"St. James," Westcliffe ordered as he climbed inside and settled back against the plush bench for the journey to his residence. Not a home. Simply a place where he resided, where he would wallow in his whiskey and contemplate why he refused to stay the night with Anne. Such a small request, but conceding to it would give her too much control over him. And he was a man who relished his freedom. He'd gone too much of his life without possessing either control or independence.

His father, damn him, had left behind little except debt, two sons, and a widow who understood the ramifications of her dire circumstances well enough that, without delay, she'd chosen as her second husband a man with a more powerful title and a good deal more wealth—the Duke of Ainsley. She'd blessed him with an heir, and five years later, he'd left her a widow—one who no longer relied on anyone for anything.

It was years before the same could be said of Westcliffe.

He'd been dependent on the kindness and generosity of his youngest brother, Ransom Seymour, the present Duke of Ainsley. He may have been the last born, but he acted as though he were the first—irritatingly responsible, obsessed with duty. He comported himself with the mien of someone three times his age. Their mother had often remarked that even from the cradle, he'd given the impression that he could handle the greatest of matters. Westcliffe had found it exceedingly difficult to usurp his brother's rightful place in the sibling hierarchy when the next moment could very well involve holding out a hand, asking for favors. It was one of the reasons that Westcliffe had spent as little time as possible with his family—to avoid the reminders of the failures he'd inherited from his father, which had weighed heavily on his shoulders as he'd grown into manhood. He'd been more than willing to take whatever actions necessary to shed them.

It had been damned mortifying to go to the whelp whenever he needed anything: assistance in managing his estate, clothes, food, coins to purchase a trinket for his occasional lovers. So he'd welcomed the opportunity to be rid of his pauper's realm—only to discover that the ultimate price was a battering of his pride far worse than anything he'd previously suffered.

The wheels whirred, splashing the rainwater against the sides of the carriage. He sought comfort from the calm, constant swishing, allowing it to seep into his soul. Perhaps tonight, he would fall into a deep, untroubled sleep. Perhaps tonight, for a brief time, he could escape the blight of Claire's betrayal.

Yet the memory of it rose as bitter as bile in his throat while his carriage drew to a stop in front of his residence. He'd not set eyes on Claire since that fateful night when she'd taken his younger brother Stephen to her bed. During the intervening years, he'd received but one missive from her.

Forgive me.

To which his drunken youthful self had cleverly responded, *When you're rotting in hell.*

The man he was now would not have responded

at all. He'd have forced her to wallow in guilt and self-recriminations without a hint as to his true sentiments. The absence of knowledge was its own punishment, and she deserved to suffer.

He leaped from the carriage, only to discover that another waited in the drive, one he recognized as belonging to him. If he hadn't known, the liveried men standing about would have served as a clue. *What the devil?*

Taking the wide steps two at a time, he rushed up the stairs. The door opened just as he arrived. His butler's pale face told him all he needed to know.

"Where the hell is she?" he demanded.

"The library, my lord."

His gut tightened. His sanctuary. He allowed no one in there. Least of all her.

Tossing back his hat, cloak, and gloves, not caring if they landed in Willoughby's arms or on the floor, he strode down the hallway. He became abruptly aware that he smelled of another woman. Lilac. He considered, for a heartbeat, racing up the stairs to take a quick wash, then decided against it. He still remembered the sandalwood stench of his brother emanating from her when he'd discovered them—

The footman opened the door to the library as he approached, and he wished she'd had no warning that he was about to barge in on her. Three long years, and the silly chit dared to intrude on the life he'd created in her absence.

With fury emanating from him, he stormed into the room. He was halfway across it, having passed two seating areas, when she turned from her perusal of the books aligned neatly on his shelves.

He came to a staggering halt as though he'd taken a powerful blow to the chest. He'd fought so damned hard to forget her, to forget everything about her.

And here she was in the flesh. Slightly older yet undeniably more lovely.

Claire.

His traitorous wife.

Chapter 2

She'd not known what to expect—of him or herself—when the moment was finally upon her. A slight shiver of dread, certainly. A tightening of her stomach. But this wild pounding of her heart, this *gladness* at seeing him. It took her off guard.

If only she'd felt it three years ago, on the day they'd married. If only he hadn't terrified her then. He still did. Not only his size—so tall and broad—but the authority and determination that emanated from him. He'd always given the impression that once power was in his hands, he could wield it with uncompromising ability. She'd never known quite what to make of him. Still, she was older now. Not only in years, but in maturity.

But even so, she was unprepared for the sight of him.

His arresting face carved in disgust, framed by thick, black hair that was noticeably unstyled as though he'd only just awoken when surely he'd been up and about for most of the day and evening.

She'd heard that he'd turned to cold marble, had heard a great deal about him during the intervening years. But it hurt now to know his implacable façade might be her doing.

He changed his direction, turning away from her, striding toward a corner table where various decanters were artfully arranged. She wondered what he'd intended with his original path. It would have brought him directly to her. Surely not an embrace or a kiss.

A fist more likely. At his side, as it was now. Not that he would ever raise it to her. He'd beaten his brother nearly senseless, but he'd never touched her with anything except gentleness—even when his hold on her was firm as he'd guided her to the carriage, she'd felt no pain. And somehow that had made everything all the worse.

With his wide shoulders and back to her, she couldn't see his actions, but she heard the tinkling of glass, loud and soft, erratic, and she wondered if his unfisted hands were shaking as they poured him something to drink. Then silence. While she watched, he tossed back his head. Then the tinkling began again. When next it stopped, he faced her, one large hand wrapped around a tumbler filled nearly to the brim when she had no doubt he'd have preferred to wrap those long slender fingers around her slender neck.

"You're not welcome here," he said, his voice low, controlled, yet seething beneath the surface. "We had an understanding, an arrangement, you and I. Go back to the country estate, Claire."

"Would that I could, but I have made a promise that requires I stay in London."

"You broke the promise you made to me within hours of making it. Break this other one as well. Should be easy enough for you."

She flinched at his harsh tone. Silly of her to think that hours, days, months, years would lessen his anger with her. Tentatively, she stepped toward him, stopping when his dark eyes narrowed.

"Westcliffe, I need you to forgive me."

"I've told you the condition under which that will happen."

"When I'm rotting in hell?" She released a bitter laugh. "Do you not think I'm already there? Do you have any idea how many ladies have come to visit me, to inform me of your lovers? You are hardly the soul of discretion. If you thought to shame and humiliate me, you've accomplished your goal remarkably well."

"I take pleasure where I find it because it pleases me to do so. You are never a consideration. Quite honestly, Claire, from the moment I delivered you to Lyons Place, I've not given a single thought to you."

"That's always been quite obvious."

He walked over to a chair before the fireplace and dropped down into it, stretching his long legs out before him. Suddenly, from beneath his desk crept a dog, a collie. It slowly limped to the chair, then curled beside it. Westcliffe reached down and began rubbing the dog's head. It appeared he'd done it without even thinking, a habit, a ritual, and she wondered how many nights he'd sat there in that position with only a glass of spirits and an aging dog for company.

Not many if the rumors that continually landed on her doorstep were to be believed.

She took several steps nearer, until she could see his eyes more clearly. They were dark, almost as black as his hair, not blue or as kind as Stephen's. How could two brothers be so vastly different?

Westcliffe's features were carved by an unartistic hand: his nose a little too large, his chin a little too square, his brows a little too heavy. The wickedness he'd embraced had etched his face into a rugged handsomeness that she couldn't deny. The years had been kind, his features even more darkly appealing.

Whereas Stephen was much fairer, his hair a golden brown with streaks of blond woven through it, almost as though they played hide-and-seek, as though his hair couldn't quite determine what shade it should be. Nothing about him had ever been frightening. He'd been Claire's friend for as long as she could remember, while she'd barely known Westcliffe. She had no knowledge of his smile, no memory of his laughter. Few memories of him at all really. But then he was eight years older, and it seemed when they were younger that his attentions had always been elsewhere. He'd been off at school or spending time with his friends or chasing skirts. Or seeing to the details of his estate.

His father had perished when Westcliffe was five, and Stephen had only just turned one. West-cliffe's inheritance had been a crumbling estate and a marriage contract with Claire's father binding him to the Earl of Crestmont's firstborn daughter. She had never questioned it, but on her wedding day it had suddenly struck her as rather archaic, absolutely medieval, especially as the firstborn daughter had yet to make her appearance in the world when the papers were signed. What if she'd had the appearance of a toad?

She suspected nothing would have changed because absolutely nothing about her mattered except that she drew her first breath ahead of her sister. She'd not objected because marriage provided her with the means to move out of her father's oppressive household, where his harsh hand had taught her that a lady did not question her place or her duties. But as her wedding day had progressed, fears had bubbled up to the surface. And when she'd shared them with Stephen . . .

"Nothing happened between Stephen and me," she admitted now.

Westcliffe's harsh laughter echoed around them. "How stupid do you think I am, Claire? I found him in your bed."

"Still in his trousers when you dragged him out."

"So I arrived before he could have his way with you. Or not. I can button and unbutton with surprising haste when the situation warrants. Even if he did not take you, it does not change the fact that you were in his arms!" He came up out of the chair with a brutal force that caused the air around him to shimmer and her to step back, unexpectedly gripped by terror. He hurled his tumbler into the empty hearth. It shattered, the amber liquid splattering. Breathing heavily, he gripped the mantel. "It does not change the fact that he was in my place, and you wanted him there."

At the sight of his anguish, she couldn't prevent the tears scalding her eyes. "I don't know what I wanted. I was a child. A silly girl. He was always my friend. You I barely knew. If given a choice regarding my husband, yes, I probably would have chosen him. I don't know. I only know that I was terrified of my wedding night, and he told me he had a plan that would allow it to be postponed."

"I'll come to your bed before him. I'll hold you. Nothing more. He'll be furious at me, no doubt, but it'll gain you a reprieve. When you're ready, you have but to tell him the truth. Then all will be well."

They'd both had enough champagne and spirits to think it a brilliant plan. In the end, it had cost her a friendship and a husband. It had torn a family apart. It had destroyed all hope of happiness.

Turning his head slightly, Westcliffe slid his unforgiving gaze toward her. "You cannot have been that naïve."

"I was five days past the celebration of my seventeenth birthday with no mother to guide me. The spinster aunt who saw to my upbringing knew little more than I did. Yes, I think I could have been that gullible. And Stephen, he has always been so charming. They say he can persuade an angel to sin. I am far removed from being an angel."

With a heavy sigh, he shook his head. "What the devil do you want of me, Claire?"

"I want you to give me a chance to truly be your wife, not the caretaker of your estate."

He turned to fully face her, his features hard and callous. A shiver skittered along her spine as his gaze slowly, leisurely roamed over her. She quite imagined he was envisioning her without her clothing. Perhaps she deserved his unkind regard, but she wouldn't back down. For her sister's sake, she would suffer whatever punishment he deemed necessary in order to get beyond this insufferable state of their marriage. To a point. She'd not let him force himself on—

"So you're now willing to welcome *me* into your bed?" he asked, mockingly.

She should have come during the day, when such a possibility wouldn't be an option because she knew bedding took place only at night, but she'd thought it would be easier to face him within the shadows. Her mouth was suddenly dry, and she could find no way to dampen it, so her voice was scratchy when she said, "I'm willing to be your wife in more than name."

He studied her a moment longer before demanding silkily, "Unbutton your bodice."

Her hand flew to her throat, her fingers skimming over the buttoned collar of her serge traveling dress. She glanced hastily around. "Here?"

"We're alone. Well, except for the dog, but Cooper is not one to interfere or gossip. If you truly know of my reputation as you claim, then you know I don't limit my bedding to bedchambers." He jerked his chin toward her. "The buttons, Claire."

At that moment, she despised him almost as much as she had when he'd exiled her to his ancestral estate. "I hate you!" she'd yelled, as he'd departed the manor after informing her that she would stay in residence there while he returned to London. His dark laughter had echoed along the hallways and followed him into the stormy night.

Now, she wanted to turn on her heel and march from the room. She wanted to tell him to rot in hell. Instead, she tilted her head defiantly, met his cold stare with one of her own, commanded her fingers not to tremble, and forced them to loosen one blasted pearl button after another. Strange how she'd not noticed the chill in the air until the material parted. It seemed to take hours before her fingers finally reached the last button at her waist.

She thought so much distance separated them, but he reached her in five long strides, bringing with him the scent of lilac. He'd come here not from his club but from another woman's bed. Tears once again burned the back of her eyes, but she blinked them away. She'd not let him see how much he could devastate her without even trying. For the first time, she thought she might finally know what he'd experienced on that long-ago night. It shamed her that she'd been so young and self-centered not to have realized it immediately.

He did deserve his revenge, however he meant to exact it. She would do anything to put the past behind them.

His gaze still on hers, he placed one finger on the hollow at her throat. A challenge. A dare. So be it. She'd not retreat. He would see she was not the ninny she'd once been. She'd had three years of managing his household at the estate. It thrived beneath her watchful eye, and he'd never even had the decency to thank her—the ingrate.

He dipped his gaze and trailed his finger down, his hand slipping beneath the cloth, further parting it to expose the swell of one breast above her chemise. She barely breathed as his other fingers joined the first to skim over the exposed flesh. She was only grateful that he'd lowered his gaze, so he couldn't see the anticipation mixed with fear that was no doubt clouding hers. How could he stir these unwanted sensations with something as simple as a touch?

His fingers moved slowly up, then back down, across one way, then the other.

"Tell me, Claire, is all of you as enticing?"

Her gaze clashed with his, and to her mortification, the heat of passion consumed her. Had she ever seen so much fire in eyes so dark? Yet, beneath it all, she could see the mockery. He wanted her to desire him, so he could punish her all the more. She was certain of it. She'd created this villain—with a moment's weakness, with a gossamer dream of a life far different from what had been unfolding before her. She'd wanted to change her path and had been stumbling along it ever since.

She deigned to ignore his smoothly delivered taunt, certain he would have his answer in short order. Her heart beat erratically, her breathing refused to settle into anything resembling normalcy. She'd heard he was skilled at seduction, a master at eliciting pleasure. Strange how her knees suddenly wobbled. It was the lack of air. She thought she might swoon.

"You said you were in London because of a promise. What promise?" He sounded as though he were on the verge of strangling.

What promise indeed? Why am I here? She shook her head slightly to clear it, to focus on his question. "My . . . my sister. Beth. Father has arranged for her to marry Lord Hester, despicable man, so much older than she. With Father's blessing, she has one Season to find another prospect. I know what it is to marry a man you barely—"

"Are you saying he forced you to marry me?"

"I'm saying I had no choice. How could you think otherwise when you were fully aware of the contract, when you never courted me or asked for my hand?"

His fingers jerked over her skin, his eyes probing hers as though he sought evidence of deception.

"So you will be a wife to me in order to save her? You could accomplish your goal by staying elsewhere in London."

She considered telling him everything, but she didn't think it would sit well. The ladies were not happy that her husband ran wild through the boudoirs, that he gave their own husbands the notion that a man owed no fidelity to his wife. In order to receive invitations to the balls, in order to help her sister be accepted into Society, she had to bring her own husband to heel. But instead, she said, "You have influence. I must take my place beside you in order to properly introduce her into Society."

"Which you no doubt see as a noble sacrifice."

Her patience snapped. "For God's sake, Westcliffe, I've asked for forgiveness, which you withhold, and I've told you that I wish to be your wife in all matters. Why must you make this so blasted difficult?"

"Because I no longer want you for my wife."

Her heart slammed against her ribs, her stomach dropped to the floor as he stepped away. She'd never even considered that he'd refuse her. That he'd make it difficult, that he'd make her pay for her youthful indiscretion—yes. But to not want her at all? He needed an heir. He needed a wife. He had a wife.

"It's late. I'll have Willoughby prepare a guest room for you," he said, his voice flat, back in control. "We'll discuss this situation in the morning."

He began striding across the room.

"Where the devil are you going?" she called out after him.

But he didn't answer, didn't even glance back as he made his exit from the room. Sinking to the floor, she allowed the tears of humiliation to flow at last. How was it that her life had become such a frightful mess?

Chapter 3

Damnation! As his carriage clattered through the streets, Westcliffe could still feel the heat of her alabaster flesh against the tip of his finger. What had he been thinking to dare her so? She was still remarkably naïve not to realize the full extent of her betrayal and the lengths he'd go to in order to make her suffer.

He'd anticipated marriage to her as he'd anticipated nothing else in his life before or after. He'd known that at long last he'd acquire the funds that would set him free of Ainsley. But it had been more than that. In spite of how it might have all appeared, her damnable dowry was only a small part of the reason he'd honored a preposterous contract, the terms of which his solicitor could have no doubt relieved him with very little effort.

From the moment his mother had married the Duke of Ainsley, Lyons Place—Westcliffe's ancestral home—had been relegated to a lost manor, of no consequence. Its upkeep cost more than the income it provided, so it was left to languish, while the family took up residence at the magnificent Grantwood Manor. It was there that he'd first caught sight of the girl who would one day become his wife.

He couldn't deny the pleasure he'd felt when he'd initially glimpsed her smile. His own mouth had twitched when he'd first heard her laugh. While she'd played with the others, he'd watched from afar, and he'd known, *known*, in his heart and soul that she could help him bring Lyons Place back to what it was meant to be. It could become again a place where a family would gather. It would no longer be shunned and forgotten.

He would no longer be shunned or forgotten. There were times when he felt like an outsider in his own family. Perhaps because he'd always fought to keep his distance, not to readily accept another man as his father, regardless of the other man's goodness. The eighth Duke of Ainsley could not replace what Westcliffe had lost.

He'd been convinced Claire could somehow fill the void. He'd taken such damned care in preparing himself for his wedding night, bathing again, shaving again, donning fresh trousers and a silk dressing gown. He'd planned to be gentle with her, to take such care. He'd had no intentions of rushing her.

Then he'd walked into the bedchamber and seen his brother in his place, and once again he'd been struck with the realization of being worthy of nothing—not even his own wife would remain loyal to him.

He became acutely aware of his hands aching. They were fisted so tightly—as to almost push bone through skin. He unfolded them as his carriage came to a halt. He belonged to several clubs, but Dodger's Drawing Room was his favorite haunt. Its owner, Jack Dodger, had risen from the streets to become a powerful man. He understood a gentleman's needs—although he had recently dispensed with his girls. Marriage no doubt was taming him.

But no matter. There were brothels aplenty if a man was in need of a warm body. At the moment, Westcliffe simply needed to be away from his residence. He strode through the gambling room and went into the recently renovated tobacco room, where men enjoyed a cigar or pipe along with their liquor. He took a chair in a corner sitting area.

At Dodger's, customer preferences were memorized by liveried youths whom the owner had pulled from the streets and given employment. No one was left to wait for more than three minutes. Westcliffe didn't even look up when his favorite brand of whiskey and a cigar were quietly set on the table beside him.

He did look up when a gentleman sat in the chair next to his. He glared, but his brother paid him no heed.

"Thought I'd see you here tonight," Ainsley said. "So how did you find Claire?"

Westcliffe arched a brow at him, and his brother merely shrugged. "She came to my residence earlier, thinking that you still lived there. She was quite surprised to discover that you had purchased a residence of your own. Do you not communicate with your wife?"

"No." Westcliffe reached for his glass, relished the slow burn as he swallowed the caramel-shaded smoky-flavored brew. He set the glass down, right side up, a signal that it was to be refilled. Promptly, it was.

Ainsley grabbed his own drink and leaned forward. "Why is she here?"

He'd always wanted to dislike Ainsley—simply on principle. He'd been born with everything: wealth, a powerful title, his mother's love, and his father's adoration. But he couldn't help but admire him because he'd always been such an affable fellow, willing to help when needed, never keeping accounts on what was owed. Sometimes it irked knowing that his youngest brother was the best of them. "Apparently her sister has one Season in which to find a suitor, or their father will force her to marry Hester."

"What has the man got against his own daughter?"

Westcliffe gave his brother a wry grin. "If you're so appalled by the notion, why don't you offer for her?"

"Good God, no! I've only just reached my majority, taken my seat in the House of Lords. That's ample accomplishment for one year. I do not need to add taking a wife to my list of achievements."

Westcliffe hardly blamed him. He'd have not married so young if he'd not been desperate for funds. But no matter when he'd married, he'd have honored the right to marry Claire that his father had reserved for him.

Ainsley sipped his brandy, tapped his snifter. "I thought Claire looked well. Hale and hearty actually. I'd say she spent a good deal of time roaming over your estate."

"I didn't notice." The lie rolled easily off his tongue. He'd noticed every detail about her. Her upswept blond hair. The gentle slope of her throat. The fire in her sunset blue eyes when he'd ordered her to unbutton her bodice. She'd wanted to tell him to go to the devil. Three years ago, she'd run from him. Tonight, she'd stood up to him. What had happened to strengthen that backbone?

But he'd noticed more. So much more. The heat of her skin against his finger. The quiver of her muscles as his touch lingered. Her rose scent wafting enticingly around her.

He'd spoken true. He no longer wanted her as his wife, but that didn't mean he didn't want her beneath him. Traitorous wench. How could he desire her? Because she was a woman, and he was a man. It was as simple as that. It had nothing to do with the blue of her eyes or the fine figure she presented. Or the defiance. Women desired him, granted his every wish in an effort to please and tame him. But in the end, they bored him with solicitousness. Claire infuriated him.

He reached for his glass, having lost track of how many he'd emptied while he and Ainsley sat there. The liquor swirled through him, as did the memories, the past and the present nudging up against each other. Only now, having seen her tonight, looking back did he realize how very young she had been on the day they'd married.

More sixteen than seventeen. Why had he and her father thought that a single day, the celebration of her birth, would change her from a girl into a woman? She'd been thinner then, but now she possessed more womanly curves. Then she'd not been so far removed from the swing.

"I know the situation with your wife is none of my business—" Ainsley began.

"No, it's not."

Ainsley sighed. "Is that why you avoid me? Because you don't want to know my opinion on the matter?"

"Our paths seldom cross because I have matters that require my attention."

"Based upon the rumors, most of those *matters* involve women."

Westcliffe clenched his jaw. "Are you judging me?"

Ainsley shook his head. "No. Can't say I wouldn't do the same under similar circumstances. Only I'd be more discreet."

"Not if you care nothing for the woman."

"She's still your wife. That should garner her at least some consideration."

He had no plans to get into a debate regarding his indiscretions. Claire was the one who'd initially set the terms of their marriage. He'd accepted that it was unlikely he'd ever hold her love, but he'd been convinced he'd have her loyalty. And then he'd walked into her bedchamber and realized even *that* would be denied him.

He remembered so clearly the words he'd spoken when he'd delivered her to Lyons Place. "You've made it abundantly clear that you hold no affection for me. So be it. Ours shall be a marriage in name only until I decide otherwise. You shall reside here and I in Town. Until you give me an heir, I expect you to keep your knees tightly clamped together. Find yourself with a child that is not of my loins, and I shall destroy your reputation, and while the law may force me to accept it as mine, rest assured that society will not."

He'd been walking toward the door when she'd yelled, "I hate you!"

And he'd forced himself to laugh so she wouldn't know that at that moment he'd hated himself as well. He'd never wanted to be cruel, but she'd forced him to turn his back on her. His fury had known no bounds, and his pride had demanded that on this matter he would take no crumbs.

Over the years, he'd had his servants send reports. He knew about her infrequent visitors—an occasional lady, her cousin, her sister. No gentlemen. She spent a considerable amount of time alone, except for servants. Little wonder she was so devoted to the estate. What else did she have to do with her time?

"Do you remember when her family would come to the estate?" Ainsley asked, falling into his habit of arbitrarily shifting conversations around. Westcliffe, however, knew there was usually a method to his brother's methods. "She was always such fun."

"And yet you always hid from her."

"It was part of the game."

Westcliffe remembered once—she couldn't have been more than seven, while he was fifteen. He'd been sitting in a chair in the library reading when she'd barged into it, searching for his brothers. He'd given her a harsh glare, and she'd promptly retreated.

"I knew you could make her leave!" Ainsley—all of eight—had gloated as he scampered out from beneath the desk where he'd been hiding.

Westcliffe hadn't been quite as happy with the results as Ainsley. He was afraid he'd frightened her. He'd been torn. He knew someday he was to marry her, but he also knew he had to look out for his brother.

"What are you reading?" Ainsley had asked.

"*The Last of the Mohicans.* It's about life in America."

"Isn't it the same there?"

"No."

"Are you going to travel there?"

"I can't. I have responsibilities here."

Responsibilities that had always weighed on him, duties that would be easier to bear with the dowry that came with marriage to Claire. He'd never questioned it, never doubted it, never wondered if she did.

"I always liked her," Ainsley said now. When Westcliffe glared at him, he shrugged. "Not as much as Stephen did, of course. They were inseparable until he discovered what was hidden beneath skirts and found interests elsewhere."

He didn't need the reminders.

"So what are you going to do about this situation with Claire?" Ainsley asked.

Westcliffe answered with brutal honesty. "Haven't a bloody clue."

Claire wandered through the residence. She'd not taken the time before Westcliffe's arrival, because she hadn't wanted to be caught snooping, so she'd waited for him in the library. But now, alone again, she wanted to get some sense of her husband. He had an eye for finely crafted furniture, but everything appeared haphazardly arranged. In the parlor, she moved a large lamp from a small table to a sturdier one. Then placed a miniature statuette on the first table. Such a small adjustment, but it balanced the room a bit. Why did she care anyway? She wasn't going to be staying. He'd made that perfectly clear. She should leave tonight, but where the deuce would she go? Her father didn't have a residence in London. He abhorred the city. Claire would have to give serious thought to her next plan. But not tonight. She was so weary, yet she was fairly certain she'd not be able to sleep.

Hence the aimless wandering. What struck her the most about the residence was that there were no family portraits. She supposed they were all at the estate. The occasional painting here depicted a dog. The most poignant one showed a dog curled up beside a casket. She didn't know why she was so troubled by it, why her husband enjoyed such gloomy images. This residence possessed a loneliness that seemed to settle over everything. She pushed a small sofa nearer the fireplace, to create a sitting area that was a little cozier, then wondered why she bothered. It was her nature she supposed. She'd done the same with the manor. She wanted each room to welcome and embrace its occupants.

She went to move a chair and stopped herself. "Leave it," she muttered. "Once you truly begin, you'll be here all night, and you have no idea when Westcliffe will return."

Or if he even would. She'd handled everything so poorly. It was time to consider another plan. But there were so few options. She'd considered them all when Beth had first approached her about providing her with a Season. Their mother had died, no other woman would tolerate their father's ill temper.

Claire had suggested their cousin Chastity, who had married in December.

"She's with child and won't be in London," Beth had informed her.

"You might ask Westcliffe's mother, the Duchess of Ainsley."

"She's scandalous. Word is that she's taken up with an artist. She won't have time for me."

Who remained? Certainly not the aunt who had raised them. Seeing no other choice, Claire had consented to giving her sister a Season.

Beth had hugged her tightly. "Oh, thank you, thank you. You have saved me from a fate worse than death."

But now Claire couldn't help but wonder at what cost to herself.

She was embarking on this endeavor with as much trepidation as she had her marriage.

The ceremony had taken place at Ainsley's country estate. In the small chapel just down the road from the manor. A gathering of Great Britain's most illustrious families had been in attendance.

The exchanging of their vows and all that followed had been a haze until Westcliffe escorted her from the small church and settled her into the white open carriage to journey back to the residence for a celebratory breakfast. The fog had lifted and reality had set in when he'd muttered, "Damned glad that's done with."

Her heart had sunk clear through the floor of the carriage, to be left behind on the road, trampled by horses and carriage wheels. Her husband desired this arrangement no more than she did.

What an unfortunate state of affairs, she thought hours later, as she walked through the elaborate gardens, having finally escaped the festivities that had continued throughout the day. While traditionally, the groom and bride would have left by then on their wedding trip, she and her husband were staying the night at Grantwood Manor because it was far nicer than his ancestral estate. At least for now—until her dowry allowed him to put matters to right.

Soon she would have to retire to the bedchamber to await him. Her husband.

She'd barely recognized the tall man who'd stood beside her at the altar. The last time she'd seen him, paid any notice to him, he'd been gangly, almost scrawny. But now at five-and-twenty, he had achieved a height that added grace to his slender physique. Humor, lightheartedness, joviality, however, continued to elude him.

When her cousin Chastity had arrived in London the previous spring to experience her first Season, she had wasted no time in informing Claire of the latest gossip concerning her betrothed. Apparently, he had developed quite the reputation in the bedchamber. She tried to draw comfort from knowing he wouldn't be a bungling fool when he came to her bed, but all she seemed capable of realizing was that he would bring far more experience with him than she wished him to have. How could it not be intimidating to know that he had lain with women far lovelier, and perhaps far more adventuresome, than she?

Anytime she imagined lying on the bed while he raised the hem of her nightdress—as her spinster aunt, Mary, had warned her that he would—her heart fluttered madly like the bird with the broken wing that she and Stephen had nursed to health and sent back to the sky. It had been frightened. She'd felt it trembling against her palms, had known it simply wanted to be released. She felt that way now—if only she were free.

"Claire?"

She spun around, her heart filling with gladness. "Stephen."

He was so incredibly handsome standing there in his dark jacket, waistcoat, and gray trousers, his cravat perfectly shaped. His blond hair was a trifle disheveled as though he'd recently plowed his fingers through it, but then it always gave that appearance. Even when he was outfitted in his finest, he did not appear nearly as put together as Westcliffe. With Stephen, there was always a bit of a tousled look as though he'd only just risen from bed, as though he didn't take his role in life as seriously as his brothers did. Three men who shared the same mother but little else.

He cradled her jaw with one hand, pressed his forehead to hers, and chuckled, his whiskey-scented breath wafting over her cheek. "What are you doing out here, sweetheart?"

"Trying to gather my courage."

Swaying slightly, he reared back. "For what?"

She felt the heat suffuse her face, but he was her friend. Had been forever. She could tell him anything. "My wedding night," she whispered.

"Ah, yes, consummation."

"Westcliffe terrifies me."

"He terrifies everyone. It's that perpetual scowl he wears as though he's not happy with anything. But not to worry." He leaned in as though to impart a secret. "He's very skilled when it comes to the bedchamber. Not as skilled as I, of course, but then no one is."

She saw no humor in his remarks. "Stephen, you make it sound as trifling as a game of cards."

He seemed momentarily taken aback, then his blue eyes widened. "Are you crying? Good God, sweetheart, don't cry. You know I can't deny a weeping woman anything."

"I'm not crying," she said, swiping at the tears trailing down her cheeks. "It's just that"—she spun away from him—"I barely know your brother. And the things that will . . . pass between us . . . I don't know. I only wish I were more comfortable with him."

"Tell him. Tell him you're not ready to be a wife."

She turned back to him. "Do you think he'll listen?"

"No, unfortunately. He needs this marriage, Claire, needs the dowry that comes with it. He'll want to ensure nothing will take it from him. He'll no doubt feel obliged to, well, to do his duty."

Duty? Was that all it would be to him? No passion, no fire? Just cold duty?

He touched her cheek. "How truly frightened are you?"

"Truly, truly."

"Well, then. We just have to ensure that he doesn't want you tonight."

"How do we do that?"

He gave her a devilish grin. "Do you trust me?"

"With my life."

"Good girl. Then listen carefully. Prepare yourself for bed, place a lamp in the window when you're ready, then leave it all to me."

And she *had* left it all to him, she mused now. She'd not wanted to take responsibility for meekly accepting her marriage, so she gladly accepted his offer to make everything all right. In the end, they'd done little more than step onto a path leading to disaster.

She didn't want to make that mistake again, but God help her, she didn't know how to avoid it.

The residence was quiet when Westcliffe returned. Servants all abed, and with any luck, his wife was as well. He supposed it would behoove him to stop thinking of her as such. He walked past the parlor. Something caught his eye. He doubled back. A lamp had been left burning on a small table, but that hadn't drawn his attention. The room appeared somehow more welcoming, but he couldn't put his finger on exactly why it was.

Inhaling deeply, he detected the faint scent of roses. Claire had been in here. What had she done? Or was her mere presence enough to bring warmth to his residence?

Don't be ridiculous. It's because someone left the damned lamp burning.

He extinguished the flame, sending the room into shadowed darkness, the only light now coming from the entryway and the outside gas lamps. Why did the residence have a different feel to it? Because he knew she was here. It was no more than that.

He strode to the library, where no footman waited. The only one to greet him was his faithful dog, who began struggling to his feet.

"Stay, old boy."

Cooper dropped back down. Westcliffe thought he might have even sighed with relief. He poured two tumblers of whiskey before joining Cooper on the floor, pressing his back against his favorite chair. He dipped two fingers into one tumbler before extending them toward Cooper, who licked them. Westcliffe savored his own glass and released his own sigh.

Claire had blossomed into a beauty. Not that there'd been anything lacking in her when she was barely seventeen—except for loyalty and devotion—but she'd still had the willowiness of a child. She'd been as flat as a well-planed plank of wood. Now she was enticing curves. Her eyes had lost their innocence, and he regretted whatever role he might have played in that transition. Although he suspected Stephen was more at fault there. He doubted his brother had kept in touch with her over the years, as no one else in the family had received letters from him.

In anger over Stephen's betrayal and his family's disappointment in what they had considered the young man's lack of character, Westcliffe and Ainsley had purchased him a commission in a regiment. Ainsley inquired with the War Office from time to time regarding his brother's whereabouts, but then that was Ainsley's way, to want to give the appearance that he was a member of a caring and loving family when the truth was they were all much better off going their own way.

Westcliffe saw Ainsley with a bit more frequency of late. It was gratifying to no longer have to hold out his hand. He'd taken Claire's dowry and invested it, until it had grown into a substantial amount. It seemed he had a knack for determining sound investments. He'd never again be dependent on Ainsley—or anyone—for anything. He'd acquired what he'd always desired: total independence. He couldn't understand why he felt something was lacking in his life.

He remembered the satisfaction he'd felt when he'd handed over the money for this residence. It was the first thing of any significance he'd purchased without help from Ainsley. That night he'd gotten drunk to celebrate. Alone. Because he had no one who could understand how liberating it had been to require no assistance from anyone. Only now the woman who had made it all possible was sleeping here, in a bedchamber upstairs, her eyes closed, her breaths quietly puffing.

With the help of Claire's substantial dowry, Westcliffe had been able to rise above his beginnings, to become his own man, to step out from beneath his brother's long-reaching, suffocating shadow.

"What are we going to do about her, Cooper? Without her dowry, we'd have not had the means to purchase this house or make investments. And you saw the estate each time we visited. She may have avoided us"—her avoidance had actually begun to amuse him—"but I clearly saw evidence of her efforts."

His overseer, his manager, and his solicitor had often come to him with requests from Claire for funds regarding improvements she wished to make. He'd approved them all. He'd fought not to admit even to himself how much he'd anticipated their visits, reading her letters to them, knowing what she was about. She might have been a silly girl when she married him, but he'd never been able to find fault with the manner in which she'd handled the estate.

Perhaps she'd known that as long as she did a fair job of it, he'd stay in London for the most part and leave her be. Only now she needed him.

He gathered more whiskey on his fingers and extended them to Cooper, who took the offering, his intelligent gaze never leaving Westcliffe. "Damnation, you think I owe her this blasted Season for her sister."

With a heavy breath, he dropped his head back and stared at his book-lined shelves. Books and boudoirs. They entertained him. "I don't much like it when you're right. Christ." He downed his whiskey, then finished off Cooper's.

Burying his fingers in the soft fur, he stroked the one creature with whom he'd shared all his secrets, his disappointments, his dreams. He wished he could overlook what he owed Claire, send her back to the country or, at the very least, to his mother's.

But he couldn't. Damnation, he couldn't. Because the blasted dog was correct. He owed her.

Chapter 4

Claire awoke neither relaxed nor rested. Having just rung for her maid, who'd traveled with her from the estate, she lay in bed and listened to the occasional clanging activity taking place in the bathing room that separated her bedchamber from Westcliffe's. She wondered if he'd anticipated that Willoughby would see her settled into a room so near his.

She wondered exactly what he was doing. Bathing, no doubt. Perhaps shaving. Getting dressed for the day.

The last time she'd heard sounds such as the ones she was hearing now had been on her wedding night. Her maid had left her alone, and she'd stood there in her night rail, listening as he prepared to come to her. Tremors of fear had rippled through her. They'd never kissed. Their skin had never touched. She couldn't imagine him climbing into bed with her, touching her intimately. It was wrong, wrong to have something so personal happen between two people who were virtually strangers.

She started to carry the lamp to the window, to signal Stephen—

And stopped. It was equally wrong.

But he wasn't terrifying. He was safe and comfortable. Just one night, if she could gain just one night's reprieve—

So she took the lamp to the window, unlocked it, and scurried to the bed.

She lay there, listening to the movements of her husband. She'd waited too long to summon Stephen. She should have acted sooner. She heard a sound, then the window was opening. She came upright. "Stephen?"

"Shh." He smiled, his sapphire eyes filled with the deviltry that made him so much fun. He tossed his jacket onto the floor.

She'd not expected that. "What are you doing?"

"Ensuring that he leaves you alone." He quickly removed his waistcoat and nimbly unbuttoned his shirt.

"I thought you were going to talk to him. Explain—"

He winked at her. "No, sweetheart. Words will have no effect on my brother tonight." His shoes came off next and he crawled onto the bed.

"I didn't know this was what you had in mind. I think this is a terrible idea," she said. She started to scramble out from beneath the covers, but he snaked an arm around her and drew her down.

"Do you want him to bed you?" he asked.

She looked up into a face she'd trusted since

childhood, into eyes that had promised to hold all her secrets. She'd always been able to tell him everything. "No."

"Then trust me. He'll be angry at me, not at you."

He tucked her beneath him, half his body covering hers. She could feel his breath wafting over her hair.

"What if this doesn't work?"

"It will."

"How do you know?"

"Because I know my brother."

"Tell me about him, then. Help me to know—"

The door opened. Very slowly, Stephen turned his head to look over his shoulder. "West—"

Before he could even finish addressing his brother, Westcliffe grabbed him, yanked him out of the bed, and threw him to the floor.

Seeing the fury in Westcliffe's dark eyes, she bolted upright, fearful for her own life. What had she expected? Had she thought he'd simply look at them, and say, "Oh, pardon. I'll return later then, shall I?" He turned away from her. Before Stephen could get to his feet, Westcliffe had drawn him up and plowed his fist into his stomach, causing him to double over and drop to his knees.

"No!" she screamed. "Leave him be!"

But he didn't. He hit him again, sending him crashing into a table. It shattered beneath Stephen's weight. Westcliffe lifted him as though he weighed no more than a pillow and slammed his fist into him again.

She scrambled out of the bed. "No, please, you're going to kill him!"

The door leading into the hallway banged open.

"That's enough!" a voice of authority rang out from the doorway. Ainsley strode into the room. Fearlessly, he stormed over to the brawl and shoved away his older brother. "Enough, I said!"

She'd always been amazed that in spite of the fact he was the youngest, he wore a mantle of power. But at that moment, her attention was riveted on Westcliffe, who was breathing harshly, his large hands balled into massive fists at his side. She could see blood on his right, and her stomach lurched. Whether it was his blood or Stephen's, she couldn't tell, but either was too much.

"Come along," Ainsley said, pulling Stephen to his feet, one hand clamped around his arm while he used his free one to gather up Stephen's jacket and waistcoat, as though he thought by keeping himself near his middle brother, he could protect him from the temper of his older. "Out with you, puppy." Ainsley shoved Stephen toward the door.

"Dammit, you're my baby brother. I hate when you call me that."

"Then stop behaving like such a dolt."

She could scarcely blame Stephen for going so willingly when the devil remained in the room— although she would have found some comfort if he had just glanced back at her. But it was as though the play had come to an end, and he didn't consider it worthy of applause. She felt abandoned and confused.

"Get dressed," Westcliffe ordered. "We're leaving tonight."

And they had. He'd packed her into his carriage and taken her to Lyons Place. Exiled. Unloved. Unhappy.

The bitter truth was that she understood she deserved it all.

But surely three years was long enough for her to suffer for the foolishness of youth.

She could no longer hear any sounds coming from the bathing chamber. Was he soaking in the tub? He would smell very different the next time she was near enough to inhale his fragrance. It would be all masculine, earthy, and rich. She wondered to whom the lilac scent belonged. She didn't know why noticing it had been like a physical blow. She'd known he'd not honored his vows, so it should have come as no surprise that he carried the scent of a woman. She'd been married all of six months when her cousin Charity had visited and wasted no time in informing Claire of her husband's perfidy.

"It's scandalous, Cousin. He openly flaunts these liaisons. Every week he is seen with a different lady in the park—walking, riding, driving her around in his curricle. I myself have seen him kissing a woman behind a tree! And we are not talking a kiss upon the hand or cheek, but upon the mouth. It went on so long that I could scarce believe she didn't faint from lack of air. He's making a fool of you, Claire."

Because she'd made a fool of him. She'd tried to rationalize, to pretend it didn't hurt, that she didn't care—"*It is not uncommon for a man to have an affair.*"

"*Within months of his marriage, and so openly? You must return to London and take him in hand.*"

Only she'd stayed at Lyons Place and buried herself in all the matters that had needed tending to there. The estate was in shambles, and she'd set about righting it because she didn't know how to do the same with her marriage. Even now, she didn't know how to make a go of things with Westcliffe. She'd tried the direct approach, asking for forgiveness, stating that she wished to be a wife. And he'd merely mocked her, humiliated her by making her want his touch only to then withhold it. She was so damned lonely—that was the only reason he'd managed to take her breath last night.

She couldn't—wouldn't—seek out the companionship of a man until she'd given her husband his heir, and perhaps not even then. In spite of the abysmal start to their marriage, she'd never intended to stray or to see him cuckolded. She'd only wanted Stephen to comfort her. Why couldn't Westcliffe understand that? Why was he so consumed by his anger? Although in truth, she knew any man would be.

A soft rap sounded on her door, then Judith entered the room. She curtsied. "M'lady. Did you sleep well?"

"I didn't sleep at all," Claire said as she threw back the covers and clambered out of bed.

"It's the residence," Judith murmured, glancing around warily. "It's as cold as a mausoleum. It holds none of the warmth of Lyons Place."

Claire knew she wasn't talking about the temperature of the air. It was the character of the house. Lyons Place had been the same when she'd arrived. Cold and dreary. Somewhere to take shelter from the elements but not the storms of life. She had worked diligently to change that, to make it a place where happiness could abide.

She had begun to cherish her time there, but still she was haunted by loneliness and regrets. For a moment, she considered accepting the challenge of altering this residence, but what was the point? She would be here for one Season. If that long. She didn't think she could stay when her husband so despised her. But neither could she stand the thought of not helping her sister avoid the lecherous hands of Hester.

Claire chose a morning dress of hunter green, which flattered her complexion. If she was going to battle Westcliffe again, she was determined to do it in full armor. It took her an inordinate amount of time to see to her toilette and she knew she was dawdling, but she couldn't seem to help herself. Well aware of the sounds coming from next door, she knew the moment he withdrew from his room. She recognized the tread of his steps in the hallway. Half an hour later, as she made her way down the stairs, part of her hoped he'd left for the day, and another part of her wanted him to still be there, to see that she was no longer a young girl who was fearful of him.

Even if her stomach quivered at the sight of him sitting at the table in the breakfast dining room. His dark gaze homed in on her—she felt it almost like a touch—as his chair scraped across the floor, and he came to his feet.

She tilted her head slightly. "Good morning, my lord."

"My lady. I trust you slept well." His deep voice reverberated off the walls and shimmered through her. She cursed her knees for weakening at the alluring smoothness.

"Very well, thank you."

Forcing a casualness to her step, she strolled over to the sideboard and began placing random delicacies on her plate, barely giving any attention to what they were. She was unsettled, the hairs on the nape of her neck prickling as she was acutely aware of him studying her. She wanted to appear sophisticated, calm. But he still had the power to rattle her.

She walked to the foot of the table and took the seat that the footman held out for her. Deliberately, with as much of a challenge as she could muster, she lifted her eyes to Westcliffe's. He was still standing as though not quite certain what to make of her. Finally, he sat down.

He'd been reading the newspaper before she'd arrived. It rested on the table beside him. She fully expected him to return his attention to it. Her father always read while he enjoyed his breakfast. No one ever spoke during meals, so she nearly came out of her skin when Westcliffe did.

"You must love your sister very much to have risked facing my wrath."

She made the mistake of trying to appear unaffected by lifting her teacup. The brew sloshed over the sides, revealing the truth of her nervousness. If he noticed, he didn't react. As she set down the cup and fought to ignore the footman who was quickly replacing it with another, she supposed she could take some solace in the fact Westcliffe wasn't gloating at her obvious discomfort.

"I love her immensely." This time when she lifted her cup, she was pleased to discover her hand had ceased its trembling. Perhaps the trick was to concentrate on Beth, rather than Westcliffe.

"As I recall, your father does not come to London for the Season. Where did you intend for Beth to reside?"

"With me."

Across the length of the table, she could see his jaw tighten, his eyes narrow.

"I assure you that you'll barely be aware of her presence," she promised.

"Can you say the same for your own?"

His question startled her. Avoiding him was not what she'd planned. But then he'd clearly stated that he no longer wanted her. She was going to have to make the ladies understand that she had no control over the man she'd married—or she was going to have to convince him to change his mind regarding her. She was certain that confessing to them would be much less humiliating than trying to seduce her husband.

"I'm sure that can be arranged," she stated succinctly. At least until she could determine how best to handle this matter.

"Then you may stay. But I want nothing to do with you or your sister."

"You're a hard man, Westcliffe. Little wonder I was so terrified of you three years ago."

"Do not blame me for your actions."

"For my actions, no. For my fears, yes."

His eyes narrowed. "I'm giving you leave to stay here. You should be grateful."

"To stay in a residence my dowry no doubt purchased? Perhaps 'tis you who should be grateful."

He came up out of the chair so fast that she nearly tumbled backward in hers. "I am well aware of what I owe you. It's the only reason you're still here. Give your sister her damnable Season. Spare no expense to find her a husband as quickly as possible; and then I want you gone."

He strode from the room with the force of a storm. If they were engaged in a war, she supposed she could claim victory over the first battle. But seeing the anger and hatred in his eyes made it ever so bittersweet.

"No one is to disturb me," Westcliffe ordered the footman outside his library right before he closed the door behind him and locked it.

He needed to prowl, and he did just that, weaving through the library, fighting not to remember the sight of Claire taking a seat at his breakfast table, just as he'd imagined before they were married. The scene had been an idealized version of marital bliss—to have company at every meal. To look up from his paper to see her sitting there. To detect only a hint of her sweet fragrance.

He would have to find another residence for her while she was in London. He couldn't have her in his house. She would drive him mad with her nearness.

She was nothing like any of the women he'd ever bedded. Even Anne. For as much as he enjoyed her, she was nothing at all like Claire. When she walked into the room, she brought with her an icy chill. Claire brought warmth.

It was incredible, his reaction confusing. He wanted to be rid of her. He would be rid of her. As soon as her sister was betrothed.

He marched over to his desk, took his seat, dipped pen in inkwell, and began to scrawl the name of every eligible man he knew.

Following breakfast, Claire stood at the window in her bedchamber and gazed out on the lush greenery. How often had she done the same thing at Lyons Place? He'd exiled her there, forbidden her to come to London. He was doing the same now—exiling her, banishing her from his company.

She'd have to face London without him. Sighing heavily, she wondered where Stephen was when she needed him. She'd asked Ainsley when she stopped by his residence last night looking for Westcliffe—only to learn he now had his own residence. Ainsley had told her that he had word Stephen was in India. He'd shown her on a globe in his library exactly where his brother might be. It seemed so dreadfully far away.

She was on her own here, but then she'd been that way for three years. Stephen had not come to see her before he'd embarked on his adventures, nor had he written. Whether it was fear for her safety or fear of his brother's wrath, she didn't know. Nor did it really matter. It could have been any of a hundred reasons. He was a soldier now, with more important matters with which to deal.

The Season would go so much better for Beth if Westcliffe was at Claire's side. And Claire had to admit it would be much easier for her as well. Only then would she have any hope of putting rumors about her husband's romantic escapades to rest. Besides, she didn't want him with other women while she was here. She no longer wanted it when she was in Lyons Place either.

She'd spoken true last night. She wanted to be his wife. She wanted children. She wanted respectability. She didn't want people snickering about her and her inability to hold her husband's interest. She'd kept her knees clamped together as he'd ordered. She was damned well ready to unclamp them.

She thought.

She still yearned for what she had three years ago—to know him before he came to her bed. Was that too much to ask? She knew so little about him, and he no doubt knew even less about her. Why couldn't they have a courtship?

But a more nagging question was: If he didn't want her, who did he want? And could Claire offer any sort of competition? Where did she even begin?

The only person in London who could possibly counsel her was Westcliffe's mother, and she wasn't happy with Claire either.

She marched across the room and yanked on the bellpull. Her life was in a sad state of affairs because she'd chosen retreat over confrontation. She wasn't going to make that mistake again.

In spite of the queasiness in her stomach, she was determined to call on the Duchess of Ainsley.

Tessa Seymour, Duchess of Ainsley—mother to the eighth Earl of Westcliffe, the Honorable Stephen Lyons, and the ninth Duke of Ainsley—lounged on the bed with the silk sheet bunched at her waist and trailing over one hip and thigh, leaving the other provocatively revealed. Her black hair with only a hint of gray at the temples provided a covering for her shoulders and exposed one breast to the eye of the beholder. And the beholder had such gorgeous golden eyes. Before she'd commissioned this painter, she'd never seen anything like them. Soulful. But when passion ignited them, they flared like the sun.

"You're thinking again about getting me in that bed with you," he said as he stood at the window, where the light cast its brilliance over his canvas.

"How can you tell?" she asked saucily. Leo was all of fifteen years her junior. Firm and not yet gone to fat.

"Your eyes," he said. "They darken."

"So come join me then."

"I want to work on your portrait while the light is still good."

"I told you. I always come first. The painting second."

He grinned. "Ah, but I'm working on my favorite part right now. Your long, slender legs."

"Come over here, and I'll wrap them around your waist."

"Later. Right now, they're perfect just as they are. You're perfect as well."

"Is there any doubt as to why I love you?" He'd created three portraits so far, and each time he convinced her to wear less. This one was the most scandalous so far. She wasn't quite certain what she would do with it when he finished it.

"Then marry me."

She laughed. "No. I've had two husbands. That is more than enough for any woman."

"Neither was young. You deserve a young husband."

"Who will eventually grow old."

"But what fun we'll have until then."

"We have fun now. Marriage will simply ruin everything." Although her second marriage had not been too awful. Ainsley, at least, had treated her well, and she *had* cared for him. But her heart had only ever belonged to one man. The Earl of Lynnford. They'd had a brief affair while she was married to Westcliffe. By the time Westcliffe died, Lynnford was married. He'd ended their affair when he became betrothed and had remained faithful to his wife. As much as Tessa despised him for his devotion to his countess, she couldn't help but admire his loyalty.

"Now you're thinking of someone else," Leo said softly. "Who is it that always turns you melancholy?"

She brought herself back to the present. "It's your talk of marriage that has ruined my mood. Perhaps if you were to paint without your clothes on, my fair temperament would be restored."

Grinning, he set the palette aside. Before he'd removed his loosely fitting white shirt, a knock sounded on her door, and her lady's maid peered in. "The Countess of Westcliffe has come to call."

That was a surprise although Tessa refused to show it. She'd not even known the girl was in London. Well, that could prove interesting for the Season. Still, she responded tartly, "Tell her I'm not at home."

"No," Leo said, moving away from the canvas. "You should see her."

Tessa waved a hand at the maid, who promptly

retreated, closing the door in her wake. "She took two sons from me. I have no wish to welcome her into my home."

It had nearly broken her heart to realize that her second son, the one born of her heart, had grown into a man lacking in character. He'd refused to discuss his reasons for cuckolding his brother. He'd simply sat in the library, downed brandy, and acted as though his actions were of no consequence—when Tessa knew they'd very nearly destroyed Westcliffe. While she'd never felt as close to him as she'd felt to the others, by God, he was still her son, and she understood as only a mother could.

Leo walked over to the bed and tugged on the sheet, exposing her hip a little more. "It can't have been easy for her to come here."

Tessa sighed with feigned annoyance. Something about Leo prevented any woman from growing angry with him. "You're going to fall out of my good graces if you continue this path."

"At least determine what she wants."

She jerked on the sheet, wrapped it around her body, and slithered off the bed, tossing her hair back over her shoulder. "Why do you care?"

"Because I know you're unhappy with the way things are between you and your sons. Perhaps her visit can alter the situation."

"You are such a dreamer, Leo."

He approached her and bussed a quick kiss across her lips. "Visit with her. What harm can come of it?"

Her relationship with Morgan was estranged, but then it had always been difficult. She'd despised his father, and God help her, she'd had a difficult time separating her feelings for the father from those for his son. She'd been so young, barely seventeen when he was born. Then Stephen, whom she had adored from birth, had come into the world, and she'd showered him with her affections, ignoring Morgan in the process. She felt so uncomfortable with him now, out of her element. She didn't enjoy feeling like a failure, but she knew she'd been a miserable mother—at least where her older son was concerned. She pressed her body against Leo's. "Make me happy again before I greet her."

He grinned. "With pleasure."

Claire sat in the parlor, her hands clasped in her lap. It was strange to be in London. She'd spent most of her youth in the country, most of her marriage there as well. When she had come to Town, she'd visited with Charity and her friends, but she'd never truly developed any friendships of her own, so it was quite unsettling to determine upon whom to call next. She might not have to make any calls at all if she could garner the support of the Duchess of Ainsley. She might be scandalous, but with two sons bearing titles, she held quite a bit of power in her little finger.

But alas, Claire had been waiting for nearly an hour. It had obviously been a mistake to come here. The woman was sending a message. Claire would have to send one of her own. She'd not be treated so shabbily. She'd taken two steps toward the door when the duchess swept into the room, her cheeks aglow and her brown eyes alight with mischief.

"Countess. What an unexpected surprise to have you visit."

Claire detected a slight chill in her voice. She curtsied. "Duchess."

The duchess went to a table and poured amber liquid into two glasses. She extended one toward Claire. "I'd offer you tea, but I gave up the dreadful drink long ago."

"Oh." Claire took the offering.

"Please sit." The duchess indicated a settee while she, herself, lounged on a fainting couch and gazed out the window. A small smile played on her lips as a young man walked by the window. "You interrupted as I was having my portrait done."

"My apologies. I do hope you'll forgive me. I didn't think I should wait much longer before coming to see you," Claire said as she sat on the settee.

The duchess waved her bejeweled hand as though Claire's words were of no consequence. "I'm certain I can take up the pose again with little bother. When did you arrive in London?"

"Last night. Too late to call," she added hastily before the duchess could find fault with that.

Sipping from her glass, she peered over the rim at Claire as though she were measuring her and finding her sadly lacking in every regard. "So. Why have you come to call?"

"First, I wish to apologize for what happened on my wedding night."

"It is not me to whom you need to apologize, girl."

"I've already expressed my regrets to Westcliffe."

The duchess sat up, her interest obviously piqued. "Have you? You've seen him then?"

"Yes. I'm staying at his—our—residence in St. James." She took a swallow of the burning brew. "He does not seem prone to forgive, but he has granted me leave to remain in London."

"Is he well?"

She was astounded that the duchess would inquire of her regarding her son's health. She nodded. "He seems to be, yes."

"I have seen him but once since your wedding. I went to inform him that I did not approve of . . . his handling of himself while he was in London. Apparently he did not think I was one to cast aspersions regarding proper behavior." She sighed, and her eyes took on a faraway look as once more she looked out the window. "Creating scandal was much more enjoyable when I was younger."

"I've never relished it," Claire admitted. "I know the ladies are not pleased that my husband has such free rein."

"What do you intend to do about it?"

"I'm not quite certain. But I know I must earn their good graces. My sister is having her coming out, and I wish to help her as much as possible. I fear I'm not quite as schooled in the fine art of the Season, never having had one myself." She'd married the spring before she would have had a Season. Surely, in retrospect, no harm would have come from waiting a year or even six months. But her father had not seen that anything was to be gained by granting her a reprieve. In truth, she suspected he feared she might begin to have reservations about her lot in life if given too much time to contemplate it, if she had an opportunity to experience a modicum of choice, even if the choice was simply deciding with which gentleman to dance. "I thought perhaps you could advise me, Your Grace."

"Avoid it, at all costs."

Not exactly the advice she'd anticipated. "Surely you jest?"

"I find the Season to be a bit of a bother."

"I fear I have no choice in the matter. You see, if my sister doesn't find another suitor, she'll be forced to marry Lord Hester."

The duchess visibly shuddered. "Good Lord, I always want to take pruning shears to his nostrils when he's about."

Claire released a small laugh and covered her smile with a gloved hand.

For the first time since she'd walked into the room, the duchess seemed to soften toward her. "I'd hoped you'd laugh like that around my son, around Westcliffe. He's had little enough laughter in his life."

Claire immediately sobered. "We had a dreadful beginning. I was terrified of my wedding night. Stephen meant well—"

"By taking his brother's place in your bed? Stephen has always been mischievous, but that was beyond the pale. I must share some of the blame. I spoiled him, led him to believe that he should be denied nothing."

"It wasn't like that between us. Truly. We'd both had too much champagne. It seemed like such a brilliant idea in our muddled minds—just a way to delay my wedding night."

"Being honest with Westcliffe would have probably gained you more."

In retrospect, she had to agree. "I didn't know him very well. I still don't." She eased up on the edge of her seat. "Duchess, I would very much like to make amends with him."

"Then do so, girl."

"I hardly know where to begin. And as much as I'd like to know him better, it seems he's done with me. I think he merely plans to tolerate my presence."

"Then you'll have to use your womanly wiles to change his mind."

"I fear I have none."

"My dear girl, every woman possesses them. She simply needs to recognize the ability within herself. Men are very simple creatures really. They desire women. You simply must make yourself desirable."

Claire refused to let her confidence diminish with the comment. She thought she looked quite smart in her dress.

"Don't look so offended, girl."

"I'm not."

"Your face would say otherwise. You look lovely. Truly. But a man doesn't desire lovely. He desires daring. You must tease him, make him wonder how much of heaven he'll find beneath that skirt."

She didn't know if she could do it, but still she nodded, hoping the conversation would move on to another topic, before the heat of embarrassment caused her to burst into flames. She'd never spoken about intimate matters so candidly with another woman. It was unsettling simply because it was so intriguing. "There is still the matter of my sister."

"Ah, yes, the reason for your visit. I shan't make morning calls with you as I find them tedious, and as most gossip concerns me, it limits conversation. I shall, however, send word hither and yon that Ainsley will only consider invitations to balls to which you are invited."

"Does he attend balls? Is he searching for a wife?" It occurred to her that if that was the case, he might consider Beth.

"Good God, no," the duchess said. "I won't say he'll attend, only that he'll consider them. He's one-and-twenty. Still sowing his wild oats. I'm fairly certain marriage is the very last thing on his mind. Which is to our advantage, as it allows me to concentrate on yours."

"Mine?"

"It's time Westcliffe was settled, and after watching your face turn as red as an apple, I can see you need some help with the matter."

Chapter 5

 ⁓⚬⚬⁓

I cannot believe in all these years you have not invited me to visit your London residence."

It was midafternoon. Westcliffe had been studying reports in his office when his butler had announced that the Duchess of Ainsley had arrived. He didn't trust her visit any more than he trusted his wife, who was sitting in a chair beside his mother and preparing tea.

"You're my mother," Westcliffe stated succinctly, standing by the fireplace, refusing to be drawn into the unfamiliar tableau. He'd had few visitors to his residence. It was a place to sleep, eat, and work. Nothing more. "Surely an invitation is not required."

"Of course it is. How is one to know that one is welcomed?"

Westcliffe darted his gaze to the man lounging casually on the sofa. He suspected Leo was his mother's latest lover. He was tall and slender, with graceful hands and the face of an Adonis. He seemed much too angelic for his mother. Turning his attention back to her, he said, "You are always welcome in my residences."

"I shall keep that in mind." Winking at Claire, she took the offered cup of tea. *That* didn't bode well. His mother had a tendency to be conniving, and Claire's reaction more than his mother's alerted him that some sort of conspiracy was afoot. "I'm here on a rather urgent matter. You've been married all of three years, and you have yet to have your wedding portrait made."

He ground his back teeth. "I didn't see the point in having it done."

"Of course there is a point, dear boy. It is family tradition to have a portrait of every earl and countess made shortly after they are married. For posterity's sake."

"I don't recall your ever caring about the earl. What do you care of his posterity?"

"The previous earl, no. The present earl, yes. Why would you ever think otherwise?"

Before he could respond, his mother turned to Claire. "Perhaps you would be so kind as to take Leo on a tour of the rooms, so he can determine where the best lighting can be found."

Claire appeared startled before rising to her feet. "Yes, of course."

Westcliffe watched the young man follow his wife from the room. He was tempted to go after them, but what did he care if Claire was alone with a man? He didn't. The time for such caring was past. Instead, he glared at his mother. "What are you about?"

"I told you. You need to have your portrait done."

"And I told you there is no point. I intend to have this farce of a marriage brought to a legal end."

"My God. Do you have any idea of the scandal—"

"Don't be a hypocrite, Mother. If our family is known for nothing else, it is known for its unconventional flouting of societal rules. Your own scandals make mine seem paltry in comparison."

He knew she couldn't deny the charges, and she didn't even try. Rather she arched a dark brow. "And what of Claire? Is she aware of this plan of yours that will bring shame and humiliation to your doorstep?"

"No."

"I see. So it's true then. Lady Anne Cavil has won your heart."

He considered lying, considered claiming to be madly in love with Anne, but the truth was that he felt nothing for anyone. "I have no heart to be won, and well you know it. But Anne suits me."

"Well, then, what more is there?"

But the icy tone of her voice set his teeth on edge. He watched warily as his mother rose, graceful as ever. She approached him, then proceeded to brush some lint from the shoulder of his jacket. Finally, she lifted her eyes to his. They were dark—brown—but his were darker still, his had come from the man who'd sired him.

"I gave you so little love growing up. I couldn't separate you from your father, and I despised him. For whatever pain I caused you, I'm sorry. But it is not like you to be hurtful. Surely you can give Claire another chance to be your wife."

"Is that the reason you're here? To speak on her behalf? If so, you're wasting your breath, and I would beg you not to interfere."

"I'm here to see about having your portrait done." She tilted her head slightly. "And because Claire invited us for dinner."

He narrowed his eyes. "You're meddling."

"I've ignored you for a good part of your life. Don't you think it's time?"

Before he could answer, the painter walked back into the room. "I found the perfect lighting. I'm going to gather my materials from the carriage. Will you help the countess select an appropriate gown?"

Westcliffe almost answered no before his mother murmured her reply, and he realized the question had been directed at her. A gown. Not a dress with buttons clear to her chin. But a gown. Something that would lay bare the skin he'd touched last night. It would be pure torment—

"You are both going to a great deal of trouble needlessly," he said. "I have no desire to sit for a portrait."

"Don't be petulant. Even if you dissolve this marriage, there should be a portrait."

"Of the woman who betrayed me?"

"You can burn it in celebration afterward," the artist said from the doorway.

Westcliffe glared, and the man merely shrugged. "I have burned a few portraits. There is satisfaction in destroying the image of one you wish to forget."

"I see no reason to subject myself to hours of sitting—"

"Please," his mother said quietly. "For me."

Under his breath, he cursed her because that was all it had ever taken from her to gain what she needed or wanted from him. Watch out for your brothers—for me. Exceed in the classroom—for me. Teach Ransom to read—for me. Play with Stephen—for me. She was his mother, and in spite of her years of putting him last, he could no more deny her than not draw in a breath.

He didn't know why he was surprised that the room chosen was his bedchamber. He was certain the artist was conspiring with his mother to accomplish something that Westcliffe did not desire.

The furniture in the seating area had been rearranged, brought nearer to the windows, where the drapes were drawn back to allow in the afternoon sunlight. In a pale blue gown with a scooped neck that revealed the upper swells of her breasts, Claire sat on the settee. At her throat was the string of pearls he'd given her on the morning of their wedding. It had once belonged to his grandmother. If his mother hadn't put it away for safekeeping, he'd have sold it long ago. He found it difficult to be sentimental about *things* that might have been responsible for his previous state of *poverty*. He wanted to tell her that it was not a good idea to remind him of that day, yet neither could he deny that they accented her throat perfectly. Resting near her feet was Cooper.

"I thought the portrait would have more meaning for you," Claire said quietly, "if your dog was part of it."

It would ensure he didn't burn it. When he was thirteen, he'd acquired the puppy. The Earl of Lynnford, who'd become their guardian after the duke had died, had given the dog to Westcliffe as though he'd recognized that the boy had little enough in his life.

She reached up and scratched her nose. Just the edge of her gloved finger moving quickly against the tip of her upturned nose. She had such tiny features. Everything about her was delicate. He remembered how awkward she'd been as a child, chasing after Stephen, for whom responsibility was a foreign word. But he'd been popular with everyone because he'd been ever so good at playing and giving everyone a good laugh.

"If you'll stand here, my lord," Leo said, directing him so he stood behind and slightly to the right of Claire, which gave him an unencumbered view of her bared skin as well as his bed.

Was this his mother's perverse notion of matchmaking?

"My lord, you're creating a bit of a shadow . . . if you'll move in just a little closer to the countess?"

Westcliffe felt her stiffen as his stomach nestled against her back.

"Very good. Let's curl your hand around her nape—"

"This isn't going to work."

Leo actually appeared stunned. "Pardon?"

Westcliffe glanced at his mother, who was observing near the doorway. "The proximity isn't going to make me want her." He felt a tiny jerk go through Claire, beneath his fingers, as though he'd slapped her. "You're forcing me to be cruel. Claire and I have an arrangement. She is here only for the Season, then she is gone."

"Then the portrait should be done now, while she is here," his mother said.

He shook his head but stayed where he was.

"If you'll look here, my lord, a bit of profile, very good," the artist said, as though no tension resided in the room. He moved behind his easel.

"I shall be in the parlor," his mother said, and quickly vanished.

"Was this your idea?" Westcliffe asked Claire.

"No. I want it no more than you do."

"Then why are we here?"

"To please your mother. I need her assistance this Season to help me find a suitable husband for Beth."

"So you wish to acquire her good graces?"

"Precisely."

They posed for several minutes, neither moving nor speaking. He was acutely aware of her scent infiltrating his room, her warmth penetrating his fingers, her profile bathed in sunlight. He'd never noticed before, but she had three small freckles— two high, one low—on the curve of her cheek. He wondered if the sun had caught her without a bonnet. He wondered how often she'd walked over his land.

"My lord, there are some stray strands of her hair falling over her cheek," Leo said. "Would you be so kind as to tuck them up behind her ear?"

Three strands at the most. How the devil had Leo spotted them from his distance?

"You're an artist. Pretend they're not there."

"I fear I lack imagination. I paint what I see."

"But you are not yet painting."

"No, I'm outlining, but they are a distraction."

With a sigh, knowing his cooperation would help speed things along, Westcliffe reached out and moved the strands aside, his fingers glancing over her cheek. She shivered beneath his touch. Against his will, his gaze darted to the bed, and he imagined her shivering there. Unlike the artist, he had a keen imagination. He could imagine his mouth trailing over her skin—

With more force than needed, he tucked the stray strands back into place. As he did so, he noticed the faintest of scars intersecting her right brow. "How much longer?" he snapped.

"Not much. You're free to speak," Leo said.

"It actually assists me with my painting, to get a clearer idea of your character. For example, what is your favorite color, my lady?"

"Blue."

That explained the color of her gown, which even from the disadvantage of his angle he could see enhanced the shade of her eyes.

"My lord?"

Westcliffe tore his gaze from his wife and glowered at the artist, arching an eyebrow.

"Your favorite color, my lord," he said smugly.

"I see no reason to encourage your inquiries."

"Brown," Claire said softly. "His favorite color. It's everywhere in his residence. Dull and dreary. Is that how you see your life, my lord?"

"My life is seldom dull and never dreary. I simply find brown . . . peaceful." In truth, he'd never given it any thought. But his mood was often flat. He couldn't remember the last time he laughed. Anne brought him moments of pleasure, but he seemed incapable of holding true joy.

"How did you get the scar?" he asked quietly.

Her hand came up quickly, and before Leo could chastise her for moving, she'd returned it to her lap. "When I was eight, I took a tumble off my horse."

Then she'd had the scar for years. The scar, the freckles. What else had escaped his notice? He realized he was falling into his mother's trap—taking an interest in Claire he'd not meant to take.

"What are your intentions regarding my

mother?" he asked bluntly of the artist, deciding turnabout was fair play. Besides, he had no desire to delve into his own mannerisms.

Claire seemed almost as surprised as Leo. She swung her head around to look at Westcliffe, her blue eyes wide, her luscious lips parted. They were the red of a rose.

"Did he kiss you?" he suddenly demanded, not certain what had provoked the question. Maybe it was simply that her mouth appeared so damned kissable.

She appeared even more flummoxed, her brow pleating.

"Stephen. Did he kiss you?"

"No. Never." She squeezed her eyes closed. "Yes, once. I was ten. I was curious. I asked him to kiss me. He did. It was . . . disappointing."

He was trying to process her disjointed answer. She'd been ten? A child? Curious? She'd gone to Stephen instead of the one to whom she'd been betrothed? Where had he been? All the times when she and Stephen had been frolicking about—he'd been riding or reading or off doing something that put distance between them. He'd been older, had no patience for their childish ways. A man needed to know very little about a woman—only that he desired her—before he bedded her. What did a woman of quality require? He'd never given it any thought. Had assumed Claire would welcome him only because he wanted her.

"That's the only time he kissed you?" he heard himself ask.

She nodded. "Yes."

Unblinking, she held his gaze. The only sign of her distress was the reddening of her cheeks.

And she'd found Stephen's kiss disappointing. He took perverse satisfaction in the knowledge until he realized that Stephen would have been fourteen, on the cusp of childhood, no doubt still unschooled in the art of seduction. Westcliffe was damned tempted to take her in his arms and show her exactly what a kiss should be. Only the idiot painter was standing there.

"I'm losing the light," Leo said calmly. "So we're done for the day, but we shall meet at the same time tomorrow. You're not to look at the work until it's completed. You may leave if you like, and I'll set matters to rights here."

Westcliffe didn't bother to argue. He strode from the room before he did something very foolish. He needed at least two tumblers of whiskey, perhaps three, before dinner, or he'd never survive it.

Chapter 6

∽◦◦◦∽

Claire didn't recall inviting the duchess to dinner, and yet there they all were, sitting at the dining table while soup, pork cutlets, and garnished brussels sprouts were served as though the guests had been anticipated. It occurred to her that the duchess had seen to matters regarding the cuisine while everyone else was in Westcliffe's bedchamber.

It was not the room she'd have chosen. She thought the light in the salon with its floor-to-ceiling windows was better, but Leo—while she was uncomfortable referring to him so intimately, he insisted it was the only name he possessed—had assured her that the bedchamber was the only room that would do. She had stared at that massive bed, which had obviously been crafted especially for Westcliffe's size, and wondered how many women had shared it with him.

"Your décor is rather interesting," the duchess said to her son, breaking into Claire's thoughts. "Paintings and statues of dogs, but no people."

"I purchase that from which I receive enjoyment. Besides, dogs are loyal. People seldom are."

"And by 'people,' I assume you mean family."

Her husband did little more than hold his mother's gaze.

"You might say that of Stephen, and perhaps of me," she said quietly. "But Ainsley would give you the shirt off his back if you asked. He has always adored his oldest brother."

Westcliffe dipped his gaze to his plate and began to concentrate on his food, and Claire wondered if he were uncomfortable with Ainsley's adoration. She knew Stephen had sometimes felt conflicted, loving his brothers but resenting what they possessed. He was in a unique position of being the middle brother between two lords.

"I saw Ainsley last night," Westcliffe said.

"At a gambling house no doubt," the duchess stated, as though she knew exactly where they'd been.

Claire felt immense relief that they'd not been at a brothel although she was certain he'd been with someone. She didn't want to contemplate that he no longer wanted her because he'd fallen in love with someone else. Through the wisdom of years, she couldn't help but consider that his amour might be as passionate as his fury. What she'd feared as a child intrigued her now.

"I do worry about him," the duchess said. "He gambles so much."

"He was winning. He always wins." Westcliffe

slid his gaze over to Claire. "Fortune seems to smile on Ainsley."

"Do you resent it?" She didn't know from where the question had come.

His jaw working back and forth, he seemed to give it serious thought before shaking his head. "No."

His answer made her smile inside, gave her a sense of relief. It was one of the things that had always bothered her about Stephen—that he could be angry at his brothers for things over which they had no control. They couldn't help it if they were born to inherit titles and property while he was not.

The conversation drifted into more comfortable territory: the styles of the Season, which ladies were still unspoken for, which ones would be making their debut. While the duchess claimed to live on the fringes of society, she was quite well versed in the comings and goings of the upper crust.

It had been a long day, and Claire was quite relieved when dinner finally came to an end.

"We shall see you tomorrow afternoon," the duchess said brightly, squeezing Claire's hand and patting her son's cheek before disappearing through the doorway with Leo.

"Thank God that matter's done with," Westcliffe muttered. Then he shouted, "Willoughby!"

"Yes, my lord."

"Have my carriage readied immediately."

"Yes, sir."

Claire desperately wanted to ask him where he was going, wanted to ask him to stay. She didn't want to be alone. She was so tired of being alone, but she'd promised not to make a nuisance of herself, so instead she said, "I'm sorry."

He turned and looked at her as though only just remembering she was there.

"Your mother. I'm sorry. The portrait, the dinner, they weren't my idea. I went to her hoping that she could assist me in being invited to balls, in introducing Beth to society. And she is going to help. She will let it be known that Ainsley will only attend balls if we're invited—"

"I don't need Ainsley to garner invitations."

Without another word, he strode down the hallway toward his library, leaving her standing there, feeling foolish. What was she to do now? She'd thought he'd be pleased not to be bothered with courting invitations. She was about to ascend the stairs when he returned to the entryway and held out a handful of invitations to her.

"Are these to upcoming balls?" she asked, amazed.

"And dinners. And various other functions."

Taking the offering, she stared at the half dozen envelopes. "I'm not sure why, but I assumed you weren't invited to balls."

"There is not a woman in London who doesn't want to be seen dancing with me."

Her joy over finding herself with entry into the finest houses diminished. "Of course."

She heard his harsh curse, then his hand was beneath her chin, lifting her gaze to his. "Claire, I'm sorry. That was uncalled for. I'm invited because I'm a curiosity. I seldom accept."

She nodded, licking her lips. Why was her mouth always so dry when he was near? "Perhaps you would consider altering your stance for this Season."

He narrowed his eyes, and she rushed on to explain, "I should think it would go a long way to guaranteeing my sister is welcomed into society if you were to accompany us to the first ball. Of course, the sooner she is accepted, the sooner she is likely to find a match, and the sooner I may return to the country."

If at all possible, he seemed almost bemused by her explanation. "I shall consider it."

She offered him what she hoped was an appreciative smile. His gaze dipped to her mouth before returning to her eyes. She could think of nothing else to say except to ask him to stay, and she didn't think he'd be pleased with that path of conversation, so she held her silence, acutely aware of his chiseled features, his dark eyes locked on hers. She inhaled his rich, masculine scent, could almost feel the heat from his nearness.

His hand still rested beneath her chin, and his thumb slid up to stroke her lower lip. She wondered if he was thinking about their earlier conversation regarding kisses. It seemed she was able to think of little else. She imagined his kiss would be vastly different from the innocent one Stephen had given her so long ago. His mouth appeared as though it had been shaped to deliver pleasure. It was an odd thought coming from her, when her experience was so lacking.

His head dipped a fraction, her heart thundered, his eyes heated—

"Sir, your carriage is ready," the butler suddenly announced.

Westcliffe stepped back easily as though he'd been meaning to go in that direction all along. He nodded slightly. "Good night."

Then he was gone, out into the night, and she was alone.

He possessed a key, so he didn't bother to knock. He simply entered Anne's residence. No servants were about. A single lamp waited on the entryway table. He knew where he'd find her this late. He grabbed the lamp and took the steps two at a time. At the landing he set the lamp on another table and extinguished the flame. Opening the door, he entered Anne's bedchamber.

Lounging on a chaise, she was reading a book. He'd expected her to be miffed with his tardiness. But they had no set hours, no formal arrangement. He came and went as he pleased, and she welcomed him as it suited her. On occasion they attended the theater or an opera. They had planned to meet each other at various balls this Season, perhaps even to arrive together. They made no secret of their liaison.

She set the book aside and came to her feet. "I was afraid you weren't going to come tonight."

"I need you." He crossed the room in half a dozen strides, took her into his arms, and plundered her mouth. He skimmed his hands up and down her back, her sides, her bottom, acutely aware that she wore nothing beneath the silk. She moaned low. He threaded his fingers through her hair, holding her head, angling it so he could taste her more fully.

The entire day had been hell, nearly every moment of it spent in Claire's company. There was still an innocence to her, a sweetness, and yet there was also a strength. And her favorite color was blue. He'd had no idea. He knew Anne's favorite color. It was whatever was the most expensive. She loved her trinkets and her baubles. Because of Claire's dowry, he could shower Anne with them.

Claire. Claire. Claire. He didn't want to think about her anymore. But he seemed incapable of catapulting her from his mind. She was there even now. With Anne's lithe body pressed up against his. Tearing his mouth from hers, he swung away from her.

"Whatever's wrong?" she asked. He heard the confusion, her panting.

He was breathing just as heavily, his heart racing. She deserved the truth. Better to hear it from him than the gossips. He faced her, regretting any hurt his words might cause her. "My wife is in London for the Season."

He watched as displeasure crossed Anne's face. Her features were all defined lines and sharp angles, but they came together in a mosaic of beauty. "After all this time, why now?"

He knew the reasons didn't matter. He walked back over to her. "I know it'll be difficult, but her being here has nothing to do with me. She wishes to give her sister a Season."

"And you will play the role of dutiful husband?"

"I will do what I can to help her. I owe her that."

He'd never seen her with tears in her eyes. It was like a blow to his chest.

"I want to be more to you than I am," she said.

"You are everything." Reaching inside his jacket, he removed a slender black box and extended it toward her. He held his breath while she glared at the object as though it were vile. Finally, she snatched it from him and opened it. Inside was nestled a necklace of emeralds. "It's gorgeous."

She looked up at him then, more tears welling. "But it's not enough."

Pressing her body against his, she cradled his jaw. In a low, provocative voice, she said, "I will do anything to have you. Will you say the same of me?"

"Anne—"

"Be rid of her."

"An annulment is not possible. A divorce will create a scandal that—" The words lodged in his throat as she cupped him intimately and began a slow, seductive massage that he knew from experience concluded with her talented mouth doing wicked things no wife would do.

"Surely, you must admit that I'm worth scandal."

Oh, yes, she was worth scandal . . . and a good deal more.

Chapter 7

~~~~~~∞~~~~~~

Sipping a Bordeaux, Claire sat on the floor in the library and listened to the residence settling in for the night. A creak here, a moan there. She'd done the same a thousands times at Lyons Place. She'd drawn comfort from the noises, had felt she was absorbing some part of her husband's history. But here—he had very little history here.

Cooper made a small snuffling sound. He was asleep, his head resting on her lap. She wore her nightgown and wrap, her hair braided and draped over one shoulder. Having prepared for bed, she'd been unable to sleep, so she'd come in search of something to help her relax. It seemed her husband had quite the collection of spirits. The wine slid down her throat smoothly, warming her almost as much as the fire. With her back against the chair, she wiggled her bare toes and tried not to wonder what Westcliffe might be doing. It was past midnight, and Claire was fairly certain he was engaged in some sort of errant behavior. She was going to demand his fidelity while she was in London. She had dealt with overbearing estate managers and surly staff whose loyalty had been to the master of the manor rather than the mistress. She'd won them all over with a firm but fair hand. She'd dealt with unhappy tenants and villagers who attempted to cheat her.

What was one irascible husband compared to that?

She heard the *snick* of the door opening, followed by a heavy tread—

Her heart barely sped up. The wine she supposed. She was almost finished with her second glass, and her pours were generous.

"Claire? What the deuce are you doing here?"

She glanced up at him. From this angle he appeared to be a foreboding giant. It might not be the best time to lay out her rules, especially as her mouth had begun to tingle. She wondered if his kisses made a lady's mouth tingle. When Stephen had kissed her, he'd simply pushed his mouth into hers, bruising her lips against her teeth. What had either of them known of kissing then? What did she know of it now?

"Don't you remember?" she asked, striving to concentrate on the question. "I came here to give my sister a Season."

He crouched, his elbows resting on his thighs, his large hands clasped together. She couldn't help but recall the feel of those hands, his fingers especially, against her skin. He hadn't even been trying to seduce her, and yet she'd been seduced. Little wonder he'd developed a reputation in that regard.

His brow furrowed, his eyes narrowed. "Are you foxed?"

"Absolutely . . . not."

He released a dark chuckle. She didn't like the way it shimmered through her, as though they were sharing a private moment. His knees popped as he straightened and moved beyond her sight. Peering around the chair, she could see him at the table. When he turned, he was holding a glass and the bottle of wine. She moved quickly out of his sight.

"Playing hide-and-seek, Claire?" he asked as he dropped to the floor, pressing his back against the chair opposite hers, stretching out his long legs until his feet reached past her hips. "You were much better at it when you were younger."

She realized she was indeed foxed because he sounded almost amused, amiable. It could only be the influence of the wine making her think so. "How would you know? You never played with us."

Leaning forward, he filled the bowl of her goblet. "That didn't mean I wasn't aware of what you were doing."

He poured wine for himself, then settled in against the seat of his chair. She couldn't help but notice how his long fingers held the bowl of the glass—in the same manner that he might clasp a breast. These intimate thoughts had never haunted her before. They were no doubt a result of the mortification he'd put her through last night.

"You seem to have won Cooper over," he said quietly, further creating a sense of intimacy between them. Or was it simply the wine? She should stop drinking.

She skimmed her fingers over the dog's head. "I think he was simply lonely. I know what it is to be lonely. I'm certain once he wakes up, he'll return to your side."

"Were you lonely at Lyons Place?"

She lifted her gaze from the dog. She saw no mockery in Westcliffe's eyes, only true curiosity. "Wasn't that your purpose in leaving me there?"

"My purpose was to keep you out of my sight. You seemed to welcome the idea. I didn't even see you when I visited the manor."

She sipped the wine, felt it tripping over her tongue. "The first winter you were there, I could see your bedchamber from mine." The manor was built in the shape of a U. She lived in the east wing while he'd taken up residence in the west. It was very easy to avoid him. The first night, she'd peered between the draperies in her room and watched him undress. She'd been amazed by the clarity of the view. She'd watched as his body had been unveiled—toned muscles, flat stomach, rounded buttocks. He'd turned, she'd slammed her eyes closed, and when she'd dared to open them again, he was standing at the window, visible from the waist up, his arms stretched high over his head as though he'd been gripping the window casing.

"You seemed to put yourself on display. Were you aware I was watching?"

Instead of answering her, he raised a knee, draped his wrist over it, swirled his wine, and asked, "What did you see?"

"Nearly everything." Feeling the heat suffuse her face, she turned her attention to the fire and watched the low flames dancing.

"I didn't know which room you'd taken," he said. Then he taunted her, "Did you like what you saw?"

She peered at him beneath her lashes. So much easier to admit the truth when she didn't meet his gaze directly. "I was conflicted. Part of me was glad you didn't consummate our marriage on our wedding night, and part of me wondered if it would have been so awful."

"I assure you it would not have been awful. I was quite experienced by then."

"Yes, I know. I'd heard. I think that was part of what terrified me. You were accustomed to women who knew what they were about, and I was not accustomed to men."

Setting his goblet aside, he wrapped his hands around her feet, placed them on his thigh, and began kneading the soles. She'd have pulled them away, but they'd grown cold, in spite of the fire, and his hands were so remarkably warm. "I had no plans to ravish you like a barbarian."

And she wondered if he'd have touched her like

this: slowly, deliberately, sensuously, as though his thumbs and fingers were well versed in how to manipulate every aspect of her feet so her entire body felt each touch.

"As I said last night, I was a silly girl." She took a large gulp of her wine. She'd also been a coward. After catching a glimpse of him in the flesh that first winter, she'd moved across the hallway to avoid the temptation of watching him again. Afterward, she'd avoided him every time he visited, each year longer and more desolate than the one that came before. Servants alerted her whenever he came to the estate, and she kept to her rooms, to her wing. It wasn't difficult to avoid him in the monstrosity that was Lyons Place.

Last winter she'd been gazing out the window of her bedchamber when she'd noticed a man striding toward the stables. She'd asked her lady's maid who he was. Judith had glanced out the window, and said, "Why it's his lordship."

He'd looked broader than she'd remembered. Taller. His hair longer. She didn't know why she'd thought he'd remain unchanged through the years. She certainly hadn't.

But to see him now, she thought of the two of them that he'd changed the most. He'd left all evidence of boyishness behind. He was a man to be reckoned with, a man who exuded power and influence. There was a calm confidence about him that had been lacking before. He knew who he was, knew his place. It was more intoxicating than the wine. She was weary of dissecting the past. He'd said he no longer wanted her, and yet his presence, his interest in her feet seemed to indicate otherwise.

"It was very kind of you to consent to allowing Beth and me to reside here for the summer," she said.

"You make me sound as though I'm a tyrant."

She peered up at him again, only this time she met his gaze fully and gave him the smallest of smiles. "I always thought of you as one. Quite often I model my villains after you."

He arched a brow. "Your villains?"

"For my own amusement, I often write stories."

"Do I gobble up little children in your stories?"

She laughed self-mockingly, and blamed the wine for the words that escaped. "You drag the heroine away to your castle. She's not very bright. She always falls madly in love with you."

"I'm not quite certain if I should take that as a compliment or an insult."

"Don't give it much credence either way. They're just the musings of a silly girl."

"You're not a girl any longer, Claire. Last night was proof enough of that."

She'd had far too much wine because she thought the heat from the fire had jumped into his eyes. But surely that wasn't possible. "I've heard that you've taken a hundred lovers since we were married."

His dark laughter reverberated around them. "I

assure you the numbers are vastly exaggerated."

She pulled her feet free of his grasp. Cooper stirred and rolled away from her. She missed the comfort of any touch. Still she plowed ahead. "But you have taken lovers."

"Our marriage was not consummated. I was a husband in name only. You assured that when you allowed my brother into your bed. If you truly knew my reputation, you could not have expected celibacy of me."

Shaking her head, she finished her wine in one large gulp that nearly choked her. She waited as the warmth diffused through her. She met his gaze. "Who is she? The lady who smells of lilac."

"None of your concern."

"You were with her earlier."

He finished off his own wine. "I didn't want her to hear from the gossips that my wife was in London."

"But you have no qualms about your wife hearing from the gossips that you have lovers? Do you care for her?"

"I'd not spend time with her if I didn't."

"Do you intend to flaunt her in front of me?" She felt the tears burn her eyes and forced them back.

He studied her for the longest before saying, "If you knew me at all, you'd know the answer to that."

"But I don't know you, Westcliffe, any more than you know me. That is the very reason behind the debacle of our marriage." His gaze was hard, almost unforgiving, but she didn't sense that he was angry with her. Rather he was striving to come to terms with something.

Quite abruptly, he was standing over her. "No, Claire, I do not intend to flaunt her." Bending down, he lifted Cooper into his arms with all the gentleness that one would cradle a child.

Then he was striding from the room, and it was all Claire could do not to call him back.

After settling Cooper into his favorite chair for the night, Westcliffe began removing his clothes, paused, and grinned. His wife, who had feared her wedding night, had watched him undress. He remembered that first night back at Lyons Place and the sense he'd had of being watched. Little voyeur. Perhaps he should have offered to disrobe in closer proximity.

He heard the door to her bedchamber close. He should have assisted her up the stairs. She might not have thought she was foxed, but she was. Otherwise, she'd have not spoken so candidly. Or perhaps she would have. She was correct. He didn't know her. Everything he knew about her had come from a distance.

He had known that she was the one he'd marry, and he'd assumed she'd fawn over him as all women did. Christ, he'd been an arrogant bastard in his youth to think he didn't have to woo her at all. He hoped the next man in her life would take more care with her.

He finished stripping down and went to the bathing room. Using water left in the washstand, he thoroughly washed up. When he was finished, he returned to his bedchamber and clambered into bed. He was about to extinguish the lamp when he caught sight of the sheet-covered easel, set at an angle so it faced his bed. "Don't look," Leo had ordered.

"Then you shouldn't have left it, whelp," Westcliffe murmured as he stretched across the bed, grabbed the sheet, and dragged it down. What he saw shocked him. The artist had only etched in the lines, but he had a deft hand. Claire was looking up at Westcliffe with an expression of soft wonder while he was glowering down at her.

It was a formidable expression. Surely, he didn't appear that terrifying.

Easing back, he settled against the pillows and continued to study the portrait. Why had Leo chosen to capture that moment? They'd been looking at him for a good part of the sitting. He'd positioned them so the lighting highlighted their best features, so why this? Westcliffe would develop deep furrows in his brow if he wore that expression for every sitting.

His gaze came to rest on Claire. She still appeared young, wary . . . and yet defiant. She was not brittle like Anne. There was a vulnerability to her. Had he ever truly looked at her, studied her, come to know her?

He was still contemplating the artist's rendition of them when he heard a distant scraping sound. *What the devil?*

In spite of the wine that had made her lethargic, Claire couldn't sleep. Weary of rolling from one side of her bed to the other and staring at the canopy above her head, she'd decided that she might as well determine which bedchamber Beth would have when she arrived.

She'd settled on the one at the far corner, opposite the side where hers was. It provided Beth with the luxury of two sets of windows, and on days when the sun held, an abundance of sunshine. She wanted her sister's room and her stay to be as bright and cheerful as possible, and she sincerely doubted her husband would play a role in that endeavor.

Upon determining which room would best suit Beth—and place her the farthest from Westcliffe—Claire's next order of business was to rearrange the furniture. While she knew any sane woman would wait until the morning, when the footmen would be available to assist her, her very presence in Westcliffe's residence claimed her to be insane, and so she began pushing a chair from the sitting area by the fireplace to a spot in front of the window. How much lovelier it would be to sit in the sun during the summer. She was breathing heavily when she finally had the chair in place. Tucking behind her ear the strands that had worked their way loose of her braid, she charged back over to the sitting area and began shoving the next chair—

"What the devil are you doing?"

She came up so abruptly that she nearly wrenched her back. And she realized that her breathing had not been hard at all, because suddenly drawing in a breath was near impossible. Her husband stood just inside the doorway, wearing nothing except his trousers and a shirt tucked into them. Thank goodness, he'd buttoned his trousers, but he'd not buttoned his shirt, and it hung open to reveal a good part of his chest—displaying a light sprinkling of dark, curling hair. Obviously, she'd not seen as much detail as she'd thought when she'd observed him from her window that long-ago night. Or perhaps he'd only recently acquired it. But it added such an alarming allure of masculinity to his physique. His feet were bare and so large. Why did wearing boots not make them seem so big? Even from this distance, she could see that the ends of his hair were damp, curlier than usual. He should have looked boyish, but nothing about him was anything except manly.

"I, uh—" She cleared her throat. "I was preparing the room for Beth."

His dark eyebrows drew together. "Is she arriving in the early hours of dawn?"

"No, not for a few more days. But I couldn't sleep so I thought I might as well . . ." She let her voice trail off.

"What is your obsession with moving my furniture around?"

So he'd noticed the parlor, yet hadn't said anything. She wondered what else he might not have commented on. "I can barely tolerate the haphazard way it's arranged."

"Haphazard?"

"The sitting area in front of the fireplace is cluttered with chairs. Why would anyone entertain so many in a bedchamber?"

He arched a brow at her.

"A lady does not," she snapped, assuming he had been with women who entertained a good many men at one time in their chambers. "So I decided to make two sitting areas."

"And it couldn't wait until morning?"

"I couldn't sleep."

"Then read a book. Something quiet."

"I'm sorry. Did I wake you?"

Instead of answering her, which seemed to be a nasty habit of his, he strode toward her. She skittered back without thinking, cursed her cowardice, then stepped forward. For a moment, the way his mouth moved, she thought he'd been entertaining the notion of a smile. Bending down, he lifted the chair. "Where do you want it?"

"Oh . . . by the window." She stared at the play of muscles over his back, the way his shirt stretched across them, and wondered what it might feel like to run her hands over them. Like touching warm marble perhaps. Silky and smooth.

When he'd set down the chair, she hurried over and angled it in relation to the other—with his help. At his nearness, the first thing she noticed was that he no longer carried the faint fragrance of lilac that had been with him earlier. Instead, his scent was dark and masculine, true to him.

To her surprise, he continued to assist her—carrying over two tables, then rearranging the pieces of furniture that remained near the fireplace. When they were finished, she looked at the room from the doorway. "Oh, yes, that's so much more pleasant."

She walked to the foot of the bed and studied one side of the room, then the other. Smiling with satisfaction, she said, "Beth will be happy here."

"As long as she isn't so happy she has no desire to leave," Westcliffe said, standing by one of the windows, his arms crossed over his chest.

"Oh, I'm certain she'll be as anxious to leave as I am."

His jaw clenched, and she wished she could take the words back, but surely after the welcome he'd given her and the demands he'd outlined, he couldn't possibly think she relished being here.

She fought not to tremble as his gaze wandered over her. What was he searching for when he looked at her like that?

He walked forward, and she felt the back of her legs hit the bed. He tucked strands of hair behind her ear. "When your hair is not braided, it must be much longer."

"Yes."

"Is it long enough to reach your waist?"

She was having a difficult time drawing in a breath with him so near, still she managed, "Longer."

"To your hips?"

She nodded.

He dropped his gaze to her hips, then lifted it to her mouth. "Your first kiss. Why didn't you ask me to give it to you? I was the one you would marry, and well you knew it."

While his expression was still hard, uncompromising, she sensed no anger there but a dark curiosity. How could he not understand the reasons? How could she explain them?

"I was ten, a child," she said softly. "You were already a man. I saw you talking with my father and Lynnford and other adults, and you seemed completely comfortable with them, their equals. While the eight years separating us does not seem such a great span of years now, when I was ten I despaired of ever catching up to you. When you were eighteen, would you have wanted to kiss me?"

She could see him considering her words, the realization taking shape that a chasm of years had separated them in their youth. With each passing year, the chasm narrowed, until at last he didn't seem all that much older.

And then she heard herself say, so boldly that she couldn't quite believe it was her voice, "I would very much like to know what your kiss is like."

It seemed to be all the invitation he needed. Before she could react, he'd wrapped an arm around her, drawn her up flush against his body, and begun a slow, seductive plundering of her mouth. He was not forceful, but he was insistent, his tongue enticing her lips to part. He tasted wicked, of something darker than the wine she'd drunk earlier. Her body hummed, erupting with pleasure, like little bubbles in champagne, cascading through her, popping along her nerve endings. She clung to Westcliffe, because to do otherwise would see her on the floor in a pool of muslin. He took her strength while at the same time granting her energy. It was the most marvelous thing she'd ever experienced.

He released a grating growl, then his hand was cradling her cheek, his thumb beneath her chin, tilting her head back slightly, altering the angle of the kiss so that his tongue delved more deeply. Hearing a restrained whimper, she realized that it came from her. She wanted to crawl up his body, wrap her legs around him. She felt pressure building between her thighs and wanted to push herself against him. What was wrong with her? Where were all these wanton thoughts and feelings coming from?

He glided his hands over her as though intent on memorizing every dip and curve, and with each stroke her body swelled with need. Heat built, desire flourished. She'd not expected this, this rampant yearning. It was far more intense than anything she'd experienced, and the strangest thought darted through her mind: that she wished she'd had this on her wedding night. For there was no denying the powerful need to take this journey to its rightful destination.

He cupped both hands around her bottom, pressed her firmly against him, her stomach molding around the hard ridge of his desire. She thought she should have been frightened. Instead, she wanted to explore him with the same furor. Oh, he was skilled at stirring passion, and all she'd feared retreated in the wake of overpowering sensations. He was like the storm, powerful and determined, that altered everything in its path, drenching thirsts and causing leaves to dance.

There was no hope for it. Whatever he wished of her—with the penetrating stroke of his tongue, the titillating touch of his fingers—he caused her to wish for herself. She wanted to follow these sensations to their fruition. She wanted to follow him.

With an abruptness she'd not expected, he broke off the kiss. Breathing harshly, his face flushed, his brow coated with dew, his eyes burning with a terrifying passion, he ground out through clenched teeth, "What you had before was the kiss of a boy. That is the kiss of a man."

While she, gasping for breath, sank down onto the edge of the bed, he strode to the door. "Where are you going?" she forced out, her voice as weak as her body.

He stopped and glanced back at her over his

shoulder, all fires banked, nothing but icy disdain now reflected in his features. "This changes nothing between us."

Then he disappeared, and she wondered how he could be so unaffected—when, for her, it had changed everything.

Christ! Standing in the tub in the bathing chamber, he dunked what water remained in the washbasin over his head. He told himself that it was because he'd left Anne without his needs satisfied. He'd been a tinderbox of desire ready to ignite with the smallest flame. But if he were honest, it was more than that. Claire had tasted sultry, the wine on her tongue more intoxicating than any he'd sipped from a glass. Her reaction had been instantaneous, passionate, and heated. She'd not been coy. She'd not held back.

It unsettled him to think she might have given him the first honest kiss he'd ever received.

It wasn't possible. He had more than a dozen years of knowing various women's mouths, yet he couldn't recall a single one that had been more alluring, that had made him want to draw out her pleasure as well as his. He'd never wanted simply to kiss a woman over and over. He'd wanted to sit down, draw her onto his lap, and kiss her. He'd wanted to lay her down and continue playing his mouth over hers.

A kiss was a prelude, but with her it had been as satisfying as anything that might have followed.

Grabbing a towel, he scrubbed it over his hair as he walked into his bedchamber, slamming the bathing-room door behind him. He stripped out of his wet clothes, poured himself a drink, downed it, and crawled into his bed. Stuffing his hands behind his head, he stared at the canopy.

Slowly, inch by inch, his gaze followed the unwanted path until he was once again scrutinizing the etching. Leo had perfectly captured the shape of Claire's tantalizing mouth. Even now in dark gray, it still managed to ensnare him.

He could very possibly go bloody well mad before this Season saw its final ball.

Chapter 8

~∞~

Westcliffe had left word with Willoughby that he was to be notified the moment the duchess's carriage pulled to a stop in front of his residence. Therefore, he was nearly to the front door as Leo walked through it.

"My lo—"

Westcliffe abruptly halted his greeting by grabbing him by the scruff of the collar and hauling him to the parlor. The man was only a few inches shorter, but the way Westcliffe was feeling at that moment, he doubted even a man who towered over him could have dissuaded him from his purpose.

He was in a foul mood. He'd gone to bed aching with need. He'd intended merely to play his lips over Claire's, give her a sampling of his kiss, but somewhere along the way his intentions had wandered off course. It had been too late to go to Anne or any other woman. So his frustration over what had happened with Claire was still harping at him, and he needed to unload it somewhere. Unfortunately for Leo, he was about to be the unlikely recipient. Westcliffe slung the young man into the room and closed the door behind them before advancing on him.

That Leo merely straightened his attire while standing his ground spoke well of him, but it did nothing to lessen Westcliffe's temper.

"What the devil do you think you're attempting to convey with that portrait?" Westcliffe demanded.

Leo merely smirked. and sank into the nearest chair. "I told you not to look at it."

"You knew damned well that I would."

Leo shrugged as though he couldn't be bothered to care what Westcliffe thought or felt.

"That scowl does not flatter me."

"Then I suggest you not scowl."

Before he planted his fist in the young man's fair face, Westcliffe strode away, then swung back around. "Why that moment? Why did you choose to outline that particular moment?"

"Because it was the only one that revealed any emotion. I care little about the outer shell of those I put on canvas. I attempt to reveal the inner soul."

Westcliffe braced his arms on either side of the man's head where it rested against the back of the chair. "You won't much like what you'll find in my soul, so stop digging into it. You will paint as we are posed or not paint at all."

Leo's mouth formed a cunning smile. "Interesting. Yesterday you wanted me not to paint at all. Now you give me a choice. Perhaps you welcome the excuse to be so near your wife."

Did this man not recognize a threat when it was delivered? And he didn't wish to be near his wife. He did not desire her. He did not want her. He shoved himself back. "You know nothing."

"As you wish, my lord. I'm merely an ignorant painter."

The door opened, and Westcliffe moved even farther away.

"Oh, you're here, Leo," Claire said. Her gaze darted to Westcliffe, and he could have sworn her cheeks took on a pink hue before she turned her attention back to Leo. "Are we going to have another session?"

"I believe we are," Leo said, coming out of the chair.

Westcliffe watched as he approached Claire and pressed a kiss to the back of her hand. He knew he shouldn't feel any jealousy, and yet he did. He'd be rid of her come the end of the Season. What did he care who touched her, who kissed her? But for now, she was still his wife.

"Whenever you are ready, my lord," Leo said, and escorted Claire from the room.

He followed them up the stairs, his gaze level with Claire's provocatively swaying hips, hips he'd cupped last night, hips he'd pressed against his. What had he been thinking? He'd been frustrated following his visit to Anne's because the distraction of his wife's arrival had prevented him from wanting Anne. Then his wife had enticed him with her innocent request for a kiss.

She wore the same gown as yesterday, while he'd not bothered to wear the same jacket, waistcoat, and cravat. He'd assumed Leo would go skittering away. He should have known better. His mother didn't suffer fools gladly. The fact that Leo had been her companion for some time now meant the man was no fool.

But neither did it mean that in this particular matter he was not serving as his mother's puppet.

Claire was acutely aware of the tension in Westcliffe as he stood behind her, his hand resting heavily at her shoulder, his thumb grazing the nape of her neck. She wondered if he was even aware of the constant stroking. Leo had already moved on to using the oils. She wondered how many afternoons she'd be forced to endure this heaven and this hell. It was strange to find herself intrigued by her husband, to want to know so much more about him. In particular how he could act as though the intimacy of talking and later kissing had never happened, when it was all she could think about.

Suddenly, she felt the brush of his fingers over her cheek as he captured the errant strands that had once again worked their way free of her pins.

"They never seem to stay caught," she said, wishing she didn't sound so breathless.

"They say when a woman's hair will not stay pinned that there is a wildness in her," Leo murmured.

She'd thought she'd spoken quietly enough that

only Westcliffe would hear her. "I'm not wild. I'm dreadfully dull."

Westcliffe's thumb stilled, and she wanted to glance back to see if he agreed.

"You never did answer my question yesterday," he said instead.

What had she not answered?

"The one about my intentions regarding your mother?" Leo asked calmly, and she realized the question had been directed at him. "I intend to marry her, my lord."

"That way lies heartache. She has only ever loved one man."

Claire swung her head around and up to look at Westcliffe only to discover that his gaze was focused on her. Her heart stuttered, and she wondered if he'd been focused on her the entire time. What was he thinking when he touched her hair, when his fingers skimmed over her skin.

"I assume you're referring to the Earl of Lynnford?" Leo inquired.

Because she was looking at Westcliffe, she saw the flash of surprise in his eyes before he concealed it behind his arrogant mask, and she was left to wonder how much of himself he hid from others. She'd have not expected him to help her move furniture around. She'd actually enjoyed sitting with him in the library last night. She'd certainly relished his kiss.

"Why would you say Lynnford?" Westcliffe asked, his voice flat, giving away nothing.

"Just before you were married, your mother commissioned me to paint your portrait. I've been with her for three years. Since Lynnford was named guardian of her three sons, and Ainsley has only just reached his majority, I've had occasion to see Tessa and Lynnford together. You're scowling again, my lord."

She watched as Westcliffe relaxed his facial muscles. She knew she should turn her attention back to the artist, but it was so much more fascinating to observe her husband.

"Why would you settle for a woman for whom you would always be second?" Westcliffe asked.

"I would not even be second, my lord. Her sons would come before me. But you see, what matters to me is that in my heart, she would always come first. I can imagine no happier life than to always hold near what I love most."

"Then I wish you your happiness, painter. But I suspect you'll not find it with my mother."

Claire was aware of the friction in the air, hovering between the two men. She wanted it to go away. "Westcliffe, I've been looking over the invitations you gave me. Were there any in particular you wished to accept?"

His gaze came again to rest on her. "Whichever suits you."

"I don't know these people. I never had a Season. Even at our wedding, I walked among strangers. I cannot discern which balls would be the most favorable to attend."

He seemed to give the matter considerable thought before saying, "The Duke and Duchess of Greystone. I believe theirs is next week. It will no doubt be the most well attended."

She gave him a tremulous smile. "Then we shall start there."

He furrowed his brow. "Did you attend no balls?"

She shook her head. "No. When would I have? I was married before what would have been my first Season."

His thumb began stroking her nape again, and her eyes almost drifted closed in wonder at the sweet sensation. "Sometimes I overlook how very young you were when we married. So this will be your first Season as well. I assume you dance."

"Yes. Father hired a teacher. I'm not sure why. I suppose to prepare me to take my place—" *Beside you.* Not where she wanted to lead the conversation now. "I'm grateful. Do you dance?"

"On occasion."

She could not help but notice that his gaze continually drifted down to her lips, which caused them to tingle in anticipation, as though he'd lowered his head to once again take her mouth. She seemed unable to stop her tongue from slipping out to soothe them, and she could see the smoldering passion in his eyes when she did. Did it take so little to arouse him? Only she wanted so much more: love, respect, trust. She wanted him to want her to be his wife again, only she had no idea how to gain that.

But at least they were talking. Late into the night. And he had kissed her. Surely, if he found her repulsive, he'd have not lingered.

"I received word from Beth this morning," she said. "She will arrive on the morrow."

"I'll not be available until sometime in the afternoon. I have an investor's meeting."

"In what did you invest?"

She saw his hesitation, and she realized that he was not accustomed to sharing much of himself. Did he fear her hurting him again? Did he fear another betrayal? How lonely it must be always to guard one's words, to constantly shelter one's heart. Was Claire exclusively to blame? Or was there more? Was there a reason beyond his age difference that he'd always seemed at the edge of his family? He came to Lyons Place at Christmas. Why did he not go to Grantwood Manor?

"Railways," he finally muttered, and she'd almost forgotten the question. "And shipping."

"I've never traveled on the railway. Have you?"

"Yes, it's quite remarkable."

"Where did you go?"

"To the seaside. To Brighton."

"You are such a man of the world. Perhaps I shall give it a go someday."

He gave a barely perceptible nod as though he couldn't imagine that she would carry through on the notion. He had such little faith in her. Perhaps she and Beth would go next week, just to show him that she had grown bolder. She craved his attention. Such a silly thing really.

"Will you be available for dinner tomorrow? It would make Beth feel most welcome."

"I shall strive to be here."

"Lovely. I'll have Cook prepare your favorites."

Abruptly, Westcliffe jerked his attention to Leo. Claire did the same and saw the young artist was leaning casually against the bedpost.

"If you're finished for the day, you could have alerted us," Westcliffe snapped.

"I did not wish to interrupt."

"You're meddling, painter. It's not your place."

"I'm aware of my place, my lord. It's at your mother's side."

"She'll not marry you, no matter how much you may wish it."

"Then I shall be content with whatever she grants me."

Again, Claire could feel the tension between the two men. She rose. "Leo, may we postpone these sessions until the Season is under way. I have so much left to accomplish and to help prepare Beth."

He bowed. "Of course, my lady. I shall take the canvas with me and work on what I can. Send word when you're again ready to pose."

"As I'm no longer needed, I have matters to which to attend," Westcliffe stated succinctly before striding from the room.

Claire knew she should leave as well. It was not appropriate for her to be alone in the bedchamber with another man. She almost laughed with the absurd thought. She should have realized that on her wedding night.

But the door was open. And Leo obviously had no interest in her other than as a subject for his art.

"Perhaps you would do a portrait of Beth," she said, to fill the quiet of the room.

He stopped in the midst of gathering his supplies and smiled at her. "I'd be delighted." Then he glanced at the doorway. "So what happened between you and his lordship after the duchess and I left last night and before I arrived this afternoon?"

"Whatever do you mean?"

"I notice the subtleties in people. Yesterday, I believe he wanted to wring your neck. Today, it appeared he desperately wished to lay his lips against it."

She felt the heat of embarrassment shoot through her, as well as a thrilling spark. Had the kiss meant more to him than simply a demonstration? She rubbed the nape of her neck where he had continually stroked her. "I'm certain you're mistaken."

His expression was kind, encouraging, and she comprehended why the duchess wanted him in her life.

"This Season is an opportunity for your sister to secure a husband. Perhaps it will serve the same purpose for you."

Tessa lay sprawled against Leo's side. She'd had numerous lovers in her life, but only one had meant more to her than he did. She knew what

Leo wanted of her, but she couldn't grant it. She was forty-five, and he was all of thirty. Her first husband had been twenty years older than she, but no one had considered it scandalous. Yet when a woman was much older than the man, Society frowned. And while she might thumb her nose at them in public, in private she worried that they'd eventually wear down Leo's affections for her.

"How were matters between my son and his wife today?" she asked, circling her finger over his chest while he casually stroked her arm.

"I think something happened between them."

"Of course it did. She betrayed—"

"No, I mean last night. I sensed a sensual tension in the air. He tried to ignore it by bantering with me."

"Do you think he's forgiven her?"

"No, but he might."

She sighed. "He won't forgive Stephen until he's forgiven her."

"Is that what this is about, Tessa? Are you trying to reconcile your sons?"

"It breaks my heart that they are at odds. They are brothers. They share the same blood."

"Only their mother's."

She stiffened, her lungs refusing to draw in air. Raising herself up slightly, she stared down on him. "Why ever would you say that?"

Reaching up, he threaded his fingers through her hair. "I know that the previous Earl of Westcliffe did not sire Stephen. Do your sons know?"

Wrapping the sheet around herself, she moved away from him as though separating herself from him would distance the truth. "I don't know what you're talking about."

Pushing pillows behind him, he sat up. "I'm an artist. I notice the smallest of details. I have painted Lynnford. I've also painted Stephen. Did you think I'd not notice the similarities? Does Lynnford know?"

Tears burned her eyes. "You can't tell him." Her voice was hoarse, rough. "He'd never forgive me."

"Tessa, I would never betray your trust."

She shook her head. "I could scarce believe when Ainsley named Lynnford to serve as guardian over the boys in the event of his death. I fell in love with Lynnford when I was married to Westcliffe. We had a brief affair. Westcliffe did not care. I'd given him his heir, and he had his own paramour. I had only just discovered I was with child when Lynnford informed me that he would no longer be involved with me. He was getting married, and he would not betray his wife. I think he always believed that Stephen was Westcliffe's. I never corrected him." She released a strangled laugh. "They were always at odds—father and son. I think because they are so much alike, but neither of them could see it. Oh, God." She buried her face in her hands. "I have carried that secret for so long."

He wrapped a hand around her foot. "Tell me," he urged.

She wanted so much to unburden herself,

to someone, and he was so dear. "I have never stopped loving Lynnford. And I have loved Stephen all the more because he is his son. And my other sons have suffered because of it. Especially Morgan. As much as I tried, I could never feel close to him. He was so distant—like his father. Stephen was such a joy, always wanting to snuggle."

Leo moved up and folded her within his embrace. "You were a child when you had Morgan."

"It is no excuse. Morgan paid the price. I do not even know if he is capable of love."

"He is. He is simply cautious."

She tilted her head back and peered at him through her tears. "Do you think Claire could love him?"

"All things are possible."

"I do not want him to be unhappy. I've been happy only twice in my life. When Lynnford was my lover—and now . . . with you."

"Marry me, Claire."

Her heart nearly broke with his hushed plea. She cradled his cheek. "No. I am not for you, my sweet."

"I shall prove you wrong."

As he brought her beneath him, she hoped he would. But she suspected her heart would not listen.

Chapter 9

The carriage traveled through the London streets with all due haste. The meeting had gone longer than Westcliffe had anticipated it would. It was only because he wanted to ensure that his sister by marriage felt welcomed that he'd urged the driver not to dally. It had nothing to do with the fact that his wife had seemed to want him there. He couldn't have cared less what she wanted. But still he was determined to be a good host.

Usually he enjoyed the meetings with the other investors. Today he'd found it tedious. He'd been anxious to leave. It was strange to find himself arranging his time around someone else. He had made one stop following the meeting: to purchase the bracelet that matched the necklace he'd given Anne earlier in the week. He'd not seen her since.

Last night, he'd had dinner with Claire, then retired to his library to read. It had begun to rain just before evening, and he found little more comforting than losing himself in a good book while the rain pattered against the windows. So he'd indulged. Although mostly he'd heard the moving about of furniture in the rooms above his head. What was it with Claire and this constant rearranging of things?

And why did it amuse rather than irritate him?

This morning, when he'd emerged from his bedchamber, the fragrance of flowers in the hallway had nearly knocked him off his feet. He'd never seen so many vases filled with assorted blossoms, sprinkled throughout the residence as though his wife wished to bring the gardens indoors. He supposed she was doing what she could to offset the dreary earth colors that he preferred. In retrospect, perhaps he was doing the same as she, only he was striving to mimic the country. At times, he missed Lyons Place. It wasn't enough to visit only once or twice a year. But the women were not as abundant. So he'd chosen London and left Claire at the estate.

From a practical standpoint it worked well because it made it convenient when Parliament was in session. Being in London also gave him leave to take a more active interest in his investments. The meeting this morning involved a small company of a dozen investors, their railway line only one of many that crisscrossed over the countryside. Years ago, it was the small companies that had provided the means to establish railways through Britain, but now the larger companies were buying them up. They'd had an offer and were divided regarding whether or not to take it. He suspected they would discuss, argue, and contemplate for months. But in the end, they would sell. And then he would look for something else in which to invest. He enjoyed the challenge of determining the perfect investment.

But still, just like his encounters with women, something was lacking.

He glanced out the window as his carriage turned into the circular drive in front of his residence and he nearly choked. Three coaches were lined up, each bearing trunks. He could see his footmen struggling to remove one from the first vehicle. Was Claire's sister traveling with an entourage? He was accustomed to peace and quiet in his household. Claire had disrupted it enough. And now this.

Reminding himself it was only temporary, he shored up his resolve to bring a hasty end to Beth's search for a suitable husband.

He caught a glimpse of Claire standing off to one side, her arm around a young woman he didn't recognize. Beth, no doubt. He'd not seen her in years. She'd not attended their wedding.

His carriage rolled to a stop. As he disembarked, he saw Claire draw her sister protectively against her side. Dear God, did she think him a monster? He shortened his stride to give himself more time to approach and observe the newest addition to his household. She greatly resembled Claire. Her hair was slightly lighter in shade, but as he neared, he could see that her eyes were just as blue. She had

Claire's small dollop of a nose, but her lips were neither as full nor as generous. Still, there could be no denying they were sisters—whereas he and his brothers hardly favored each other at all.

"My lord," Claire began, "you remember my sister—Lady Beth."

So damned formal. Because they were not family. They were not intimate. They were not even friends.

"Naturally. Lady Beth, welcome." He bowed slightly, took the young lady's hand, and pressed a kiss to her knuckles, which caused her to roll her shoulders almost to her chin and giggle.

"My lord, thank you so much for allowing me to stay in your residence. Claire informs me that I'm not to disturb you at all, and I swear to you that I shan't. I shall be as quiet as a mouse."

"I've never known a mouse to be quiet."

Her eyes widened, and she giggled again. "I suppose they aren't, are they?"

"As quiet as a pillow perhaps," Claire said, coming to her sister's rescue, and he realized there was a protectiveness about her. He didn't know why he didn't comprehend the extent of it sooner. It was the reason she was here—to save her sister from Hester.

"Oh, yes, a pillow," Beth repeated with more exuberance than he thought the comment deserved. "A much nicer image, really, as opposed to a mouse."

"Or a grave," he said solemnly, and she blinked with incomprehension. "I've heard 'quiet as a grave,'" he explained.

"That's rather macabre."

"Then quiet as a pillow shall suffice."

She smiled, an innocent smile, the smile of a child. How old was she? Older than Claire on the day they married? Had she been that young? "Then quiet as a pillow I shall be. But you must alert me if I disturb you in the least. I am simply so excited to be here that I can barely contain my joy."

He was on the verge of telling her to try when Claire said, "Come, dear, let's see to getting your trunks inside."

"Are all of these hers?" he asked.

"There are only three," Beth said. "And a few smaller bags. I need a proper wardrobe for the Season."

"Obviously, I know nothing at all regarding what a lady needs for the Season."

"Not to worry. I have it all well in hand."

"Come along, Beth." Claire took her sister's arm as though words were not sufficient.

Beth had taken two steps before spinning around so quickly he was surprised she didn't get dizzy and swoon. "We will see you at dinner, won't we?"

"Yes, of course."

"Splendid."

He had no reason not to follow, but he waited

until both ladies had disappeared inside. God help him, he thought it would be an improvement if she *were* only as quiet as a mouse.

"I can't believe I'm here! You should have seen my eyes on the journey. I'm certain they were as round as saucers. I was so young when I visited London with Father that I barely remember it. I want to see everything while I'm here."

They were sitting at the dining table with Westcliffe at one end, Claire at the other, and her sister between them. He was astounded that she managed to eat with her incessant prattling. He wasn't particularly irritated; simply amazed that she could speak for so long about absolutely nothing of any consequence. He was growing weary simply from listening. He couldn't imagine trying to carry on a conversation with her.

"Oh, I do hope that I have good fortune in finding a suitor. I don't suppose you know which of the lords are available."

He was taking a healthy swallow of wine when her attention came to bear on him. Setting his glass aside, he reached into his jacket pocket. "Yes, as a matter of fact, I've compiled a list."

His gaze darted to Claire, and he saw a flash of gratitude in her eyes. He wondered, if like him, she was already longing for a quieter dinner.

"Oh, this is absolutely marvelous. Claire, look." Beth set the paper on the table between her and her sister. "There are so many. Surely, surely I shall find one who suits." Tears glistened in her eyes when she glanced back at him. "I cannot thank you enough."

He wasn't quite comfortable with her appreciation. "I cannot vouch for their willingness to marry."

"I want someone who is pleasing to the eye," Beth said. "Do you consider all of these men handsome?"

He fought not to scowl. "I take little notice of their appearance."

"Do you know them, Claire?" she asked.

"I fear I do not, so we shall discover together if they are men of character."

"I prefer that they be men of wealth. Westcliffe, do you know of their financial situations?"

"No."

"You have a nice dowry, Beth," Claire said. "You do not need to concern yourself with their finances."

"Of course I do. I do not want a man to marry me for my money. If he has wealth, then I shall know for certain that he is marrying me for *me*."

"Whether he be rich or poor, Beth, he shall want to marry you for you."

"Father doesn't share your confidence."

"Don't be so melodramatic. He'd have not given you a Season otherwise."

The ladies settled into silent eating for all of fifteen seconds—he knew because he counted. He'd made a wager with himself that they'd not reach a minute of quiet before dinner was over.

Then Beth announced, "I can think of nothing worse than being married to Lord Hester."

"He's quite well-off as I recall," Westcliffe said. "And I believe he's only forty."

Beth glared at him. "My life will be ruined."

Such drama. Perhaps he would move to a hotel for the Season.

"I notice that Ainsley is not listed," Claire said, her eyes dancing with amusement. Was she teasing him? Or was she sensing his impatience with the banality of the situation? Granted, Hester was not particularly charming, but neither was the man an ogre.

"I can vouch for his unwillingness to marry," Westcliffe informed her.

"That is unfortunate," Beth said. "What fun we'd have if we were all in the same family!"

"I can scarcely imagine it." He heard a cough designed to cover a laugh coming from the other end of the table. He glanced at his wife. She was far too amused, and he found himself wishing that she'd released the laughter.

"Beth, dear heart," Claire began, "I believe you must curb your enthusiasm somewhat lest you frighten the young men away."

"Oh, I shall behave with the utmost decorum in public. But we're family. Surely a bit more levity is allowed."

"As long as we are not upsetting Westcliffe's digestion. I daresay he's not accustomed to the flightiness of young ladies."

"I daresay he is if the rumors I've heard from Cousin are to be believed."

He watched as Claire took great interest in the food remaining on her plate while her cheeks burned a bright red.

"I assure you, Beth," he said quietly, but firmly, "there is no truth in the rumors regarding me and young ladies." *Older ladies, mature ladies certainly. But young ones? No, not for some time now.*

Beth took the paper he'd given her earlier, folded it up, and tucked it beneath the sash at the waist of her dress. "I'm so grateful to hear it. I didn't believe them. Not really." She gave him a pointed look. "Truly, why would you seek out the company of another when you have Claire?"

Why indeed? And he realized that while she'd heard rumors of his indiscretions, she wasn't aware of her sister's. Not unusual. As those who knew about it—the members of his family—were not prone to gossip.

"When Claire showed me around the residence, I noticed that you had a pianoforte. To show my appreciation for all you've done for me thus far, may I play it for you this evening?"

Surely she couldn't speak while she played. "I would like that very much."

Within five minutes, Westcliffe realized that he shouldn't make assumptions about young women. Beth could indeed play and speak at the same time, and she seemed intent on revealing the history of each tune that tripped lightly from her fingers.

"Did you think she would be silent while playing?" Claire asked quietly as she handed him a snifter of brandy.

"The thought had occurred."

She smiled with obvious amusement and something inside him shifted, teetered, made him feel as though his world were tilting. He'd always liked her smiles, but he felt as though this was the first truly genuine one she'd given him since she'd arrived. He didn't know what to make of it or his feelings about it. He held tightly to the snifter, knowing he was in danger of crushing the glass, but he needed something to anchor him. Her eyes were soft, as though they were friends sharing an intimate secret, and he wondered if they'd appear the same if they were sharing darker intimacies. He felt an absurd desire to take her mouth, to—

"Claire, please come turn the sheets of music for me. It ruins my playing to have to do it myself. You could even sing while you're over here. Have you heard her sing, my lord? She has the voice of a nightingale."

Claire's luscious mouth twisted as she rolled her eyes. Was she embarrassed by the praise? Or was she simply unaccustomed to receiving it? He'd certainly never complimented her. Anne could barely stand to go five minutes without hearing words of adoration, and if he wasn't extolling her virtues, she was—constantly reminding him of her worth.

Claire took her place, standing near enough to

where Beth sat so she could easily follow along with the music and turn the pages aside. Observing the sisters so closely together, he noted that Beth possessed a youthfulness that had long since left Claire. He thought of the manor and how much more efficiently things were managed there now. No leaking roofs. No dirty windows. No overgrown gardens. She'd even purchased a couple of mares. According to the groomsman, she loved to ride. He'd never gone riding with her. Had done nothing of any consequence with her actually.

His musings were interrupted as the sweetest voice filled the room. Claire was singing. He'd never thought anything would be more beautiful than her laughter. He'd been wrong. Of late, he was discovering that he'd been wrong about a great many things. Her broad smile was almost a perfect match of Beth's, and yet Claire's seemed brighter. There was a joy, an easiness about her that he'd never seen. She was still wary of him.

He'd never played with her, he'd barely spoken to her. She'd always seemed like a child. Last night, when she'd spoken of the years separating them, she was correct.

He'd only recently begun to recognize her as a woman. Even on the day they'd married, he'd considered her a young girl, barely a woman.

Swallowing his brandy, he found himself wondering if he was as responsible for the debacle of their marriage as she.

* * *

Unbelievably weary, Claire walked through the garden in the moonlight, with the occasional gaslight illuminating her way. She'd forgotten how Beth could wear her down. For a while, she'd feared her sister's excitement would not calm enough for her to fall asleep. But eventually she'd closed her eyes, and soon after she'd ceased her prattling. Growing up, they'd shared a bed, and it had always amazed Claire that Beth would fall asleep talking and immediately upon awaking, begin speaking again. Sometimes even completing a sentence or thought from the night before.

She'd also forgotten how delightful it was to sing. With no audience, she'd stopped lifting her voice in song. Only tonight had she realized that she was audience enough. She came to a startled halt at the sight of the shadowy figure sitting on a bench near the roses. "Westcliffe. I thought you'd left."

When she returned downstairs after seeing Beth to bed, she'd not seen him in the library, a bit perturbed with herself because she'd actually been seeking his company. She'd assumed that he'd gone to spend the remainder of his evening with Lilac—or whatever the deuce her name was. It had astounded her that he'd stayed in residence the night before. She'd warned herself not to grow accustomed to his presence, and yet she couldn't deny the spark of gladness at the sight of him.

"No, just out for a walk with Cooper. This is as far as he can get these days."

She'd taken her turn about the garden going in the opposite direction. She wondered how long he'd been sitting on that bench. "Where is he?"

"Lying beneath the rosebush over there. Not certain why he favors it, but he does."

"Perhaps he has a bone buried in the vicinity."

"I suppose that's as good an explanation as any." To her immense surprise, he slid over and said, "You're welcome to join me."

She considered excusing herself and going on, but it was such a lovely night. And they seemed to have reached some sort of truce. She sat, but the bench was narrower than she realized. He lifted his arm and set it along the back, the action seeming to free up a little more space for her. "I'm sorry about Beth," she said softly. "She's simply so excited about London and her Season. She won't talk quite so much once she settles in."

Feeling his fingers stroking the sleeve of her dress, she wondered if he always felt a need to touch a woman when she was near. She wished it was she he desired, wished she knew how to bring that result about.

"She seems so remarkably young. How old is she?" he asked.

"She'll be eighteen come November."

"Considerably older than you when you married."

He seemed mystified by the knowledge. "Not so much. Half a year or so."

"Still, you did not appear so young. Perhaps because I was as well."

"And now we are so terribly old."

His smile, so white, flashed in the shadows. She wished it had stayed longer so she might have had a chance to commit it to memory.

His fingers continued to thrum over her arm, and she wished she were wearing the gown that had no sleeves. Oh, it did seem to be a night for wishing. But the evening air was cool, and she'd have been shivering by now.

"Willoughby informs me you arrived with only one trunk," he stated as though she'd been involved in something untoward.

She was taken aback. "Why ever would he discuss my trunk with you?"

"Because I inquired. Your sister requires three trunks for the Season, and you do not?"

She laughed lightly. "She is in the market for a husband. I am not. I have a gown to wear to the balls, one for dinner. It's enough."

"Have another made. Have half a dozen. My wife doesn't need to wear the same gown to every affair."

"I don't need them. No one will be paying any attention to me."

"I care not. I can well afford it."

She fought back her disappointment because she'd secretly hoped that he'd confess that *he* would pay attention to her. She saw no point in arguing further. She'd simply not go to the dressmaker's. "At the estate, I can see the stars so clearly.

The same cannot be said here. When the fog is not in the way, the lights seem to be."

Silence eased in around them. She found comfort in it. She could scarcely remember what it was about him that she'd feared.

"I can't recall if I ever told you how much I appreciated how you managed the estate," he said.

"I didn't think you'd noticed."

"I noticed."

She sensed true gratitude in his voice, but he also seemed uncomfortable offering the praise, so she sought to put him at ease. "I enjoy it. It fills my days, gives me purpose."

"Perhaps the next time I visit, you'll not go into hiding."

She fought back her smile. "Perhaps I'll give you a tour. I suspect there are things you overlooked."

"I doubt it. What I noticed most was the . . . warmth." He shook his head. "I can't explain it, but I can feel it happening here. Must be the heat from the friction generated by you moving all that furniture around."

Was he teasing her? She was startled by the pleasure she took in it. Releasing a light laugh, she admitted, "I don't know why I do that so much. But I always have. I think perhaps it's because the placement of furniture is something I can control. I could never control my father's temper or the force of his hand when he struck me—"

"He struck you?"

She felt the heat of shame burn her cheeks. "When he was not pleased with me, yes."

"Did you think I'd strike you? Is that why you feared me?"

"Oh, no. You terrified me but not in the manner my father did. With you, it was more . . . an uncomfortableness regarding the intimacy we'd share. I simply wanted to know you a bit better."

His hand came up, settling at the nape of her neck, his thumb coming around to stroke the delicate underside of her chin. Heat traveled down to her toes. The gown without sleeves might have sufficed after all.

"Tell me, Claire, if you'd had a Season, what would you have looked for in a suitor?"

She peered over at him, surprised by his interest. She wondered to what degree Beth's arrival had put their situation into a different perspective for him. "I would have wanted someone who made me laugh, I think."

"Strange you should say that as I always thought your laughter was your most compelling feature. Stephen was adept at making you laugh."

"Yes, he could. His was such a fun-loving nature, although he could be a bit of a scamp."

"A scoundrel, more like. But he has always charmed the ladies."

"No more than you."

"I seem to have failed in that regard when it came to you."

"I think only because I was still on the cusp between being a girl and a lady."

Curling his fingers, he grazed his knuckles lightly over her cheek. "Observing your sister tonight made me realize exactly how young you were when we married. But now you're certainly no longer a girl."

They sat there for what seemed like forever, the only motion his slow stroking of her face. They were enclosed in shadows, only a hint of distant light to outline their silhouette, and yet she could feel the intensity of his gaze—as though he were striving to understand every aspect of her, as though nothing mattered more than this moment between them. She thought she was beginning to understand how women fell so easily under his spell.

When a lady had his attention, she had all of it.

"We should probably go in," he said quietly.

She nodded.

"The fog should roll in soon," he continued.

She nodded again, not at all anxious to leave, wanting to explore what was happening between them without any words, as though they were communicating on a more primal level. Her heart thumped erratically, and she desperately wanted him to lean in and kiss her.

Was he nearer? Was he going—

"It's late," he said, abruptly standing and breaking the spell.

For an insane moment, she almost flung her arms around him, lifted up onto her toes, and kissed *him*. He'd said he no longer wanted her, even though his recent actions seemed to indicate otherwise. But if he rebuffed her, she'd die of mortification.

He gave a low whistle, and she heard the rustling of plants as the dog limped out and fell into step beside his master. She was amazed at the consideration Westcliffe gave Cooper, his steps shorter, slower.

"Why not carry him?" she asked.

"When stairs are involved I do. Otherwise, well, the old boy has some pride."

Like you, she thought. She'd never considered before what it had cost him to need her dowry, then to find his brother in her bed. How was it that in only a few nights, she was coming to understand him far better than she had in all the years that had come before?

Chapter 10

Dinner was a dreadfully dull affair. He wondered why he'd never before noticed. The only noise was the occasional scraping of silver over china. He was half tempted to suggest Anne hire an orchestra for his next visit. He could hardly countenance that he missed the incessant chattering when he dined with Claire and Beth although he knew it was the laughter that most pleased him. Claire was releasing it more frequently. Sometimes it resembled the tinkling of crystal chandeliers caught in a slight breeze, and other times it sounded as though it rose from the well of her soul.

He'd not expected to miss it so much when he'd decided to join Anne for dinner this evening. He'd been neglecting her, and the guilt had begun to gnaw at him. She'd not asked for this intrusion on their plans for the Season.

"We could go to Paris," she suddenly said, and he jerked his attention away from the wine that was almost the red of Claire's lips, realizing with regret that although he was in attendance, he was still managing to neglect his paramour.

"We could go to Paris," she repeated as though she understood that he'd not been paying attention. "Your wife and her sister can stay in your residence, have their Season, and we'll return when they're on their way back to the cows."

"Is that your opinion regarding my estate?"

"I did not mean to insult. I've never been to your estate, so I have no opinion of it." She gave him a smile. "Paris?"

"I can't. I have matters I need to see to here."

He watched as displeasure crossed her face. She began slathering butter on her bread. "Then stay with me in my residence while she's in London."

"I'll not have her chase me out of my own house," he said. He'd paid a high price to possess it.

"I doubt you want me to be jealous either." She set her bread on the plate, and the knife clattered beside it. "I don't like that she's here. Already, our time together has been diminished." She heaved a sigh. "Perhaps I should have her to dinner."

For some inexplicable reason, Westcliffe's gut tightened. "I have no desire to flaunt what we have in front of her."

"You worry about hurting her?" He said nothing, and Anne laughed. "You could only hurt her if she cared for you, which she does not."

He ignored her biting words. The one thing he could say about Anne was that she was not demure. She was the most carnal creature he'd ever known, up for trying anything. Her sexuality always shimmered just below the surface, and it took very little to spark it to life. She credited his skills in the bedchamber, but he suspected it had more to do with her adventuresome spirit and the fact that she possessed no inhibitions at all.

She picked up her wineglass and swirled the red contents. "You will stay the night, won't you?"

"Not tonight, no."

"Then you'd best send me a very nice trinket tomorrow." She rose and, with a swish of angry skirts, began to walk from the room.

Reaching out, he grabbed her arm. "Anne—"

She looked down on him with the damned tears wallowing and threatening to spill over. He slipped his free hand into his jacket pocket, removed a velvet box, and set it on the table. "I will make everything up to you. I promise."

Capitulating quickly, she snatched up the box and opened it to reveal a diamond choker. "You do have such good taste." She slid her gaze to him. "You will understand if I must mope for a bit."

She glided from the room, and he was left to wonder why it was suddenly so difficult to appease two women: one he wished to be with, the other he did not. It should have been simple.

Instead, it seemed remarkably complicated.

During the fourth afternoon following Beth's arrival, she was presented at court—their father's rank having guaranteed her a presentation. The following days included a whirlwind of activity. In spite of the fact that she'd brought three trunks, Beth had bemoaned her lack of a truly exquisite gown for the first ball she'd attend. It had taken little to cajole Westcliffe into agreeing to purchase one for her—on the condition that Claire had one sewn as well. She'd not bothered to argue against it because on further reflection, following the night in the garden, she'd determined the gowns she did possess were sadly out of style. She'd also become determined to garner her husband's attention, and for that she required an arsenal of flattering clothing. The dressmaker and her ladies were working diligently to ensure that all the items purchased were finished as quickly as possible. So she and Beth spent a portion of their days involved in fittings. Then they shopped for hats and gloves and shoes.

Claire couldn't deny the joy it brought her to see Beth so hopeful and happy. But the first ball would be the true indication regarding her likelihood of finding a suitor.

Having only just awakened from a short nap, she had Judith assist her with her dress and hair. She was grateful for how busy she was helping Beth prepare for her Season. Westcliffe was often off seeing to business during the day. The evenings were a strange mixture. With rare exception, he joined them for dinner. What most surprised her was his tolerance of Beth's company. On occasion, he would play chess with her. More often she entertained them with the pianoforte. On the few evenings when he did leave the residence, it was always late—after Beth was abed. Claire would lie in her bed listening for his return. Some nights, he was as quiet as . . . the grave. And others he was as loud as an ox. On those nights she suspected him of being three sheets to the wind.

They'd settled into a comfortable tolerance. But since the night in the garden, she never found herself alone with him. Not for want of trying on her part. Strange to think that in such a short time, she had no desire at all to avoid his company. He still scowled too often, was far more serious than she thought any person should be, but she couldn't deny that he intrigued her.

After Judith finished arranging her hair, Claire walked down to Beth's bedchamber, only to discover it empty. Beth had obviously awoken from her nap sometime earlier. With a few discreet inquiries to servants she passed in the hallways, she picked up her pace and headed toward the library. As many times as she'd told Beth not to bother Westcliffe when he was there, her sister seemed intent upon not listening. She didn't seem to comprehend that if she fell out of his favor, her Season would come to an abrupt end.

But as she neared the open library door, she was as annoyed as she was surprised by the laughter, deep and masculine, floating out through it. Annoyed because it was not a sound he shared freely with her. Surprised because it was rich with the enjoyment of life.

Entering the library, she came up short at the

sight of her sister waving her fan in front of her face, opening it, closing it, touching it to West-cliffe's shoulder.

"Please," she pleaded.

His eyes crinkling, he smiled and shook his head. Had she ever seen him so relaxed, so obvi-ously enjoying himself? "The ones I know are not ones with which you need to become familiar." His gaze suddenly shot past her to land on Claire, and her heart began a strange gallop. "Ask your sister."

Beth glanced back at her, rolled her eyes, and released an impatient sigh. "She'll be of no help. She didn't have a Season. She knows nothing of flirtation."

She grew uncomfortable under his formidable gaze. He studied her as though he'd just discov-ered something profound.

"So what are you two about?" Claire finally asked, anything to break the tension that was mounting.

"I'm trying to learn the language of the fan, and your husband won't help. Claims he doesn't know anything that a respectable woman would use."

"I suspect that's true." She forced a lightheared-ness into her voice, and, based upon the sudden twitch of his mouth, she suspected he appreciated what she wasn't saying. That respectable women were not his forte. "But you are in luck, dear sister, because I do know various messages that the posi-tion of a fan can convey."

"Truly. That surprises me." But even as she spoke, Beth extended her closed fan.

"Just because I didn't have a Season doesn't mean I wasn't prepared." What she wasn't prepared for, however, was her husband hitching up one hip and settling on the corner of his desk, as though anticipating a show. "Come, Beth. I'm certain my husband is busy. We should adjourn to the parlor where—"

"Stay. Present your lesson here. Perhaps I'll learn something," he said laconically.

"I find it difficult to believe that you don't already know everything you need to know about the fan."

"As I confessed to Beth, nothing I know about it would be used in polite society." His eyes held a challenge and a glint of amusement.

With a flick of her wrist, she opened the fan and quickly closed it. "You are cruel."

His expression darkened. "Am I?"

She'd thought him so in the beginning, because he'd seemed so hard and unforgiving, but he'd done nothing to make Beth's stay unpleasant. Even her own was no longer as difficult as she'd anticipated. He possessed a kindness she'd not envisioned. She swallowed hard. "That's what the gesture conveys."

"Why would I ever use that?" Beth asked.

"Because some men are cruel. They take advantage and hurt you."

"I should think that if they took advantage or

hurt me, that waving a fan at them would be the very last thing I'd want to do," Beth said. "I believe I'd very much prefer to punch them."

Westcliffe chuckled. "No need. Simply inform me, and I shall see to the matter, for both of you."

She knew firsthand what sort of beating an unfortunate fellow would take if Westcliffe was displeased, yet she couldn't deny the warmth that spread through her because he'd see to her honor. She touched the fan to her right cheek. "Yes." To her left. "No."

"What are the questions?" Beth asked.

"Across the room, a man might catch your attention, then tilt his head toward the terrace, perhaps wanting an assignation."

"Oh, I see."

"The answer should always be no," Westcliffe fairly growled. "If you wish to retain your reputation, which I highly recommend if your intention is to find a suitable husband."

"If I said yes, I suppose you would deal with him for inviting me to sin in the first place," Beth said.

"Most certainly," he assured her.

Claire was amazed that her sister could be so at ease with this man. How was it that she had failed to recognize the truth about him when she was that age? She snapped the fan closed. "I wish to speak with you." She extended it toward her sister. "Closing the fan does signal that you wish to speak with someone. And I do wish to speak with my husband now—privately. We'll continue the lessons later."

"But—"

"Later, Beth. I'll meet you in the parlor."

"I can't imagine that anything you have to say—"

"Beth."

She gave a little pout. "Oh, all right. But we'll have to continue *much* later, as we're going to the park. We were simply waiting for you to awaken from your nap."

"We?" Claire repeated.

"Yes. Westcliffe has consented to accompany us. It would be good for us to be seen out and about before the ball tomorrow night. I shall grab our hats and parasols while you have your little discussion." Waving her fan, she fairly waltzed from the room.

"You're going to have to keep a close watch over her," Westcliffe said.

"Yes, I fear so."

As though needing to put distance between them, now that they were alone, he hoisted himself up, walked around his desk, and took his chair. He lounged back in it, his dark gaze riveted on her. He arched an eyebrow. "You wished to talk?"

Whatever she'd meant to discuss with him escaped her mind as one overriding thought dominated. "The park? We're going to the park? People will be about, will they not?"

"A good many people will be about."

She nodded absently. Knowing the ball would be difficult, that her husband's indiscretions were not secret, she'd been preparing herself for it. But this moment seemed too soon.

As though reading her thoughts, he said quietly, "It'll make tomorrow night easier."

"I had hoped all the attention would be on Beth, but I suspect there will be some speculation regarding me—us."

"You must have anticipated that before you agreed to give her a Season."

"She's very difficult to say no to."

He gave her a wry grin. "So I've discovered."

Her mouth suddenly dry, her stomach a tangle of knots, she suggested, "You and Beth could go without me."

"You're going to have to face them all sooner or later, Claire. Would it not be better when it is not with the press of bodies, and escape is a tad more difficult?"

She realized he'd given it thought and drawn conclusions about the unconscionable position he'd placed her in. At that moment, she hated him for not being discreet. But neither could she deny the role she'd played in bringing this about with her childish behavior years before.

She bobbed her head. "Yes, of course. I can see the advantage to this."

"If you grow too uncomfortable, we can easily leave and quickly."

"All right, then. To the park we shall go."

* * *

The landau was beautiful, black with red trim, pulled by two matching grays. Claire and Beth faced forward, while Westcliffe and Cooper had their backs to the driver. The dog sat on the seat more alert than she'd seen him since her arrival.

Beth could barely sit still. "You will tell me if you see anyone of consequence."

"Everyone here is of consequence," Westcliffe assured her.

"Do you think people are wondering who I am?"

Determined to focus on her sister and not herself, Claire squeezed her hand. "I'm sure they are, dear heart."

"But there are so many people. What can you tell us about them, my lord?"

"I am not one for gossip, but do you see the couple in the white landau with the white horses?"

"The woman with the striking red hair?"

"Yes. That is the Duke and Duchess of Greystone. It is their home we'll be going to tomorrow night."

"From a distance they seem nice enough."

"Until she married the duke, she was a bookkeeper at a gentlemen's club."

Beth's eyes widened. "How scandalous!"

"They are closest to those with questionable pasts. I daresay you'll see several of them at the ball. Neither the duke nor the duchess tolerates anyone speaking ill of someone within their residence. If it is gossip you seek, Beth, I fear I suggested the wrong ball for us to attend."

Claire sat there, too stunned to speak. His gaze met hers for the span of a heartbeat. She saw understanding within the dark depths, perhaps even an apology, although that might have simply been her imagination. What she did know was that at the first ball they attended, she might not be the fodder for gossip and speculation that she'd feared. Afterward, certainly, but others around whom scandal stirred would serve as an initial distraction. She could scarcely signify that her husband had suggested that particular ball as a way to spare her some mortification. It was more likely that he was most comfortable with those who created scandal with the ease that he did. But whatever the reason, she was not dreading attending the ball as much as she had been an hour earlier.

A rider on a sleek brown horse approached, and the driver brought the carriage to a halt. Grinning broadly, the Duke of Ainsley swept off his top hat and bowed from the waist. "Countess, a pleasure to see you."

"You as well, Your Grace."

"Lady Beth, when did you grow up?" he asked.

"About the same time as you, I suspect," Beth said, smiling brightly.

Then he turned his attention to his brother. "Westcliffe."

"Ainsley."

Claire couldn't believe the formality between the brothers.

"Cooper, how are you, old boy?" Ainsley reached

out and petted the dog with his gloved hand. "Heard Lord Chesney had a litter of pups recently."

"Wonder how Chesney pulled that miracle off?" Westcliffe said laconically. "He should be studied. It's not every day a man gives birth to dogs."

Claire bit back her laughter. Her husband did seem to have an odd sense of humor. It didn't often show itself, but obviously it lurked.

Ainsley narrowed his eyes at him. "Must you take everything so literally? His collie had them. Cute pups. I was thinking of getting one, but I'm leaning toward a setter." He looked over at Beth. "Do you like dogs, Lady Beth?"

"Most certainly. Especially the setter."

"Well, then, I shall keep that in mind when I make my choice. It was good to see you." He tipped his hat. "Good day."

He cantered away. Beth turned in her seat.

"Beth, don't turn to watch him," Claire scolded.

"Why? He is such a fine figure of a man. Do you think anyone noticed that he stopped to visit with us? It wouldn't hurt at all if someone thought he were interested in making a match."

"Courting is a slow ritual, Beth. You must have more patience with it."

"But it is so hard."

Before the landau could again be on its way, a barouche drew up beside it. Claire recognized the woman as Lucy Stuart, Lady Morrow. She was a friend of Claire's cousin Charity. They'd played together on occasion. Last Season she'd married the Earl of Morrow and had promptly paid a visit to Claire to inform her that she didn't approve of Westcliffe's philandering. She was one of the ladies advocating that Claire bring her husband to heel— as though that were easily done.

"Countess, what a pleasure it is to see you in London . . . with your husband." She blinked her brown eyes repeatedly as though she had a speck of dust in them. Her black hair was tucked up neatly beneath a hat with a brim so wide that her husband was forced to sit leaning to the side to avoid it. He greeted everyone, then turned his attention to their surroundings as though he were merely an ornament to his wife.

"Lady Morrow, how good it is to see you. You remember my sister, Lady Beth."

"Yes, of course. The family resemblance is uncanny. I'd not heard you'd arrived for the Season," Lady Morrow said.

"I was not aware my wife was required to inform you of her business," Westcliffe said smoothly.

Beth gasped, Lucy's eyes turned round as saucers, Morrow continued to look elsewhere, and Claire's stomach dropped through the floor of the carriage. Still, she felt compelled to force out, "Beth and I have been extremely busy." She hated herself for it, but she knew that, unlike the Duchess of Greystone, Lucy would spread rumors, and she needed her to at least think she and her husband were on their way to making amends. "Westcliffe and I are having our portrait made—and that's terribly tedious and time-consuming."

"Yes. Quite." She looked at Westcliffe, then back at Claire. "I'm glad all seems to be well. You must come to call." She bid her adieu, and they were racing away.

"I never much liked her," Beth muttered.

"She can influence your Season, Beth."

"Ainsley can influence it more."

Claire was aware of a frisson of tension radiating from her husband. If she'd learned one thing of any consequence in the short time she'd been in London, it was that he didn't like being beholden to his youngest brother. "I believe Westcliffe is providing all the influence you need. After all, he is the reason we have a ball to attend."

His voice had a more relaxed edge to it when he ordered the driver to continue on. The drive through the park was more pleasant than she'd expected. No one else stopped to speak with them, but there were the occasional nods and acknowledgments directed at Westcliffe. Because he was with them, she had little doubt that some would assume all was well with their marriage. Others might see it as a tentative beginning. And a few might see it for what it truly was: an act.

Although for the life of her, try as she might, she was having a difficult time seeing it as an act. For her, it *did* feel more like a tentative beginning.

Chapter 11

Sitting in the library, drinking his whiskey, waiting on the ladies to finish preparing themselves for the ball, Westcliffe became lost in thought. He'd never considered what effect his carousing would have on Claire if she ever returned to London. Out of sight, out of mind. But he'd seen the distress quickly cross over her face when Beth had mentioned going to the park. And he'd recognized his responsibility in causing it. In hindsight, stupid of him not to realize his actions would have an impact on her.

Three years ago, like her, he'd been young, lacking judgment, and controlled by fears, but unlike her, he'd also been controlled by ambitions. His fear was that he was lacking in what was required to hold on to a woman. His manhood had been threatened, his very sense of himself. He'd strived to become so deeply buried in pleasure in all its forms that he'd forget the betrayal, that he'd no longer think of the wife he'd left at his estate. That whatever faults might reside in him would become insignificant.

Instead, they'd only been magnified.

His pride would never allow him to set it aside for another's happiness. Yet Claire had done exactly that. He'd seen it when she'd agreed to the jaunt in the park, and he expected to see it on display again this evening. She knew of his wicked reputation, and yet tonight she would stand beside him—no doubt with her head held high—so her sister might avoid marriage to a man she had not chosen.

His wife was remarkable. Tonight would not be easy for her. While those who gossiped were not favored at the Duchess of Greystone's affairs, it would still flourish in darkened corners and balconies. He didn't envy his wife what she would endure for her sister's sake. It humbled him to wonder if he'd ever do the same for his brothers.

Knowing that the ladies would soon be joining him, he'd dispensed with his usual ritual of closing the door, so their light laughter, tittering, and footsteps traveled to him shortly before they entered. Setting his whiskey aside and rising to his feet to welcome them, he found himself without words at the sight of them.

Beth was lovely in a white gown with a spray of white roses adorning her upswept hair. But Claire was stunning in a lavender silk gown with a décolletage baring her shoulders and allowing the merest hint of her breasts. A pearl comb and loops of pearls adorned her hair.

"You don't like them," Beth blurted.

He worked to regain his faculties. "Pardon?"

"Our gowns. Do you hate them? Do they make us look so awful?"

"Quite the contrary. You're both exceedingly lovely."

"Then we must be off, or we'll be late."

"I've told you, Beth, that it's fashionable to be late," Claire said, giving her sister an indulgent smile.

"That's the most ridiculous thing I've ever heard. Why issue an invitation with a time on it if you don't want people to be there *on time*?"

"I fear we will be a tad late," Westcliffe said, "as I have a matter to which I must attend."

"Oh, Lord," Beth whined rolling her eyes.

No matter how young Claire had been when they married, he couldn't imagine her throwing such tantrums at the smallest of inconveniences. He couldn't imagine her throwing a tantrum at all. He walked to his desk, opened a drawer, and withdrew a black velvet box. "I thought a lady about to embark on her first ball of her first Season should have something by which to remember it."

He extended it toward Beth.

Her eyes widened, and she smiled brightly. "Oh! For me! Oh! Thank you." She hurried across the short distance separating them and eagerly snatched the box from him. Opening it, she gasped. "Oh, it's lovely! Oh, Claire, look. A pearl bracelet. Help me put it on, will you, please?"

She smiled at him softly, and in her blue eyes, he

saw the gratitude for what he considered a small gesture—and what she obviously considered so much more. It gave him a sense of accomplishment such as he'd never before experienced.

"Of course, I'll assist you," she said, coming to stand between him and Beth, near enough that her rose fragrance wafted toward him. He could see the pearl loops in her hair swaying gently with her movements as she bent her head to see to her sister's needs. What of her own?

When Claire was finished, Beth continued to exclaim about the beauty of the gift and walked over to a lamp, turning her wrist one way and another to better admire it in the light. Claire looked at him, and mouthed, "Thank you."

"It's your first ball of your first Season as well, isn't it?" he asked, reaching back into the drawer and withdrawing another velvet box.

Tears welled in her eyes, and he watched as her delicate throat worked while she swallowed. "I wasn't expecting . . ."

And he realized that made it all the more enjoyable to give it. Every other woman in his life had expected the trinkets and baubles.

"Well, open it, Claire, for pity's sake, and let's see what it is," Beth demanded.

"Oh, yes, of course." She'd managed to blink back the tears, but her hand was trembling when she took the box. Inside on a bed of velvet was a circlet of sapphires. "Oh, it's beautiful," she whispered, in awe.

"You'd mentioned that you favored blue," he said.

Smiling warmly, she nodded. "Yes."

"It is lovely," Beth said. "Pity you can't wear it tonight, unless you change your gown."

"Don't be ridiculous. Something this exquisite can be worn with anything."

She began to lift it out.

"Allow me," he said, taking it from her and draping it around her wrist. Although she wore gloves that rode up her arms and curled around her elbows, he could have sworn he felt her pulse thumping as he secured the clasp. Then he found himself looking down into her eyes, could sense her studying him. He didn't know what had possessed him to purchase the pieces. He'd been shopping for something for Anne—a reward for her patience—when he'd spied the piece and thought of Claire. He didn't want her to make more of it than she should, so he'd purchased a bracelet for her sister as well. "Just something to remember the night by."

She stepped back, nodding once more. "Again, thank you."

"May we leave now?" Beth asked, her impatience obvious.

He gave a low chuckle as he reached into his pocket for his gloves. "Without further ado."

During the carriage ride, Claire couldn't stop touching the bracelet. He'd given her a gift on their wedding day, but she was fairly certain it had been an obligation. This gift—what did it signify?

He'd taken her breath when she'd walked into the library and seen him in his tight black trousers, gray waistcoat, and blue double-breasted tailcoat. He looked magnificent. Even with his black hair styled, he still exuded a roughness that was appealing on a primal level. She couldn't imagine that there was a woman in all of England who wouldn't want him. She certainly did. But it was more than his good looks that appealed to her. She'd not expected the care and attention he took with Beth. She'd certainly not expected this slow shifting in their relationship.

She again touched the bracelet. In all honesty, she'd dreaded what tonight might bring for her. Pity, shame, gossip. But his simple gesture had laid all her worries to rest. She would make it through tonight. Beth would have her ball, her Season, and she would find someone to replace Hester.

Carriages were lined up in the drive leading to the Greystones' residence, and it was several long minutes—during which Beth repeatedly suggested that they simply leave the carriage and walk—before they arrived at the front. A liveried footman opened the door and handed them down. Claire couldn't deny the tautening of her stomach as she climbed the steps to the entrance. Her heart steadied when Westcliffe placed his hand on the small of her back. It was only a brief touch, but it was enough.

They left their wraps in the parlor before

proceeding on to the grand room where the dancing was taking place.

Claire knew it was rude to gape, yet at her first sight of the room she seemed unable to help herself. The ballroom was far more magnificent than anything she'd imagined. The crystal chandeliers were alight with what must have been a thousand candles. So many flowers scented the room that Claire was fairly certain not a single bloom remained anywhere else in London. But it was more than the gilded mirrors, the orchestra playing from a balcony, the beautiful gowns, the glittering diamonds. It was the atmosphere of joy and gaiety. Here there were no worries. Nothing except fun.

She was startled to hear, "Lord and Lady Westcliffe and Lady Beth Michaels!"

Where before devastation at the reality of her position had engulfed her, tonight she felt an almost unheralded sense of pride as she descended the stairs with Westcliffe's hand laying lightly, almost possessively, against her back. If the years continued to be as kind to him as they'd been so far, as he grew older, ladies would swoon from the mere mentioning of his name.

At the foot of the stairs, he formally introduced her and Beth to their host and hostess: the Duke and Duchess of Greystone. They were a handsome couple, and she had no doubt they adored each other—it was clearly telegraphed in each glance, every touch.

Westcliffe then led them over to an arrangement

of chairs near some potted fronds. "I'll return in a bit," he said, and before she could respond, he'd walked away.

The reality of their situation began to take hold as no one approached.

"Do you know anyone to whom you can introduce me?" Beth asked after a while, and Claire heard the rising panic in the high pitch of her voice.

"I'm looking."

"No one is going to ask me for a dance."

"Be patient, Beth."

But even she had begun to lose hope when the Duchess of Greystone walked over with a young gentleman in tow. "Lady Westcliffe, Lady Beth, Lord Bentley has asked for an introduction."

His introduction seemed to signal a mad dash, because Beth was suddenly catching the attention of every eligible young buck in the room. Within half an hour, so many introductions had been made that her dance card was completely filled.

"Lady Beth, have I arrived too late to snag a dance?" The question was asked smoothly, as though an answer in the affirmative would be equivalent to receiving Cupid's arrow through the heart.

Beth beamed up at Ainsley. "Your Grace, I fear you have indeed." She waved her dance card in front of his face. "Can you believe it?"

Claire grabbed her sister's wrist and pulled her hand down to her side. "Beth, don't be obnoxious."

"But I cannot believe how popular I am. Oh,

listen!" Dramatically, she set her hand to her ear. "The first waltz. Lord Bentley."

As though she'd summoned him with her excitement, Lord Bentley appeared and escorted her sister to the dance floor. After all of her worrying, Claire couldn't believe that the night would go so well.

"And what of you?" Ainsley asked.

Claire shook her head lightly. "I'm not the one having the Season." She touched his arm and held his green gaze. "Thank you so much. I know your promise to attend has helped matters where Beth is concerned. I didn't expect you to appear."

"My mother may not hold with the value of promises, but I do. And if my brother is too daft to ask his wife for a dance, allow me the honor." Bowing slightly, he extended his arm.

She shook her head more vigorously. "Oh, no, that would not be wise."

"Afraid he might get jealous?"

"More afraid, I think, that he won't." She lifted a shoulder. "I'm not even sure what I meant by that. But in either case, I believe one of us would get hurt."

"By that logic, he should be storming over here now simply because I'm talking with you." Leaning near, he winked. "I promised our hostess I'd dance once before I left. I'd rather it be a married woman. Don't want to give any unmarried young misses hope. And if you don't dance with me, I'm doomed to spend a rather boring evening here, and if word gets around that I've stopped attending—"

"Oh, all right," she said, laughing. "Although in truth, Westcliffe receives invitations to balls."

"But not as many as I garner."

Unfortunately, the music ceased. Beth returned to her side, where the charming Earl of Greenwood made his appearance and whisked her away.

"He'll be a marquess someday," Ainsley said as he gallantly escorted Claire to the dance floor. "I suppose you know that already."

With a proper distance between them, he took her into his arms, and they began to circle the dance floor.

"Actually, I'm acquainted with very few of the nobility—only those I met when we visited your estate and a few on my wedding day."

"Old men, then."

She smiled. "For the most part, yes."

"Lynnie's friends mostly."

Lynnie. The Earl of Lynnford. Their guardian.

"Should you refer to him so informally?"

"Oh, yes. I've taken my place in the House of Lords. He would expect it."

"What of Westcliffe? I suppose he's sitting there now." She'd never given it any thought before.

"He's been there for some time. Takes his duties very seriously. It's the reason he married you, isn't it?"

She lifted a shoulder.

"Do you ever wonder if perhaps there was another reason?" he asked.

"Such as?"

"Perhaps he liked you."

"He had a funny way of showing it. He never spoke to me."

"He's really quite timid, you know."

Nearly bursting out with laughter, she caught the glimmer of teasing in his eyes. "Oh, yes, I'm sure at this very moment he's hiding beyond a potted frond."

"On the contrary, he's in the corner, quite visible, glaring."

She nearly lost her footing and stumbled over her feet.

"Don't look," he ordered, just as she began to turn her head.

"We should end the dance now," she said.

"Don't be silly. I'm enjoying it far too much."

"You're enjoying antagonizing him."

"That, too."

"Please."

He gave her an indulgent smile. "I don't need you to protect me. I'm quite capable of looking out for myself."

"He has a rather nasty punch."

"Which he'd never use on you."

"But he would on you."

"Not if I stand up to him. That's the thing about Westcliffe. Never takes his anger out on those who stand up to him. You should give it a try sometime."

Thankfully, two beats later, the music ceased. With a great deal of relief, she allowed Ainsley to escort her back to the area where she would meet with Beth. Surreptitiously, she searched for Westcliffe, but she wasn't as tall as Ainsley, and so many people were in attendance that it was difficult to see around them.

When they arrived at their spot, Ainsley took her gloved hand and pressed a kiss to it. "Thank you for allowing me to fulfill my obligations here. I know a lady who will very much appreciate my ability to arrive earlier than planned."

A lady who was not at the ball? She idly wondered how much of a *lady* she could actually be, then chastised herself for doing exactly what she didn't want done of her. "Does your mother know of her?"

He gave her a devastating grin. "God, I hope not."

He left her then, and at that precise moment, across the ballroom, Westcliffe stepped into her line of sight. She did hope that Ainsley walked quickly, because based on her husband's expression, he was fully capable of committing murder.

Westcliffe grabbed two flutes of champagne from a passing footman. He'd only taken a few steps when Ainsley nearly collided with him.

"So, are you going to dance with her?" Ainsley asked.

"*Her?*" Westcliffe repeated. "First ball of the Season, there are probably more than a hundred women in attendance. Did you have a particular *her* in mind?"

"Your wife."

"You danced with her. I'd think that would suffice."

"She's quite accomplished."

"So I noticed."

Ainsley smiled, blast him. He'd wanted West-cliffe to notice.

"She didn't want to, you know," Ainsley murmured.

"What's that?"

"Dance with me. She was afraid it would anger you."

"Smart girl."

"Not a girl. More of a woman I'd say."

His jaw clenched, and he had to fight to unlock it. "I suppose you'd know, holding her as you were."

"I was most respectful. Poor thing was afraid you might strike me."

"I might yet."

"No, you won't. Enjoy the evening."

As his brother strode away, heading for the stairs, Westcliffe regretted that he couldn't go with him, that he had obligations here. He continued in the direction he'd been heading before Ainsley's interruption.

As he neared Claire, he was struck once again by her beauty. When they'd first arrived, he'd been caught unawares by her amazement when her blue eyes had widened as they'd walked into the ball-room. Quite honestly, he didn't understand why a woman would want a Season if she didn't need one. Claire had been betrothed. Why go through all this nonsense? He'd thought he was saving her from a fate worse than death.

Just as he did, he suspected that many a man considered tossing a rope over a nearby chandelier and hanging himself when attending one of these affairs.

She smiled at him as he came to stand beside her.

"Champagne?" he asked.

"The last time I drank champagne, my judgment was not at its best." Still, she took the offered flute and sipped delicately.

He was not yet ready to joke or tease about that night. It could still cut him to the quick, so he said instead, "I see your sister is dancing."

"Yes, can you believe it? Her card is completely filled."

"And what of yours?"

"Nary a name. Which is fine. I didn't come here to dance. I just want to see Beth happy."

The orchestra began to play another tune, one Westcliffe recognized. He'd known there was always a chance that someone would ask Claire for this dance before he did, but he had little doubt that one well-practiced look would have had the blighter scurrying away. His *practiced* look had even terrified his wife when she was a girl. Terrified everyone, in fact, except for his brothers. Perhaps because Stephen, damn him, had caught Westcliffe practicing in front of a mirror and shared his find with Ainsley. They'd both decided that pretended anger was no anger at all. Unfortunately, they'd yet to learn when he was truly angry and how to avoid bringing forth his wrath.

"Will you honor me with this dance?" he asked.

Her eyes widened considerably. Quickly reclaiming herself, she gave him a nod.

He took her flute, setting it and his aside. He escorted her onto the dance floor, and suddenly she was in the circle of his arms. He couldn't remember the last time he'd danced, but he didn't recall feeling as though the lady matched him perfectly. He wondered if it might have been best to have left her playing the part of wallflower.

"I love 'Greensleeves,'" she said quietly, as though the silence between them began to unsettle her.

"I know."

Her eyes widened again. He hoped she never took it upon herself to take up cards. She'd lose a fortune.

"How do you know?" she asked.

"Whenever you visited, it was the only song I recall your playing on the pianoforte."

She laughed lightly, and something inside him twisted. Her laughter had always had the strangest effect on him, had always comforted and made him long for things at the same time.

"It's the only song I've ever mastered," she said. "I think I was born with all thumbs and no fingers."

He tightened his hand around hers, acutely aware of the fingers splayed on his shoulder. "I assure you, you have lovely fingers even if they do not agree with the keys of the pianoforte."

"A compliment and a gift. I daresay this is a magical night."

He frowned. "I've complimented you before."

"Have you?" She arched a brow as though she expected him to provide an example.

Damnation, his mind had gone blank. "I'm certain I have."

She gave him an odd smile that was either sad or chastising or perhaps a combination of both. "You seldom spoke to me before we were married and certainly not often afterward."

If he'd been sitting, he'd have shifted uncomfortably in his chair and reached for his whiskey. "What is there to discuss?"

"The things you favor. Your hopes, your dreams, your plans for the future. I don't know. What do couples discuss? I've heard enough rumors to know that I was not your first lady. What did you discuss with the others?"

"We never talked. Our mouths were busy with other things."

He took a perverse pleasure in her blush. Leaning near, he said in a low voice, "You shouldn't ask questions to which you truly don't want the answers."

She angled her chin. "Perhaps I do want the answers. Perhaps this simply isn't the place to ask them."

"The library at midnight would serve better."

"Is that an invitation?" she asked, breathlessly.

"More of a dare, I should think."

She nodded, and he wondered exactly what her answer was. He also realized they'd stopped dancing. Fortunately, the music had ceased to play as well.

They'd nearly reached her little corner of the ballroom when Greenwood intercepted them.

"My lord," the young man said. Westcliffe felt him slipping something into his hand. "Lady Beth is an intriguing woman." He turned to Claire. "Countess, I hope you will give me leave to call upon your sister."

"Yes, that would be lovely."

"Very good." He bowed. "M'lord. M'lady."

He walked away, and Westcliffe made a move to return the item to his pocket, but he wasn't subtle enough. Claire grabbed his hand, unfurled two of his fingers. A flash of anger ignited her eyes. For some inexplicable reason he relished it.

"He paid you?" she whispered harshly.

"I paid him. A fiver to dance with her."

"You paid him?"

"I paid them all. A young buck is always in need of a bit of pleasure funds. You wanted her night to be memorable didn't you?"

Before she could respond, he walked away.

She'd been horrified by his actions. He'd originally planned to stay and talk with her, but he hadn't wanted to get into an argument.

He watched as a couple of elderly matrons approached her. He suspected they were more interested in her since her dance with Ainsley than in her dance with him. No doubt they wanted to gain an introduction for their daughters. A bachelor duke was always highly sought after. Little wonder Ainsley had made an early exit. Westcliffe did not envy him having to fend off so much unwanted—

Anne nudged him as she came to stand beside him. "I saw you dancing with your wife. You told me you never dance at these affairs."

With her tone of voice, she didn't try to hide her displeasure. Her face, however, gave the appearance they were engaged in a delightful conversation. She was much more skilled at deception than Claire.

"She is my wife. It seemed appropriate."

"I've never seen her before. I have to admit to being surprised by her appearance. She's rather . . . unimpressive."

Unimpressive? He thought she was the most fascinating woman in attendance. She was not jaded. She still held on to a certain amount of naïveté. Strong, determined. She stood out because she was unlike anyone else there.

"It is a nice night for a walk in the garden," Anne murmured, interrupting his thoughts. She snapped her fan closed, lifted it to her mouth, and glided her tongue along its edge. He doubted his wife was familiar with the meaning of that message.

But he was. He could scarcely believe the words he was uttering. "Not tonight."

She arched a brow at him. "Afraid we might get caught? That makes it all the more fun."

His gaze never wavered from Claire. The matrons had left, and three other ladies had circled about her.

"Why the interest in her?" Anne snapped when he didn't respond to her earlier words. "Trying to make sure she doesn't slip off with someone else?"

Her derisive retort caused his gut to tighten, but strangely he didn't think Claire would sneak away for a clandestine meeting with another man. Perhaps if Stephen were here . . . but he wasn't. He was supposedly with the army somewhere in India.

Anne touched his arm gently, almost hesitantly. So unlike her. He glanced over at her. "I could make a scene," she threatened.

"Don't," he ground out. He'd not have Claire's first ball ruined.

"Then meet me in the garden. I want to thank you properly for the diamond bracelet you gave me." She lifted her hand. "It's beautiful."

"This is not the place. I'll come see you later," he said quietly.

He could read her displeasure as though she'd taken pen and ink to her features. Finally, she gave a barely perceptible nod. "I shall be waiting in anticipation."

Chapter 12

Claire couldn't deny that she wanted Beth's first ball to be memorable. But to pay young gentlemen—

"Tonight was the most wonderful night of my life," Beth said as she twirled around her bedchamber as though she were reliving the moment when some swain had held her in his arms. "Who would have thought I'd be so amazingly popular? I don't know if there is any lady who danced as much as I did."

Claire's chest tightened. She didn't want to ruin the illusion, but hurt was certain to follow. Westcliffe couldn't pay the men at every ball. "Tonight might have been an exception, Beth. The men were curious. Yours was a new face in the crowd."

Beth flopped back on the bed the way that they'd fallen in the snow when they were children intent on creating angels. "I shall most definitely be spared from marrying Lord Hester. I have no doubt."

"I simply don't want you to be disappointed if

your dance card isn't filled at the next ball."

Beth popped up and smiled at her. "You worry about things before there is a reason to worry." She walked around the bed and yanked on the bellpull to summon her maid. "You worried that living here with Westcliffe would be awful, and it's not," she continued. "You worried that we'd not receive invitations, and we have an abundance of them." As she glided by, she tweaked Claire's nose. "You are such a worrier. But all will be well. Even between you and Westcliffe. You seem to have his attention now."

She wished she could be so certain. But she didn't wish to discuss her doubts with Beth, so she simply said, "Sleep well, sister," and let herself out of the room just as the maid was entering.

She was exhausted from the night, from all the emotions running rampant through her. She'd danced twice. Strange, she'd always felt comfortable around Ainsley, and yet it was the dance with her husband that stayed uppermost in her mind. The strength she'd felt in his hold, the sureness of his steps. When she was seventeen, he'd seemed like such a bully, and now she saw him as a man. One with responsibilities he did not shirk.

He knew her favorite song. He'd given her a bracelet to commemorate her first ball. And she'd noticed him talking with the most gorgeous woman she'd ever seen. She'd made the mistake of asking one of the ladies talking with her who she was.

"Lady Anne Cavill. Until recently, she was seen about town with your husband."

She'd almost asked, "How recently?"

She considered preparing for bed, but words needed to be said. And Westcliffe had issued a dare even though it was long past midnight.

She walked down the stairs. The only sound echoing around her was the ticking of the clock in the grand entryway. She made her way along the hallway that led to the library. She was grateful to see no footmen or other servants about.

Of course, perhaps her husband wasn't either.

But when she opened the door and peered inside, Westcliffe was lounging in a chair, near the windows, a tumbler of whiskey in one hand and the ever-faithful Cooper curled at his feet.

Westcliffe watched her approach. He'd told Anne to expect him, but he'd also issued an invitation to his wife and, for some unknown reason, curiosity had harkened him to remain a bit longer, to see if she would appear. She sat in the chair beside him. He reached for the extra tumbler of whiskey he'd poured earlier in anticipation of her arrival and handed it to her. She took it and sipped gingerly.

"Beth . . . she"—Claire released a heavy sigh—"she thinks every night will be like tonight."

"No reason it can't be."

She arched a brow with a look of annoyance. "You intend to pay gentlemen at every ball to dance with her?"

"I can well afford it."

"That's not the point. She thinks they see something in her—"

"Perhaps they do. Greenwood wasn't the only one to return the fiver."

Sitting up straighter, she leaned toward him. "Truly?"

With only two lamps lit, she was mostly in shadow, and yet there were so many things about her to notice at that moment. The brightness in her eyes that outdid the glow of the lamps, the hint of her bosom, the creamy smoothness of her skin, the flush of her cheeks. But what caught his attention the most was the wayward curl that had fallen over her forehead and tapped against the small scar that bisected that delicate eyebrow. Without any thought at all, he captured it between his fingers and tucked it behind her ear, allowing his bare knuckles the luxury of skimming over the silky curve of her cheek.

Her breath caught, but she didn't jerk back. He wondered if she'd remain as still, as brave, if he moved his mouth toward hers. She was nothing at all like Anne, and at that particular moment he was glad. Every moment spent with Anne was a game of enticing her, of keeping her satisfied. She grew easily bored. They shared no quiet moments. Everything was innuendo. Each conversation was wrought with naughtiness and conjecture.

He realized that he'd stayed here, hoping for Claire because she would expect nothing of him.

"How many admirers does she require?" he asked, trailing his finger over the slope of her throat, lingering for two rapid beats of her pulse, before retreating, not wanting to admit the pleasure he'd found in so simple and so brief an exploration.

He watched her throat work as she swallowed, and as though finding her mouth dried, she turned to the tumbler, gulping a bit more than usual, swallowing again. Had he ever been so enticed by a woman's throat?

"One, I suppose," she rasped, "if he's the right one."

"How will she determine he's the right one?"

"She'll fall in love with him."

He couldn't help himself. He laughed. Apparently, her innocence knew no bounds. "Love is an emotion dreamed up by women. Men lust. They need. They desire. Women make men want them. Women call it love."

"You're quite cynical."

He touched his glass to hers. "Quite."

Claire hated hearing that. There was something in him that called to her, even without his trying. "I noticed tonight that you seemed to give an inordinate amount of attention to Lady Anne Cavill."

He studied her for a moment before saying quietly and without emotion, "You should know that I intend to ask her to marry me."

She'd obviously swallowed too much whiskey too quickly. His words made no sense, and neither did those coming out of her mouth. "You intend to ask her? To extend a courtesy to her that you never extended to me?"

He said nothing.

"I suppose it's moot as you're already married," she felt compelled to point out.

"Yes, we'll need to discuss that at some point after the Season is over."

"We can discuss it now."

He shifted in the chair to better face her. "Very well. I propose we seek a divorce."

She stared at him in shock. The bracelet, the dance, the kiss, the way he looked at her of late— they all meant nothing. An elaborate ruse. A game. "Do you love her then?"

"I have a care for her, yes."

"That's not what I asked. Do you *love* her?"

He reached back, grabbed the bottle, and splashed more whiskey into his tumbler. "I'm incapable of love."

"Why?"

He released a harsh bitter-sounding laugh. "It's enough that I am. And before you ask, no, she doesn't love me either."

"How can she not?"

With a quick shake of his head, he downed the whiskey and refilled his glass. "Surely you can determine the answer to that easily enough."

Only she couldn't. The man she'd married had been harsh, hard, but she'd have not described him as bitter. She'd done this to him. Made him callous.

"I'm not easy to love," he finally answered for her, each word delivered with a biting edge to it.

But you could be, she wanted to say. Instead, she held her tongue on that matter and addressed a more pressing issue. "If we get a divorce, I'll be completely ruined. No man will have me. I'll never have children."

"I no longer give a damn. I'm weary of this life, of the loneliness, of—"

She didn't know what possessed her, but she tossed what remained in her tumbler on him. Anger erupted on his face. Three years ago, she would have cowered, now she wanted to reach for the bottle and smash it over his head. He was weary? He was lonely? He was in the midst of people while she was surrounded by naught but land. Her life—

She shrieked and came out of the chair as his whiskey splashed over her. "You cur! You call yourself a gentleman?"

"You call yourself a lady?"

"Damn you! May you rot in hell!"

She wasn't certain where she'd planned to strike him or even if she'd really intended to. She only knew that she raised her hand—

He rose in magnificent ferocity and grabbed her wrist, twisting her arm behind her back, bringing her up flush against him. "To borrow your words, do you think I'm not already there?" he demanded.

She was breathing harshly, the fury emanating from the core of her being. She realized it wasn't that he'd tossed his liquor on her—it was that he was going to cast her aside . . . after everything. In such a short time, she'd begun to have hope that there was a chance for them. They'd talked, they'd moved furniture, they'd worked to give Beth a night she would remember. He'd been kind to Claire. Generous. He'd made her want him.

"I hate you," she rasped.

"I know."

Then he did the strangest thing. He touched the curl of her hair, the one that would never stay pinned, the one that always played with her irritating scar, and he tucked it gently behind her ear.

"I know," he repeated, just before he lowered his head and licked the amber liquid that dotted her bosom.

Warmth swirled through her, its movement through her body mirroring his hot, velvety tongue as it journeyed over her flesh. Her knees grew weak, and if not for Westcliffe's arm banded around her back at the waist, she was fairly certain she would have embarrassed herself further by ending up as a puddle on the floor. Why was he doing this, and why did she want him to continue?

His words echoed through her mind: *What you had before was the kiss of a boy. That is the kiss of a man.*

He'd left her with such longing after the scalding kiss he'd given her, but he'd only given her a sampling. The fire, the fury, the passion in him that she'd always feared . . . when released, they stirred her in ways that she'd never imagined that a body, a soul, even a heart could feel.

The first night here he'd also given her another sampling of what he could deliver with the simple touch of a finger. And here again, another sampling: the velvet caress of his tongue. Only she was growing weary of sampling. She wanted the entire meal.

He'd mocked her earlier reference to love—but could anyone experience such stirring, the giving or the receiving of it, if not even a hint of love, of caring was involved?

This was not lust—but if it was, God help her, she wanted more.

Finally, he began to lift his head, and before he was at his full height, she reached up, holding his head in place, and sampled the whiskey that clung to the bristle at his jaw. It was more flavorful, its richness enhanced by the saltiness of his skin.

His gaze held hers for the longest, searching for what—she didn't know. When he finally released her, she dropped back into the chair, irritated that he had the uncanny ability to make her too weak to stand while he seemed to gain strength from the encounter.

"We'll continue this discussion after the Season is over," he stated succinctly, his armor back in place, his emotions tethered. He spun on his heel and strode from the room.

Glancing down, she realized he'd missed a drop. She almost called him back to see to it. Instead, she brought her feet up, curled in the chair, and gazed out into the darkness of the garden.

She didn't want a divorce. He spoke of it as though it was a simple matter, but it was costly and involved, and fraught with scandal. She'd only ever heard of one couple being granted a divorce, and the woman had moved to France to escape the humiliation of it. Besides, she didn't want an end to this marriage. Perhaps she was prideful, not wanting to be so easily thrown over for another woman.

But it was more than that. Recently, she'd begun to catch rare glimpses into the man she'd married, and she couldn't deny that he fascinated her. She wanted to know him as fully as a woman could know her husband.

Even if it meant that the seduction would be left to her.

He did not want his wife!

Damnation, he did not. But bloody hell, he couldn't stop thinking about her.

Westcliffe sat in a dark corner at Dodger's, drinking fine whiskey almost as quickly as it could be poured. He'd intended to go see Anne, but he'd come here instead. The fragrance of roses wafted around him, and he had no desire to have it replaced with the scent of lilac. What an absurd thought.

But it was there all the same. Claire was uppermost in his mind, and it wasn't fair to Anne for him to seek her out under those circumstances.

Whatever had possessed him to sip from Claire's skin earlier?

It had been the fire in her eyes. He'd seen it often enough before they were married, when she would get in an argument with Stephen. It was the fire that intrigued him. It had been totally absent on their wedding day, as though somehow, with the taking of his name, she'd lost the very essence of herself.

Tonight Beth's excitement over the damned ball had caused a measure of guilt to prick his conscience. Would it have been such a terrible thing to allow Claire to have a Season? He'd seen no sense in it. She'd been betrothed to him before she was born. She wasn't in need of a suitor. Even the ever-practical Ainsley had agreed that nothing was to be gained by avoiding the inevitable. Although in hindsight, perhaps his brother had simply been ready to stop handing coins over to Westcliffe. Or more likely, not yet interested in the marriage market, he viewed balls as a waste of a man's time.

Claire had looked so lovely this evening. He'd been glad when she'd not changed out of her attire before joining him in the library later. He'd enjoyed gazing on her—until the subject of Anne had come up. When Claire had tossed his good whiskey on him—

He gave a low chuckle. He'd reacted without thought. What gentleman tossed liquor onto a woman? What sort of gentleman retaliated at all?

He would have to apologize. Perhaps he could

convince her that licking her clean had been the apology, but each sweep of his tongue had only caused his body to grow more taut. That he was able to walk out was a true testament to his determination.

He'd been surprised by her anger at the mention of a divorce. Yes, it was an act of last resort, but how many years did they have to live apart before admitting that they would never live together? He'd have thought she'd have welcomed the end to their marriage. She was young enough that by the time it finally came about, she could still marry. Surely she desired someone with whom to spend her nights.

Yes, there would be scandal. It would be impossible to avoid. But they were already the fodder for gossips with him living in London and her in the country. At least an end to the marriage would eventually bring an end to the gossip.

It wouldn't be easy at first, but . . . well, it seemed nothing of late was ever easy.

Chapter 13

The flowers began arriving midmorning, during breakfast. From half a dozen gentlemen. Beth was simply beside herself with glee.

Claire gave Westcliffe a questioning look. He simply shook his head and shrugged, hoping she'd understand that he'd had nothing at all to do with them. He was well aware, of course, that when a gentleman was interested in a lady, he expressed that interest by sending her flowers. He'd sent flowers to other women, never to his wife.

As Beth popped up from the breakfast table to welcome each bouquet's arrival, Westcliffe shifted uncomfortably in his chair. His haste to marry Claire had denied her this excitement, this reassurance that she was sought after.

He'd not meant to be cruel, but it was another nail hammered into his coffin of guilt.

She seemed to take as much delight in the flowers as her sister, but when she reached up and touched Beth's hair, drawing her in for a quick hug, he realized that what pleased her was the evidence that her sister had caught the attention of several gentlemen.

She was happy for Beth because Beth was ecstatic.

It was a somber realization to recognize that he'd never felt the same about his brothers' successes, had never basked in their accomplishments. Rather, he'd resented Stephen's freedoms—no responsibilities to hold him down—and Ainsley's position and wealth that had come to him through no effort of his own.

Claire truly loved her sister, wanted her to have whatever would bring her the most joy. And at that moment it was an assortment of roses. Only a beast would not know that a gentleman sent roses to a woman as a sign of his affections.

Westcliffe felt rather like a beast.

"Beth, do come finish your breakfast," Claire said.

"I'm not hungry any longer. Can you believe all the flowers we've been sent? My word, where shall we put them all?"

"We'll have no trouble finding suitable places for them. But you must eat."

"I'm going to go make a list of who sent me flowers and write down all I can remember about him."

With that, she quit the room. Westcliffe didn't think she even saw the indulgent smile her sister bestowed upon her.

"Are you certain you're not responsible for this avalanche of blossoms?" she asked.

"Absolutely not. I could never afford all this."
He cleared his throat, and began stirring his tea,
which was a pointless activity as he used neither
sugar nor milk. "At least not three or four years
ago."

Her gaze found and captured his, and in them
he read the query. In spite of how much it galled
him, he heard himself confessing, "Every shilling
I had to spend came from Ainsley."

She glanced down quickly, but not before he
saw the understanding, the sympathy. It was the
reason he'd never said anything. He wasn't certain
which he detested more.

When she looked back up at him, she had control of her facial features. *Yes, sweetheart, I shall
always know what you think,* he thought.

"That's the reason my dowry was so important,
the reason you didn't annul the marriage immediately after . . ." She shook her head as though
the words were too painful to say. "I'm beginning
to have a clearer understanding of how you must
have felt. I can barely stand the thought that last
night, you went to her—"

"I didn't."

Her mouth opened slightly.

"I went to the club," he said. "I got foxed. In all
honesty, I've gone to see her only once since the
night you and I sat on the floor in the library. And
then it was only for dinner."

"Why?"

He shook his head. "I don't bloody well know.

Your apology, your sincerity—it just seemed wrong to continue as though you weren't here." It was harder to carry on with her here—her presence a constant reminder that he did indeed have a wife. He'd always planned to honor his vows. He knew his father hadn't, knew his mother had suffered because of it.

"Thank you," she said quietly.

"For what?"

"For taking a care with my feelings. It will make it easier to be here, to go forward."

"Do not misunderstand, Claire. I still desire a divorce."

"But not until after the Season ends. And the fewer rumors surrounding us, the better Beth's chances of finding a suitable suitor."

"Good God! Rumors about us could flourish, and she'd find a suitor. Did you not see the flowers?"

She laughed. "I daresay, we're off to a good start. What say we go to Cremorne Gardens this evening? It would be good for Beth to be seen about."

He tilted his head slightly. "I suppose you mean to go early, before the less-reputable people arrive."

"We shall absolutely go early." She gave him an impish smile. "Although perhaps we will also stay late."

"Not if you wish her to marry. Reputations are ruined when the hour grows late."

"Then we must take pains not to remain longer than is prudent."

* * *

Anne was pouting. It wasn't the first time he'd seen her out of sorts. She'd first approached him almost two years ago, desiring him to be her lover. But she was married at the time to the younger son of an earl. Knowing what it was for a man to find his wife with another, he couldn't bring himself to have a liaison with a married woman. Then her husband had taken ill and died. She'd been Westcliffe's companion for the past six months—as soon as she'd come out of mourning.

"I waited half the night for your arrival," she said caustically. "I assume you will at least be joining me for dinner tonight."

He'd never found her so unattractive. Before, he'd tolerated her little fits of temper, assumed they were a woman's prerogative. Lord knew he'd grown up seeing his mother display enough of them.

But today, Anne gave the appearance of pettiness. Coldness. He thought of Claire tossing the whiskey on him. Anger should be accompanied by fire. He could handle that. But cold . . . he'd never realized that he didn't much like it.

"Unfortunately, I'm taking my wife and her sister to Cremorne Gardens."

Anne lounged on the fainting couch, staring out the window with such intensity that he was surprised the glass didn't shatter. "You've been to see me only once since that whore of a wife—"

"Claire is not a whore."

"She took your brother to her bed. Don't tell me you've forgiven her."

"She is not your concern, Anne."

"I don't do well alone, Westcliffe."

He tried not to compare his wife—who'd had three years of solitude—to this woman. Claire had never complained. God knew she had a right to.

"The sooner her sister is married off, the sooner things will return to normal," he said, not willing to admit that he wasn't certain he yearned for normal any longer.

"Normal?" She came off the couch with self-righteousness etched in every move. "Did you inform her that you want a divorce?"

Why was he angry at her for being furious? She had a right. She was his lover, but this summer was not what she'd expected or hoped for. He knew that. He knew tolerance was needed. Still.

"Yes," he bit out.

She nearly staggered back, in surprise he assumed. "What did she say?" Her voice was once again soft, sweet.

He strode to the window and glanced out. "She worries about scandal."

"She should have thought of that before."

"She was a child before." Coming to Claire's defense so easily and without thought surprised him.

"Surely you're not excusing her behavior."

He turned around. "No, but until the matter with her sister is taken care of, and I can see to bringing an end to my own marriage, I think it is best that I not . . . pay court to you."

"You expect me to wait with bated breath for your return?"

"I expect you to understand how difficult all of this is and that it requires my full attention to bring it to fruition." He crossed over to her, gave her a look of longing, and gently touched her cheek. "Anne, we will be together soon, I promise."

"I'm not certain you completely understand how badly I want you. I miss what we had together. I miss you."

"I miss it as well." Taking her in his arms, he held her. Always before he'd felt the stirrings of desire. Strange, how all he felt now was a keen interest in leaving.

Chapter 14

Claire had heard of Cremorne Gardens but had never visited. Her father had never been too keen on sharing the sights of London with his daughters. And the aunt who had helped with her upbringing after her mother died had never favored walking—*aching joints, you know*—and the gardens were designed for walking.

She'd taken great care in preparing for the evening, selecting a dress that was not quite as revealing as the gown she'd worn the night before but still designed to display the barest hint of cleavage. Beth was more modestly attired, but then she was still a maiden, whereas Claire was a married woman—one who was determined to garner her husband's attention. Presently, they were strolling with her arm intertwined with his.

"I suppose if you spot a gentleman who would be appropriate for Beth to meet that you'd make an introduction," Claire murmured quietly.

"No gentleman I know would be appropriate." He wore a burgundy jacket and dove gray trousers. Being seen with him brought her both pride and pleasure. He strode through the gardens with such confidence. She didn't recall him exhibiting so much in his youth, perhaps because he'd always felt beneath Ainsley's thumb—not that she could imagine Ainsley lording his position over his brother.

But she could envision Westcliffe resenting having to ask his youngest brother for so much as a farthing. She'd only ever considered what marriage had meant for her, she'd not taken into consideration what it had meant for him. He'd gained a certain amount of freedom, perhaps absolute, to be his own man.

And within hours of taking on the responsibility of a wife in order to address the responsibilities that came with his position, he'd found her within his younger brother's arms. At the time, she'd thought only of her own fears and needs. How little she'd known about Westcliffe. How much more she was coming to know.

She should have come to London sooner. She shouldn't have docilely accepted his edict that she remain at the estate.

"Oh, may I have some lemonade?" Beth asked brightly, holding out her hand like a child before the answer had been given.

Westcliffe looked at Claire. "Would you care for some?"

"No, thank you."

He withdrew a coin from his pocket and handed

it to Beth, who fairly skipped over to the table where beverages were being sold.

"I don't think I was ever that young," Claire said.

"You were."

She looked up at Westcliffe questioningly. His jaw was clenched as though he wished he'd held his tongue. "When was I?" she asked softly.

He shook his head as though he had no answer, then he said, "You were fifteen before I realized you could walk. You were always chasing after Stephen, running to elude your sister, leaping over flowers—"

"I was dancing," she said haughtily.

He arched a brow at her, and she relished this moment of teasing each other. In spite of his claims to want a divorce, she couldn't help but hope she could somehow change his mind. "How could you notice all that? You were around so seldom."

"I was around enough."

"Why did you never join us?"

"I was the oldest. Playing was . . . beneath me. My father was not with us that long, but he taught me that with my rank came great responsibility. I must never do anything that would give the impression I was unworthy of the title I would someday inherit and the courtesy title I was born possessing. I envied Stephen his freedom to play, to play with you. You had the most amazing laugh." He cleared his throat, as though suddenly uncomfortable. "I'd have not given your sister a coin had

I known it would take her so long to purchase a lemonade."

She didn't know what to say. His words humbled her. He'd no doubt expected her laughter to fill his house once they were wed. "I didn't know," she finally said, devastated by all that he'd revealed. "I didn't know you watched, I didn't know . . . I didn't know you."

Before he could respond, if he would have responded, Beth reappeared. "You two look so melancholy. I swear you are the most boring of creatures. Come, let's have some fun."

She led the way as though she were the leader of a parade.

Westcliffe seemed to think their conversation was over, perhaps to be forgotten. But Claire wanted that moment remembered. She squeezed his arm, and when he glanced down on her, she gave him a secretive smile. "You know, should you ever long to hear my laughter in the future, you should know that I'm terribly ticklish. Unfortunately, it is only one spot. I wonder if you'd have any luck in finding it."

Before he could respond, she released her hold on him and hurried to catch up with her sister, wrapping her arm around Beth's, walking briskly along as they had when they were younger. When she glanced back, it was to see Westcliffe standing like a statue in the middle of the path, staring after her. She couldn't judge his expression, but she did hope she'd given him something to think about.

*   *   *

Westcliffe studied Claire in the shadowy darkness as the first burst of fireworks filled the sky. Anyone else watching might have thought she had the joy of a child, but there was nothing childish about her. She had matured since the day he'd taken her as his wife.

In her expression, he saw pleasure, a woman's pleasure, and he couldn't help but wonder if the same satisfaction would fill her face when she lay replete after lovemaking. He remembered the way she'd looked when he'd kissed her the night when he'd discovered her rearranging furniture. Ravished and ravishing, like a woman who'd had her senses awakened. The hardest thing he'd ever done was walk out of that room.

He would not take her to his bed, dammit. He wouldn't search for that ticklish spot. He would not.

She made him feel things he didn't wish to feel. A gentle stirring in his heart that could destroy him if it wasn't returned. Anne was a much better choice. Her eyes never welled up over silly gifts. She didn't smile because of something he'd done for another. Her flirtations carried no innocence. Her fury was brittle. It didn't heat him with desire. She didn't have a damned ticklish spot. She was safe. If she left him, if he found her with another man . . .

He'd be angry. He might even punch the fellow. But he could easily walk away and never look back. He'd invested none of his heart and none of his soul.

From the moment he'd left Claire at Lyons Place, he'd continually looked back. That was the reason he'd taken numerous lovers. To forget her, to replace the memories of her, the hope for happiness he'd placed in her.

Now here she was, enticing him with her smiles, laughter, and flirtation. Even her anger lured him. He'd be within his rights to lay her down on a bed and have his way with her. She was still his wife. But once he did that, she'd be soiled goods. What man would want her? Three years ago, he wouldn't have cared. Hell, a month ago, he wouldn't have cared. He'd have thought she deserved to suffer.

But now he found himself wanting to protect her from gossip, scandal, and himself—a man without the ability to love.

As though suddenly aware that her sister was spellbound by the spectacular display of colors dotting the sky, she eased away until she was beside him. Placing her hand on his arm, she urged him away from the crowd until they stood alone in the shadows.

"Thank you for bringing us. I know Beth was disappointed that Greenwood didn't call today. I think this outing was the perfect remedy to her melancholy."

Rising on her toes, she brushed a kiss near the corner of his mouth. It took every ounce of willpower he possessed to hold himself perfectly still and not turn into her movement, not capture her mouth and give her the blistering kiss his body demanded of him.

"Did you enjoy the evening?" she asked.

Strangely, he had. He'd never been to the Gardens when decent folk were about. It was much more entertaining later—or at least in his youth he'd found it so. God, he was getting old when he took as much pleasure in the modest gowns as he did in the indecent ones.

Or perhaps it wasn't the gown so much as the woman inside it. The dress wasn't cut nearly as low as the ball gown she'd worn the night before, yet it was just as enticing, if not more so. Perhaps because his tongue knew exactly how silky smooth her skin was.

No, she was no longer a girl. That was evident in the way she stood there, challenging him—to do exactly what he wasn't sure. Kiss her perhaps. Or take her farther into the shadows. He wasn't half-tempted.

A hundred white lights burst through the sky, and in their reflection, he saw the errant strands of her hair that always seemed to work their way loose of any pins or combs. He reached for them, to tuck them back into place—

Another burst of fireworks, followed by the accompanying boom—

Fiery pain ignited through his upper arm. "Damnation!"

Grabbing his arm, he felt the warmth pooling through his fingers.

"What? What happened?" she asked.

"Good God, I think I've been shot."

He'd been shot.

His assumption wasn't confirmed until they returned home because the obstinate man wouldn't let Claire look at his arm. He had allowed her to tie his handkerchief around it, for what little good that did.

After giving the crowd a cursory glance, he'd decided it was too dark and the crowd too immense to begin a search to determine who might have fired a pistol. He'd ordered the ladies to stay near him as they made their way to the carriage, then decided his proximity put them in danger and told them to hurry ahead.

Beth had complained incessantly because they were leaving before the fireworks extravaganza was over, but Claire hadn't told her the reason for their hasty departure because she hadn't wanted to worry her. As for herself, she was petrified. How she managed to keep her legs moving was beyond her. She kept looking back at Westcliffe, urging him on—torn between shielding her sister and dropping back to protect him.

It wasn't until they were safe in the residence that Claire told Beth what had transpired—and only then because she needed Beth to go to her room while Claire saw to her husband. Beth had nearly swooned until Claire had shaken her and told her to get control of herself. She had no time to deal with theatrics. She had to see how Westcliffe was.

He'd immediately called for his manservant and retreated to his bedchamber. By the time she'd finished dealing with Beth and joined him there, he was sitting bare-chested in a chair while Mathers was dabbing at the crimson furrow in Westcliffe's upper arm.

Westcliffe glanced over at her as though she were to be given no more consideration than a fly that had entered his domain. "It's just a gash. Nothing to worry over. Go on to bed."

"Nothing to worry over? Someone tries to kill you—"

"We don't know that he was trying to kill me."

"Why would he shoot at you?"

"We don't even know that he *was* shooting at me. I just happened to be what he hit."

"No one heard anything because of the fireworks, and if they did, they would have just thought it was noise accompanying the show," she speculated. The perfect cover. But still it made no sense that anyone would want to kill him. She walked forward and took the cloth from the servant. "We should send for a physician."

"It's nothing more than a flesh wound." Westcliffe took the cloth from her and pressed it against the wound.

She snatched the cloth away. "I should see to it. I'm your wife."

"You'll get blood on that dress—"

"I already have blood on me."

He looked at her then, truly looked at her. The concern that flashed briefly in his eyes was deeper than any she'd ever seen. She'd known he was a man of strong emotions—she'd experienced his anger and his passion when fueled by anger or drink—but this was something else, and she realized he possessed a wider range of feelings than she'd ever given him credit for.

Taking the cloth from her, he slowly came to his feet and began wiping the blood that had splattered on her chest. Each stroke was so gentle, but his hand was larger than the cloth, and the edge of it grazed her skin. She thought she must be some sort of weak, wanton woman to be so distracted by his touch at a moment like this, when his arm was bleeding—or *had* been bleeding. It appeared that the wound had stopped seeping. Still, it needed to be bandaged. She'd get to it in a moment, when he ceased his ministrations.

She'd caught glimpses of his chest before, but only in the shadows, or at a distance, or only through the narrow V of a shirt. In the light, with no shirt, he was really quite lovely. Firm and muscular. She wondered what sorts of activities he engaged in to keep himself so. He had a fine sprinkling of hair that narrowed down and disappeared beneath the waist of his trousers. Trousers that presently sported a large bulge—and she realized that he was as affected by touching her as she was by being touched.

Swallowing hard, she lifted her gaze to his face, struck by the intensity with which he concentrated, as though he would allow no speck of blood to remain on her flesh. His touch was so unexpected, so delicious.

Gathering her courage, she pressed her hand to the center of his chest, surprised how the springy hairs curled around her fingers as though intent on holding them there forever.

To her chagrin, he stilled his ministrations. "We're developing a rather nasty habit here of having me clean you up. I must confess to preferring the whiskey."

"How can you be so calm?" she asked.

"What is to be gained by being otherwise?"

"It would at least make me feel better to know you were angry or incensed."

"I was before you walked in and distracted me." He stepped back.

"Let me wrap your wound," she urged.

"My manservant can see to it."

"He seems to have disappeared." The servants were well trained in that regard. She didn't wait for Westcliffe to argue further. She simply picked up the cloth that the servant had set aside and began to wrap it around his arm, securing the wound. She could smell the sweet scent of sweat. Perhaps he was human after all, to have sweated some, not to have been completely calm.

"Why the worry, Countess?"

She jerked her gaze up to his. What was he asking?

He cradled her face with his large hand. "If I were dead, so many of your problems would be resolved. No divorce, no scandal."

"You idiot. Do you really think I would prefer you dead?"

Before he could respond, certain that anything he might have said would have been more ridiculous than anything he'd already said, she rose on her toes and covered his mouth with hers. She didn't know where she'd gathered the courage and she'd fully expected him to set her back on her heels.

Instead, his arm came around her, lifting her slightly higher, as his mouth began hungrily to devour hers. She ran her hands up into his hair, pressing herself closer until her breasts were flattened against the wide expanse of his chest.

Oh, God, she wanted to feel every inch of him, wanted the freedom to run her hands over all his flesh, all of it. To think that tonight someone could have so easily taken from her what she had yet to know, to experience. In less than a second, within a heartbeat, all could have been lost.

Because she'd been too afraid to give what they might have had together a chance. Because she'd looked at Stephen and seen the familiar, and not been brave enough to reach for the unknown.

She wasn't certain when she'd begun to care for this man. Perhaps when she'd first recognized the torment that her selfish actions had brought him. Perhaps when she'd watched his lonely figure walking over the moors with only a dog as his companion. Perhaps when he'd welcomed her sister into his home. Perhaps when she'd caught glimpses of a tenderness hidden behind a scowl or an expressionless façade. She couldn't identify a single moment, but, somehow, moments woven together had given her a glimpse of what her life could be. Tonight, it had almost been snatched from her.

His low growl reverberated through his chest, vibrated through hers. Her hair tumbled down. She'd not even been aware of his removing the pins, so lost was she in the sensations running through her. His kiss was as powerful as he was— it demanded, insisted, required that pleasure rise and be celebrated.

Tearing her mouth from his, she dragged her lips over his neck, tasting the salt of his sweat. She nipped at the vulnerable skin at his collarbone. She wanted to taste of all of him. She wanted—

Shoving her away, he staggered back, turned, and grabbed onto the mantel as though it alone gave him the strength to stand. Breathing harshly, he bowed his head. "You should leave."

She took a tentative, trembling step toward him. "No, I want this."

"If I take you—" He shook his head. "It would be unfair to take you, then seek a divorce."

"I don't want a divorce."

Shaking his head, he closed his eyes. "Tonight, emotions are high. In the morning, there will be naught but regret."

"You're wrong. I want—"

"I don't." He slammed his hand against marble. Then he was gripping it again, his knuckles turning white. "I don't. Not like this. Not because a brush with death has us wanting to feel alive. You deserve a man who wants you because it is you. God help me, it has taken me long enough to realize that."

"And you are not that man?"

"I don't know. I only know that taking you to my bed tonight would be a mistake, and if you do not leave, that is exactly what I am going to do."

"I'm not going to leave."

"So be it."

He turned around. The agony on his face nearly brought her to her knees. Then he strode past her, leaving the room, leaving her behind.

Chapter 15

The Honorable Stephen Lyons wished he were dead. Whenever he moved, his skull felt in danger of splintering into a thousand shards. The room carried the musky scent of glorious sex. Like a blind man, he gingerly searched the sheets for the bare bottom of the lovely lady with whom he'd shared the night, but she'd apparently already taken her leave. Just as well. He had to report to the War Office this morning. He wondered at the time.

Squinting, he rolled over to grab his watch only to see a man sitting in the shadows. He jerked upright at the unexpected visitor, then grabbed his head as pain reverberated through it. "Damnation. What the devil are you doing here?"

"I could ask the same of you, puppy," Ainsley said. "You're supposed to be in India."

"Devil take you! I've told you not to call me that."

"But it suits." He glanced around the shabby room. "Your accommodations are not to be desired."

"They're temporary." Just someplace to stay when he had a bit of leave. Tossing back the sheets, not bothering to hide his nakedness, he clambered out of bed and lumbered to the washbasin. He displayed the cocky mien for which he was so well-known, the one that irritated the devil out of his brothers—brothers who possessed the one thing he never would: a title. He resented their power and influence. Splashing the cold water on his face, he shivered and reached for a towel. Drying off as he went, he wandered back over to the bed, sat down, and flicked the sheets over his hips. "How did you find me?"

"I have my ways."

"I've always suspected there is more to you than shows on the surface. So *why* did you feel a need to find me? I've not been frequenting your circles. As a matter of fact, I've been working very hard not to draw attention to myself. So why the bother?"

"Westcliffe's been shot."

"Good God. I'm now the earl?" He'd wanted the title for as long as he could remember, but he'd never expected to have it. He'd not wanted to pay this price for it. Christ! He shook his head. "Why would someone kill him? Was it a hunting accident?"

"I didn't say he was dead."

He snapped his gaze over to his brother, only to find him scrutinizing him with those sharp green eyes of his. He knew women who bought emeralds simply because they matched the shade of Ainsley's eyes. Women had fawned over his brother from the cradle.

"You were truly taken by surprise," Ainsley said quietly.

"Naturally, I was. It's not every day that someone is sh—bloody hell! You're here because you think I did it."

"The thought occurred."

"Why would I do that?"

"Just as you stated. To gain the title."

"He's my brother."

"You cuckolded him."

He sighed deeply. "It wasn't like that."

"You let everyone believe it was. Suppose you explain."

He wished his head would stop aching, wished his brother would leave, wished the woman hadn't.

Ainsley leaned forward, resting his elbows on his thighs and grasping his hands. In spite of the fact that he was the youngest of the brothers, he'd always given the impression that he was the family patriarch. He had the more prestigious title and family heritage, and he had wealth. He'd given Stephen a generous allowance until the fiasco with Claire. "Why did you do it, Stephen? You can't have believed your family would forgive you for so flagrant a betrayal—"

"Mother did."

"She's the reason you're still in England." It was part question, part statement.

"It's astounding the influence she has. I truly had no idea."

"Why?" Ainsley persisted.

Stephen rubbed his brow and sighed. "Claire didn't want to be married. Not really. She was terrified of Westcliffe. So was I, truth be told. He'd always been so deadly serious. I thought if he found me in her bed, he would do exactly what he did. He'd exile her to the country estate. He desperately needed her dowry, so I knew he wouldn't seek an annulment. When Claire was ready to be a wife, she could explain things to him."

"And you truly believed he'd forgive her?"

"I was twenty-one and drunk. I believe in my invincibility and wisdom when I am drunk."

"I can scarcely believe Claire went along with this."

"She'd just turned seventeen. She'd never been in the London ballrooms. She had no sophistication. And . . . I didn't tell her everything."

Ainsley glared at him.

He released a deep breath. "I didn't explain that I was actually going to get into bed with her, not until I did. But I knew it would convince Westcliffe my intentions were dishonorable."

"He beat you to a bloody pulp."

"I know. I was there. Got a scar on my chin and one near my eye."

"You are a bloody fool."

"I love her, Ainsley. Not with passion or desire, but with a purity that doesn't characterize my experiences with other women. It's a brotherly devotion toward a sister I suppose. She has always been my friend, and I hers."

"Why didn't you simply tell Westcliffe how she felt?"

"He'd not listen to me. There has always been a strain between us."

"You could have told me."

"You're my baby brother."

"Idiot," Ainsley muttered.

Stephen shrugged. "In retrospect, I can't argue that."

Ainsley studied him for a long moment. "She's in London, you know."

"Claire?"

Ainsley nodded.

"Are things well between her and Westcliffe then?"

"Not quite, but they're not so awful either. He could scarcely take his eyes off her at the ball the other night."

He couldn't stop the smile from forming. "Well, then, perhaps all will turn out well."

"You're to stay clear of her, puppy."

"Absolutely. I want her to be happy. That's all I've ever wanted." He furrowed his brow. "So, who do you think shot him? Or perhaps more importantly, why?"

"Haven't a bloody clue."

The laughter echoing beyond the windows interrupted Westcliffe's concentration. Normally he would have been irritated with the distraction, but instead he was intrigued. It seemed to bring a lightness with it that made his office less gloomy. It flittered away, leaving behind a silence that wasn't quite as oppressive as before.

Only when he heard the trilling again did he realize that he'd paused in his work and leaned back in his chair, waiting in anticipation for the merry sound to enter his domain once more. He'd never brought ladies, not even Anne, to his residence. It had merely served as a place to study his accounts, consider his investments, discuss business with those who saw after his affairs. A place to sleep, to drink, to reflect.

It felt very different with Claire in residence. And even though hers wasn't the only laughter filtering in, he was fairly certain that he had accurately identified which belonged to her. It struck a chord deep within him that he didn't particularly want plucked.

Rising from his chair, he strolled to the window and looked out on the gardens. Lord Greenwood had arrived earlier. After a rather boring ten minutes of sitting in the parlor, doing little more than listening to the ticking of the clock on the mantel and addressing the occasional question about literature preferences, Claire had suggested they retire to the garden in order to appreciate the lovely sunshine. He'd not been surprised she'd prefer the light of the sun.

Westcliffe had excused himself to see to matters that required his attention. Business. Business always came first. It was his father's edict. Even at five, Westcliffe had taken his father's words to heart, determined to live up to his expectations. Only now did he realize that even then he'd longed for his father's approval, had searched for some evidence that he was as worthy as the babe who then received all of their mother's devotion.

And continued to do so. From Ainsley he'd learned that their mother had arranged for Stephen not to leave England's shores, although jolly good for him, he had an alibi for the night that Westcliffe was shot. In the two days since, he and Ainsley had both made several inquiries, but nothing had come of them. As far as Westcliffe knew, he had not a single enemy. If a cousin were after the title, he'd have to kill Westcliffe and Stephen. That seemed improbable.

They'd spoken with an inspector at Scotland Yard—Sir James Swindler. Based on the information they had to share, he could only advise them to keep a watchful eye. Nothing indicated that there was anyone who would wish Westcliffe dead. It could have been an accident. Some young buck showing off with a pistol. Without further evidence, the inspector was stymied, and as he had a reputation for being the best, if he could not help, Westcliffe certainly had no plans to behave as though his life were in danger.

Although he was having a difficult time believing he'd walked out on Claire when she'd been so willing to come to his bed, but making love to her would have been very unfair to her when he still wanted out of the marriage. A strange stance for him when he was not opposed to enjoying the delights of any willing woman. But Claire deserved more than to be treated with so little regard. While she might have indicated she'd changed her mind, he hadn't. She wanted to avoid scandal. He wanted a wife he could trust. With her, he would always doubt.

Claire was holding her mallet, shaking her head. From this distance, he could still see her indulgent smile. Apparently Beth was having difficulty holding her own mallet properly, as Lord Greenwood was standing behind her, manipulating her hands. Croquet was an opportunity for innocent flirtation, and it seemed Greenwood was a man who took advantage of opportunities.

As Beth clumsily tapped the ball, sending it away from where it should go, Claire's laughter rang out, and Westcliffe shifted his attention back to her. He wondered exactly where that ticklish spot was.

She was modestly dressed, her skirt swaying as she walked over to take her turn at bumping the ball. He imagined cornering her behind a trellis, skimming his hand along her calf, wiggling his fingers over the backs of her knees. Yes, that was where she'd be ticklish. Or was the sensitive spot higher up, on the inside of her thigh.

How did she even know she had a ticklish spot? Who'd first made her aware of it? Stephen perhaps? Fury roiled through him with the thought, shoving aside the pleasantness that had begun to work its way through him.

He didn't even realize he had stridden to the door and opened it until he was standing on the terrace. Claire had moved aside, giving the couple a moment to discuss strategy—although Westcliffe doubted whatever they were discussing had anything to do with the game. Based on Beth's smile and blush, Greenwood was no doubt whispering sweet words to charm her.

Claire glanced over her shoulder at Westcliffe, issuing an invitation with her eyes. He would have simply given her a nod and returned to his office if the invitation hadn't suddenly turned into a challenge. He needed a bit of fresh air anyway, so he strolled over as though nothing about his actions were of any consequence.

But as he neared, he wondered if touching the underside of her breast—her left one, the one nearest her heart—would cause her to giggle. But he didn't want her giggling—he wanted her laughing. Full, rich, and vibrant.

"What do you know of Lord Greenwood?" she asked, when he was near enough that she could speak quietly in order not to be overheard.

"He sits a horse well."

She laughed, the sound that had delighted him only minutes ago now irritating him because it came at his expense—and he wasn't even certain what he'd done.

"I've been on a fox hunt with him," he said

brusquely. "It's important to sit a horse well."

Her laughter subsided, but her smile only grew until her blue eyes were twinkling. If it were night, they'd be competing with the stars.

"It doesn't tell me how he might treat my sister."

"It does," he argued, "more than you realize. A man who sits himself well in the saddle will no doubt . . ." He let his voice trail off before he completed the inappropriate thought: *ride a lady as well*.

"You sit a horse well," she said, the brightness in her eyes darkening with passion as though she'd known exactly where he'd intended to take his earlier musings. "I've watched you when you visited the estate. You have such confidence, such command of the horse. I assume you exhibit the same sort of command in all situations."

"Your elbow," he blurted, to change the direction of the conversation, but hardly serving to alter the road on which his attentions were traveling.

Another small burst of laughter as her eyes widened. "Pardon?"

"The inside of your elbow. Is that your ticklish spot?"

He wasn't quite certain that he'd ever seen her exhibit such triumph. "I will never tell you, my lord. If you wish to know, you shall simply have to go exploring."

She started to walk off. Grabbing her arm, he swung her back toward him. "Don't tease me, Claire, unless you're willing to accept the consequences."

She took a step toward him, rising on her toes until she was almost in his face. Her breathing was harsh, her nostrils flaring. If there had been a trellis nearby, he'd have had her behind it in a heartbeat. "How do I convince you that I am?"

Chapter 16

To Claire's disappointment, Westcliffe had left her in the garden without giving her a chance to convince him of anything. As she lay in bed, she wondered what he'd been thinking as he'd walked back to his office. She wasn't aware when he left the residence. She only knew he hadn't returned for dinner.

When she was younger, she'd learned from Stephen that the most effective seduction was subtle, that it should occur without one realizing that it had taken place until it was too late. Strange how now that Westcliffe was willing to grant her freedom, she didn't want to have it. No, that wasn't exactly true.

She no longer saw marriage as little more than legal shackles. He was not the overbearing young man he'd once been. The years had tempered him. He'd been little more than melted ore, to be finely crafted, but within the center of whatever he might be was a flaw, a remnant of what she'd done to him, how she'd hurt him.

She could hardly blame him for doubting her

now. But she didn't want an end to their marriage. It would bring with it mortification. In that regard, nothing had changed during the intervening years.

Except her. She was no longer willing to be a wife in name only.

So many things to consider, so many plans to make. Yet she was so tired. A bit of warm milk. A good night's rest. And in the morning she would begin anew, would plot her strategy to remain the Countess of Westcliffe.

The house had settled in, everything was so quiet that she didn't bother to grab a wrap. She simply padded out of her room and down the hallway. She came to a quick stop outside the door that led into her husband's bedchamber. She couldn't recall hearing any movement coming from the room. She didn't want to contemplate the sting to her pride that came with the realization that he was probably finding solace in another's arms. Nor did she want to admit that she desperately wanted to be the woman in whose arms he nestled. If he did ever succumb to her charms, she would demand fidelity. Perhaps that was the reason he refused her—he knew she would take no less than total commitment.

She hurried down the stairs, wondering if she should detour by the library, see if he was there.

What did it matter? The only thing that mattered was that he wasn't in her bed.

She made her way to the kitchen, surprised to see a lamp on the table where Cook usually went about preparing meals. She'd left a mess. Seared meat remained in the skillet. It would be rancid by morning, although at present its aroma was quite enticing.

But there was no one in the room working. Perhaps someone was expecting a late-night visitor. However, when she went to set her own lamp on the table, she became aware of a soft murmuring.

She had a quick thought—*retreat, leave now*—but her curiosity got the better of her. Bending slightly, listening intently, she identified the corner of the room from which the low sound came. Peering around the corner of the table, she saw Westcliffe sitting on the floor, a bottle of whiskey at his side.

Cooper was nestled against his thigh, a plate of meat scraps—some raw, some cooked—set before him. Westcliffe's hand was buried in the fur along Cooper's neck. He was the one murmuring, encouraging the dog to eat, and she realized that in all likelihood, he was the one who had prepared a meal and left the washing up to someone else.

She hadn't meant to make a sound, but she must have because Westcliffe looked up at her, and her heart nearly broke at the sight of his red-rimmed eyes before he averted his gaze. As quietly and unobtrusively as possible, she padded over and knelt beside Westcliffe. "Is Cooper ill?"

His hand resting heavily on the dog's back, he nodded. "Simply far too old. The veterinarian says things are no longer working properly. Cooper's in pain, miserable. He's offered to put him down, but I thought he should have a last meal. He won't eat."

She covered his free hand, which was resting

on his thigh, surprised when he turned it over and tightly laced his fingers through hers. "Is that where you were earlier? With the veterinarian?"

He nodded. "Then I took him for a lengthy carriage ride, but even it couldn't restore his enthusiasm."

She wished he'd come to her. She wanted so badly for him not to feel that he had to go through moments like this alone.

"Fifteen years," he said quietly, "he has been my companion. Loyal beyond measure. He has accepted me, faults and all. Always happy to see me."

Tears burned her eyes and throat. This gentle, mourning soul was a side to him she'd never seen. "How did you come to name him Cooper?"

"James Fenimore Cooper. My favorite author. I always thought that if I had been born second, I'd have traveled to America and lived the adventures of a frontiersman."

"I suspect it's much more romantic in a book than in life."

He gave her a half smile. "I suspect you're right." He released a deep breath and the hold on her fingers. "I'm going to take him outside."

Her chest tightened. "And do what with him?"

"I should think he would like to lie in his favorite spot, beneath the roses for a bit. I'll send for the veterinarian in the morning."

"The ground will be cold this time of night. Wait here while I gather some blankets."

"Don't be ridiculous. You should go to bed."

"I'm not going to leave you to go through this alone." Before he could object, she hopped up and hurried off to gather blankets from a closet in the hallway. When she returned to the kitchen, Westcliffe was holding the dog in his arms, murmuring to him.

He had told her that he was incapable of love, and yet here was evidence to the contrary. He had a great capacity for love.

Grabbing a lamp and opening the door for him, she followed him out into the garden. The large rosebush to which he led her was in a distant corner, near a wall, near the bench where they had sat and talked one night. She arranged the blankets. Sitting down, she rested her back against the stone while Westcliffe made Cooper comfortable. The scent of roses wafted on the air.

"You should go in," Westcliffe said quietly when he settled in beside her.

"I'll be fine."

The lamp provided enough light that she could see Cooper's head resting on Westcliffe's thigh as he ran his long fingers through the dog's coat. Unexpectedly, she felt Westcliffe's arm come around her, drawing her near.

"Come closer, you must be cold," he said, and she wondered if his true reason had been to provide her with warmth or because he'd welcome a bit of comfort for himself. She burrowed herself against him, inside his jacket where the heat from his body had been captured.

"Your sister seems to get along quite well with Lord Greenwood," he said quietly, and she understood his need to distract himself from sorrowful thoughts.

"And he with her. In truth, I feared she'd find the Season a disappointment. She says I'm a pessimist, always fearing the worst."

"Yet you always persevere."

"I must confess that I did not come to London simply for her. I came for myself as well."

"To have the Season you never had?"

"No," she said softly, her heart hammering with the truth, wondering how he might take it. "To truly be the wife I never was."

She thought he would stiffen, perhaps turn away. But he held her nearer.

"I never thanked you for what you did with Lyons Place," he murmured. "Since you've been seeing after it, it is a . . . pleasure to visit there. It is almost what I had always hoped it could be."

"What is lacking?"

"Noise. Small footsteps echoing along the hallways. Laughter. Whispered secrets. It is too quiet there."

"Do you not relish the quiet? I was under the assumption most men did."

"Silence reminds me too much of sitting before my father's casket. I was only five, but I sat there all night. I thought perhaps he would come back if I did. I know my mother did not care for him, but I never doubted his affection for me."

"It's difficult to lose a parent," she said. "I was not allowed to go to my mother's funeral. I was always afraid that she somehow knew, that it made her sad, made her doubt my love for her."

"Children should not lose parents," he said quietly.

"Parents should not lose children." She squeezed his hand. "And people should not lose their dogs."

"No, but I have."

Sitting up, she thought she could see a well of tears in his eyes. "Is he gone then?"

He nodded.

"At least he was not alone."

"But now I shall be." He released a quick bitter chuckle. "I'm quite the selfish bastard, aren't I? Would you mind giving me a few moments alone?"

"No, of course not. I shall fetch a servant to help you see to him."

"Have him bring a shovel. I shall lay Cooper to rest here beneath the roses."

Her throat thick with tears, she nodded, rose to her feet, and headed to the house. She wanted to do so much more, but she knew he was not ready to welcome more affection or caring from her. He thought he was now alone, and she realized she needed to try so much harder to make him realize how much she'd come to care for him.

She needed to show him, make him understand, that he wasn't alone. That a collie named Cooper wasn't the only being to love him.

Chapter 17

L ord Greenwood has the most astounding sense of humor," Beth said, as their carriage journeyed along Regent Street.

They'd visited a milliner and a dressmaker. Of a sudden Beth was in want of a new gown to wear to the Countess of Claybourne's ball next week. And she required a new hat for her walks in the park with Lord Greenwood.

Both items purchased contained something that no other item in her wardrobe did: a shade of blue, which was Lord Greenwood's favorite color. Claire found herself wondering what Westcliffe's favorite color was. She'd thought it brown, but she was no longer certain. Quite honestly, she couldn't envision him taking up any thought with something so trivial.

"He constantly makes me laugh," Beth continued.

From the moment they'd left the residence that morning, she'd been lauding Greenwood's attributes.

"Do you think it wise to settle on one man so early in the Season?" Claire asked.

Beth gave her a look that conveyed she thought they should make a stop by Bedlam to drop off her sister. "When he is perfection, of course."

"No man is perfection, Beth."

"What are you saying?"

"That perhaps you should strive to discern his imperfections."

"There you are again, always looking for the worst. If you seek it, you shall find it."

"I simply think that a man's flaws determine whether or not he is easy to live with."

"And what are Westcliffe's flaws?"

"He is passionate in all things."

"And that makes him difficult to live with?"

"When his anger is sparked, but it does not make him intolerable. Our father, on the other hand, when he is angry—"

"Oh, God, please do not liken Greenwood to our father. He does not compare."

"It is only that while he is courting you, he is showing you only his better side. Were you to marry him, you would see all sides of him. I think it better to see all sides before you marry him."

"If you'd seen all sides to Westcliffe, would you have married him?"

Claire glanced out the window at the shops and busy walkways as the driver directed the carriage onto one street and then another. "I think I would have—yes."

And she would not have feared him at all.

"Have you come to love him then?" Beth asked.

"I have come to discover that he is very different from what I thought."

"That's not an answer."

"It's all I'm willing to provide at the moment."

"I find it amazing that Westcliffe is so much darker in temperament than Ainsley, and yet they are brothers. I should expect them to be more alike."

They had stopped to visit with Ainsley before going to the dressmaker. He had a way of making them feel welcomed. Claire had a question for him, and to her delight, he knew the answer. "They have different fathers, and their inheritances were very different, which in essence gave them different lives."

"Greenwood will inherit his father's title; he'll be a marquess."

"Very commendable."

"I do not think he is after me simply for my dowry."

As Westcliffe had been. He'd have not married her without the dowry, which he'd made plain enough. But that did not mean that they could not be happy. "I should hope not."

"How is a woman to know?"

"The greater question, I should think, would be: Does it make a difference?"

"In my esteem of him, no. I enjoy his company." She glanced out the window as the carriage drew into the drive of a residence. "Who are we calling upon?"

"Lord Chesney."

"Why ever are we calling upon him?"

Claire smiled as the carriage came to a stop. "Do you remember Ainsley mentioning that Lord Chesney had a litter of pups?"

"No."

"Well, he did. That day at the park." Which was the reason she'd had them stop by Ainsley's earlier—to garner the address. "And I'm in need of a puppy."

He was not a man who allowed his emotions to rule, but in the three days since Cooper's passing, Westcliffe could not deny that melancholy nipped at his heels in much the same manner as Cooper had when he was a puppy—always getting underfoot, tripping him up.

He kept telling himself that it was only a dog, but Cooper had been his friend. He knew of no one who was always as happy to see him as Cooper had been.

Although sitting in his library, he couldn't help but think part of his doldrums were brought on by the investment report he'd just received. Damnation, one of his investments was floundering. He had to right this situation immediately because he would not—could not—hold out his hand to Ainsley again. With the pages spread over his desk, he took a blank piece of parchment from the desk drawer, dipped the pen into the inkwell, and began scrawling out solutions to his investment woes. What he might sell, where he might invest with more success.

The door opened, and he fought not to groan as his intense concentration was shattered. Now was not the time for interruptions. Unfortunately, it seemed he was the only one aware of that.

He came to his feet as his wife walked into the room, holding something behind her back. Whatever it was required both hands. She looked like a mischievous young girl as she strode toward him. Before any damage to her feelings could be done, he said, "Claire, now is not a good time for visiting."

She gave him a gamin smile. "But I have something for you."

She came to a stop before his desk. "Do you want to guess what it is?"

He wished it was not so, but he was not in the mood for games. "Claire—"

Then out from behind her back, she brought a tan-and-white puppy, a collie. He'd have recognized the breed anywhere. His reaction came fast and furious, with no thought, no consideration. "Why in God's name would you get me a dog?"

Startled, she opened her mouth, closed it. Shook her head. "Well . . . to replace Cooper."

"Do you think something I have loved for almost half my life is so easily replaced?"

"I thought Fenimore would help fill the hole—"

"It cannot be filled, and it is certainly not your place—"

The tapping of water on paper stilled his words as horror swept over Claire's face. She pulled the dog back into her embrace, which only served to send an arc of dog piss over the corner of his desk.

"Did you have him drink a bloody lake before you brought him in here?" he demanded to know.

"I'm so sorry."

He looked at the mess on his desk. Life's sweet mockery. His life was a cesspool. "Bloody hell."

Knowing full well that a servant would be in to clean it up, he strode past Claire.

"Where are you going?" she called after him.

"Riding."

"But the dog?"

"I don't want him."

During times like this he missed not being in the country. It was damned difficult to urge his horse into a gallop when people and conveyances swarmed over the streets. Even the parks didn't allow for the sort of hard riding he craved because people strolled hither and yon.

Good God, he was in a foul mood.

Finally, he made it to the edge of town, where there were fewer houses, buildings, and people. He gave the horse its lead and let it race down the road as though they had someplace to go and only a limited amount of time in which to arrive.

When the horse was lathered, Westcliffe took

pity on him. Stopping, he dismounted and walked him over to a stream. Crouching while the horse drank, Westcliffe stared at London in the distance. He'd not ridden nearly far enough, but the truth was that it was impossible to do so.

He was trying to outrun himself.

He didn't want his wife to show him a kindness because it would be all the more difficult to let her go. He'd set his sights on starting the proceedings for a divorce at the end of the Season, of starting his life over with Anne, but he couldn't see Anne sitting with him on the cold ground while he waited for his beloved pet to cross over into the next life. He couldn't imagine her delight at bringing him a puppy.

If he'd not turned to anger, he might have wept at the sweetness of the gesture.

He had fought so long to be strong, not to need anyone, especially anyone in his own family—because they always seemed to disappoint—and yet, there he was finding himself needing Claire.

And that awareness terrified him, made him more vulnerable than he desired to be.

Anne cared only about Anne. He knew where he stood with her, would always know. They shared few emotional ties. It was the physical that bound them.

With Claire, there was so much more. She was like the river flowing before him. He could study the surface all afternoon, but unless he waded into it, he'd have no idea what ran through it.

Claire's flirtations were innocent, naïve, and touching. She did not possess the sophistication of other women with whom he'd been intimately involved, and yet he had a sense that she would be far more satisfying. The thought of taking the steps to learn the truth terrified him. Yet he had to admit that the more time he spent in her company, the more he yearned to have her. But everything would change.

Shoving himself to his feet, he grabbed the reins. "Come on, old boy. Back to town we must go."

"Oh, Fen, please go to sleep."

It was after two o'clock in the morning, and the puppy was whining and yelping as though his heart were breaking. Claire had placed him on a mound of blankets in a box in her bedchamber because somehow the little rascal had already managed to steal her heart, and she couldn't stand the thought of handing him over to a servant, who might ignore him.

It was obvious Westcliffe didn't want him. He'd not arrived home until long after supper, and based upon the cigar smell emanating from his clothes and the languid look in his eyes, he'd been enjoying himself at the club. They'd passed in the hallway, and he'd said little more than good night.

At least he'd said something. She took comfort in that.

But now, sitting on the floor in her nightgown, petting the puppy, trying to comfort it, she was exhausted and desperate for sleep. She'd managed to catch a few snatches, perhaps half an hour in all.

A rap sounded on her door. Probably Beth again, asking her to silence the dog. "Yes?"

The door opened, and Westcliffe came in. Barefoot, he wore only trousers and a shirt that was half-buttoned. It wasn't even properly tucked in. The hem just flowed around his lean hips. His hair was disheveled, sticking up at the back on one side. He was all rumpled, and she thought he'd never looked more delicious.

"Oh, I'm so sorry. Is he keeping you awake as well? I've tried everything. Warm milk, taking him for a walk. I'm at my wit's end."

His feet made not a sound as he walked over the carpet, which surprised her as his feet were so large, long, yet lean. He sat on the floor beside her, bent one knee, draped his wrist over it, and unfolded his fingers to reveal his pocket watch.

"What?" she asked caustically. "I just need to make him aware of the time?"

He gave her a self-mocking smile that tugged at her heart. Then he slipped the watch beneath the blankets in the box. The puppy went quiet and curled around it.

"Oh," she whispered in amazement. "Wherever did you learn that trick?"

"The servant who looked after the hounds at Ainsley's estate. When I first acquired Cooper, he was just as unhappy as this little fellow, and Mother, bless her, banished him to the stables. Of course, I'd not leave him to sleep alone, so I was there as well."

He reached toward the box, and she grabbed his wrist. "Don't wake him."

"Did I hear you say earlier that you'd named him Fenimore?"

She nodded. "After James Fenimore Cooper. It didn't seem right to name him Cooper, but as he's you're favorite author, I thought using another of his names would serve just as well."

With her fingers still wrapped around his wrist, he skimmed his knuckles over her cheek. "I owe you an apology for earlier. I'd received some unfortunate news—"

"Worse than your dog dying?"

"No, not worse than that actually. But I did not take well to the news. Some of my investments have taken a turn I'd have rather them not. It put me in a foul temper."

"They'll turn back around."

"I thought you were the pessimist."

"Only when everyone else is being an optimist. I like to be different."

"You've always been that."

She'd not seen him move, but he was suddenly nearer, close enough that his breath caused the strands that had worked free of her braid to lift slightly and tickle her temple. She'd left only one lamp burning low, but it was enough to see the seriousness in his gaze.

"It wasn't only your dowry," he said softly.

She furrowed her brow, and immediately his

thumb was pressing out the creases. "Pardon?" she asked.

"I didn't marry you only for your dowry or because of an archaic contract that was signed by our fathers. I wanted laughter in my life."

"And you've had little enough of it." She closed the distance between them, taking his mouth with a boldness that stunned her.

But she was tired of waiting for him to forgive her, tired of waiting for something monumental to happen between them, tired of waiting for him to come to her bed. Coming to her bedchamber was close enough.

Despite the tautness of her braid, his fingers were suddenly threaded through her hair at the side of her head, wrapping around to the back, holding her in place as his mouth plundered hers with far more efficiency and far less decorum. His tongue swept through, exploring and conquering every nook and cranny, every corner. Taking her cue, she dared to do her own exploring. As always, his taste was rich and flavorful.

Drawing her mouth from his, she trailed it along his jaw, his neck, until she was able to pinch his earlobe between her teeth. He issued a low groan, his hands behind her back, tugging on her hair, loosening her braid.

"Westcliffe, is the puppy the only reason you're here?" she asked with what she hoped was a sultry voice.

"No."

"Then you're here—"

"Because I couldn't stop thinking about you."

Pure unadulterated joy shot through her. She couldn't contain it, didn't want to contain it. She wanted him to see everything she felt.

But first, she had to kiss him again. Just as her lips met his, he pulled her onto his lap. Once again, he took over the kiss, deciding the direction in which it should go, and she found herself in uncharted territory. How many different ways could there be to kiss? This time he was suckling on her tongue, silk and velvet at the same time.

She tugged on his shirt, working it off his arms, lifting it to his neck. He had to break off the kiss so she could remove it completely, whisking it over his head. She expected his mouth to return to hers, and instead it went to her throat.

Just below where his mouth was, his fingers were making short work of loosening her buttons, and as the material began to part so his mouth followed the path until it reached her navel. While his tongue dipped inside, her breasts rested on the soft, thick strands of his hair. She ran her fingers through them.

Lifting his head, he slid the gown off her shoulders and down her arms. She saw awareness and anticipation light his dark eyes.

Without warning, he stood and pulled her to her feet, leaving her gown pooled on the floor. With no modesty whatsoever, he removed his trousers and cast them aside. Before she had time to completely take in his magnificence, his mouth captured hers again as he brought her flush against him, heat and hardness molding against the softness of her stomach. The sensations swirling through her were incredibly intense, but she knew no fear, perhaps because she had no reservations, no doubts.

Putting one arm at her back and the other behind her knees, he swept her up and carried her across the room. He followed her down as he laid her on the bed, his body half-covering hers, his leg wedged between her thighs. He skimmed his hand along her side.

"Where exactly is it?" he asked.

"What?"

"Your ticklish spot."

"You're mad. I can't laugh at a time like this."

"I want you to. Just once."

Releasing a burst of laughter, she raised her head and ran her tongue along his collarbone, relishing the saltiness of his skin. His arm came around her, pressing her closer to him, his hand holding the back of her head so she could linger at his throat. She nipped his skin, then soothed the spot with her tongue. His breathing grew harsher, his groans deeper. Turning herself into him, she skimmed her sole up his calf.

He was so firm, everywhere. He'd been gangly as a boy, less so on the day they married. But now he was all man, hard and muscled, toned and fit.

Pressing her back on the bed, he took his turn at torturing her by laving the side of her throat, journeying along the soft underside of her chin, then kissing his way down the other side of her throat. Each touch awakened something deep inside her, something that had been slumbering. Although she wasn't certain that was an accurate description of what she was feeling. She was holding nothing back. She wasn't afraid of him, wasn't wary of what he might deliver. For the first time, she felt up to the challenge of giving as much as she was given.

She'd seen him as a god, a man who knew his way around women, while she'd felt a novice. She'd equated physical experience with exquisite results. But she knew now that it didn't matter if she'd never touched another man intimately. It only mattered that she wanted to touch him, know the feel of him, bring pleasure to him.

She might not be accomplished, she might even be clumsy in her efforts, but they were honest attempts. The man she'd thought he was would have laughed, perhaps ridiculed her. The man she now knew him to be would appreciate her and urge her on.

He nibbled his way to her right breast, kissing the inside of it, his rough bristle abrading the skin, heightening her pleasure. With his tongue, he circled her nipple. It hardened, pearled, seemed to beg for something. She raised her hips, pressing herself against his thigh, the pleasure traveling from the center of her womanhood to her breasts, creating a tension that had her writhing.

He closed his mouth over her nipple, and she released a small cry as desire poured through her. Her nerve endings danced. Her skin had never been as sensitive. Her breasts felt swollen and heavy. Cupping the one he was suckling, he began kneading it, stirring passion that demanded something more.

She dug her fingers into his shoulders, clawed her way down his back. Growling, he pressed his rigid manhood against her thigh, and she wondered if the sensations were as unbearable for him as they were for her. She longed to reach the end of the journey, and with the next stroke of his tongue, touch of his fingers, she wanted them to continue traveling this path until it built into an inferno.

It was so close, so close. Their flesh had grown slick with the heat of their passion. She held him near while he slid his mouth across the valley between her breasts and began to give his sweet attentions to the other one. A suckle, a bite, a pinch, a stroke.

She scraped her fingernails across his hardened nipples, and he murmured, "Yes."

Lifting her head, she licked what she had scored, and he growled low in his throat as though she tormented him.

These moments were nothing like her aunt had described. There was no lying back while he lifted the hem of her nightgown. It was constant movement, constant stroking. It was giving and receiving pleasures. It was groaning while he growled, whimpering while he moaned. It was joy and satisfaction.

Again he took control, grabbing her wrists, raising them over her head, holding them firm with one hand. Her eyes captured his, and she watched as his gaze took a slow sojourn over her body. She saw the heat of passion burn more intensely as his nostrils flared, his jaw clenched. Her own breathing became labored. She thought she should have felt shame or embarrassment to be exposed like this, but all she felt was desired. He looked at her as though he'd never seen a more exquisite creature.

Dipping his head, he blanketed her mouth and his tongue delved more deeply, more passionately. Slowly, he trailed his hand down her hip, her thigh, and brought it around to rest heavily between her legs, his fingers gliding intimately—

She gasped as the pleasure speared her and shot through her until it felt as though there was no part of her body that he was not touching. Still kissing her, he swallowed her cries, her moans. He tormented her, but it was the most heavenly torture imaginable.

He returned his mouth to her breasts while his fingers elicited further sensations and cries from her. When she was near, so very near, to exploding like a thousand fireworks in the sky, he eased between her thighs and took her mouth with astounding eagerness, while she exhibited more boldness than she ever had expected of herself. It was as though they were parrying, then waltzing.

With him, there was no single movement, no repetition. Each kiss was different from the one that had come before it. Sometimes shallow, sometimes deep. Each touch was a surprise: a gentle caress, a firm stroke, a desperate urging. The dance of their bodies dictated the rhythm. What amazed her the most was that they seemed to be listening to the same music, that there were no missteps, no awkwardness. It was as though they'd been together a thousand times before while being together, truly together, for the first time.

She loved his rich, dark flavor, loved the musky scent of him heated by their passion. His skin was slick and velvety beneath her fingers, dampened by a light coating of dew.

Rising above her, with his knees, he spread her thighs farther apart, with his fingers he probed intimately. He rested his mouth near her ear, his harsh breathing echoing off the pillow. "Let me know if it hurts. I'll stop."

She nodded, even as she knew that if they stopped now, she would die from lack of fulfillment, and she was fairly certain he would as well. Why had she feared this? Why had she feared a man who would give her such consideration?

Then she felt the pressure as he pushed into her, the discomfort quickly following—

Then he gave a powerful thrust, and she cried out. They both stilled. She watched his face above hers, saw the agony outlined in his features.

Working her wrists free of his hold, she cradled his head. "It's all right."

"I didn't want to hurt you."

"It's better now." She gave him a timid smile. "Is this it then? Is this how it ends?"

He grinned. "It is far from over, sweetheart."

Before she could nod or respond, he slid a hand beneath her bottom, lifting her slightly, burying himself more fully inside her. He was thick and heavy, and she'd not thought she could take any more of him, but somehow her body accommodated his size. Then, slowly, he began to rock against her, pulling himself out, pushing himself back in, a little deeper, a little more insistent, a little faster.

The discomfort gave way to pleasure, jumping in leaps and bounds, and she was reminded of water playing over rocks in a nearby brook at the estate. The water splashed higher as the rocks got larger.

Her body tightened. She wrapped her arms around him, then moved her hands down to hold on to his firm buttocks. She eagerly met his thrusts as he pounded into her.

She lifted her gaze to find his eyes concentrating on her. His jaw was clenched, his breathing labored. There was a feral look to his features, a ferocity to the deep growls that rumbled through his throat. She thought she'd never seen anything as magnificent.

Watching him heightened her own pleasure until it became almost unbearable. She wanted to close her eyes, but he was so magnificent. And she suddenly knew what was driving him, why he was so focused on her face: He wanted to witness pleasure taking her over completely.

Then her body exploded, a thousand fireworks in every color, sparking throughout, dancing through her veins, tingling her flesh. She felt her body pulsing around him as he cried out, his thrusts going deeper, deeper—

Until he threw his head back, the tremors shaking them both. He collapsed on top of her, rose on his elbows to keep some of his weight off her. She wound her arms and legs around him, holding him near. Tiny rivulets of pleasure continued to journey through her, and she wondered how it was possible to still be conscious after what she'd just experienced.

His hands closed around her head as he held her in place and pressed his forehead to hers. "All I wanted to do was stop the damned dog from whining so I could get some sleep."

Laughing, she hit his shoulder. "Instead, you nearly woke him up."

When he lifted his head, he was smiling, the most glorious smile she thought she'd ever seen. "I never did find your ticklish spot."

"Perhaps you need to go exploring again."

"Perhaps so. But first, some sleep."

Rolling off her, he grabbed the sheet, flicked it

over both of them, and tucked her up against his side. Before she even blinked, he was gently snoring near her ear.

Claire awoke to find herself alone in the bed. She couldn't stem the tide of disappointment that slammed into her. She'd hoped that tonight their marriage had crossed a threshold, that they could truly embrace their roles as husband and wife.

Sitting up in bed, she realized she wasn't alone in the room. Westcliffe was sitting on the small sofa before the fireplace. He appeared to be staring into the empty hearth. Surely lying in bed, staring at his wife would have been more pleasing.

As her nightgown was on the floor near the sitting area, she grabbed her wrap from the foot of the bed and slipped it on. As quietly as possible she glided over to the sitting area. He was wearing his trousers but no shirt. His elbows were digging into his thighs, his chin resting on his balled fists. His gaze was indeed on the cold, empty hearth.

"Was it so awful?" she asked softly.

Glancing up at her, he released a dark laugh. "No. But you do realize it changes everything. There can be no divorce now. You were a virgin."

She knelt in front of him. "Did you think I wasn't? I told you nothing happened."

He shook his head. "I wanted to believe you, Claire—"

"But you didn't trust me." Yet he had taken her. "Do you still want an end to this marriage?"

Instead of answering her, he tugged on the strands that always fell over her scarred brow. "Why do these always seem out of step with the others?"

"Probably because I trained them to be so. I was always tugging them over my brow, trying to hide my scar."

"Why?"

"Because I thought it was hideous and made me ugly."

His finger slid down to her cheek. "Nothing could make you ugly."

"Why didn't you whisper such sweet words before we married?"

"I was too busy seeking out women who would make me feel I was worthy of love. It was always obvious my mother loved Stephen the most, and Ainsley is an irritating paragon of virtue. And a duke. *Everyone* loves a duke. He is powerful and has influence simply by his position."

"So do you."

"There are a great many more earls than dukes. We are not so special."

"You are to me. And I'm certain you are to your family."

He seemed to hesitate, then he said, "They have not been to Lyons Place since my father died. Lynnford would escort me there and explain my responsibilities. But my mother, my brothers, it was never home to them."

"Perhaps we will invite them to join us there for Christmas."

His eyes narrowed. "Have you no regrets for what happened earlier?"

"Nary a one."

"Do you want this marriage, Claire?"

"Have I not been clear enough all Season? I am ready to be a wife. Your wife. I want children."

"And what of Stephen?"

She rolled her eyes. "I have told you. He was a friend. You will never again find me in his arms."

He studied her for a moment, then he said, "Well, then, let me take you back into mine."

And with that, he lifted her into his arms and carried her to the bed.

Chapter 18

S he is quite taken with Greenwood," Claire said, as she strolled through Hyde Park, her arm linked with Westcliffe's, a short leash tethering Fen to her as he sniffed along the unfamiliar ground. She'd awoken in Westcliffe's arms that morning. While he'd slept, she'd done little but observe him. He'd seemed younger, more carefree, until his eyes had finally popped open. And then it had been as though the weight of the world settled on him.

She didn't know how to lighten his load. Their relationship was fragile, and she knew she had to tread carefully; but in time, she hoped they would share more than a bed. She hoped he would share his troubles and allow her to help him carry whatever burdens he now balanced on his shoulders.

"You don't approve," Westcliffe said.

The couple was walking several feet ahead of them. Beth was wearing a pale pink dress and her light blue bonnet. She was constantly looking up at Greenwood with adoration, and he was gazing down on her with adulation. From time to time, their laughter would waft back toward Claire and Westcliffe.

"She wanted a Season and after only one ball, she seems to be content with one suitor. She's given no one else an opportunity to garner her affections."

"Do you not believe in love at first sight?"

She snapped her head around to stare at him. "I'd have not expected that question from you. To even contemplate that love can come about so easily. No. Lust perhaps. But love? No."

"Why not?"

"Love at first sight would be love based upon only what you could see. The color of her hair, the shade of her eyes, the shape of her nose, the curve of her chin. Those are not things to love. Love must see below the surface, to a person's soul."

"But what if . . . you heard her laughter, watched the way she made the loneliest person in the room feel less lonely, saw her dance with even the most homely of men, noticed that her smile was seldom absent and always glittered in her eyes. First impressions, Countess, are not always based upon the attributes with which one is born."

"My God, I'd never realized you had poetry in your soul."

"Perhaps it is because I distract you with the poetry in my fingertips."

She laughed. "Those talented fingers have yet to find my ticklish spot."

"My desire to uncover it has lost its urgency. You're laughing more."

So was he, she realized. And his smiles were more forthcoming. He was not quite as formidable as he'd once appeared. Strange, how in so short a time, their relationship had changed to such a great extent. All because Beth had wanted a Season.

A dashing gentleman on a black horse brought the beast to a prancing stop in front of Beth and Greenwood. Sweeping his hat from his head, he engaged them in conversation.

"Who is that?" Claire asked.

"Possibly another suitor."

She squeezed his arm. She'd never expected that he'd be such a tease or that she would enjoy so much spending time with him, even engaged in an activity as simple as taking a walk through the verdant park. "His name?"

"Ah. Viscount Milner."

"Do you know him well?"

"I've played cards with him now and then. He has rotten luck."

"It's interesting to note that what a man values in other men is not at all what a woman searches for in a husband."

With a wicked grin, he capitulated. "He's a pleasant enough fellow."

"Did you pay him to dance with Beth at the first ball?"

"I did."

"And did he return the money?"

"No."

"Pity."

"You're judging too harshly. Love at first sight is often preceded by the discovery of the size of a lady's dowry."

Before she could make a scathing rebuke—even though she knew that was the way of things, as her circumstance had been—Milner trotted his horse over to them and bowed in the saddle. "My lady, my lord."

"Lord Milner," Westcliffe said. "How is your mother?"

"One day older than she was yesterday, which means she has one more ache in her bones. I daresay your mother seems to avoid the years."

"If rumors are to be believed, she made a bargain with the devil to keep her youth."

The young man laughed before giving Claire what she was certain was his most charming smile. "Lady Westcliffe, I was hoping you would allow me to call on your sister tomorrow."

"We would be delighted with your company, Lord Milner."

"Jolly good. Until tomorrow then, I bid you good day." Settling his hat into place, he cantered away.

Westcliffe lowered his head to hers, his breath skimming along her ear. "Are you happy now? Your sister has another suitor, a choice."

"I want her to have a choice."

"Because you didn't," he said quietly.

The darkness had returned to his gaze. She did not wish to pursue this path. "I simply want what is best for her. I want her happiness."

"A choice does not always guarantee that."

"A poet *and* a philosopher. I learn more about you every day." She hoped her teasing would return the lightheartedness to their walk.

"And I about you."

His eyes darkened with desire, and she thought he was probably thinking about last night more than any other day that had come before. Thank goodness, Fen started tugging on his leash, apparently wanting to explore the brush at a nearby tree.

"What do you think he's found?" she asked, irritated that she could be so affected by him with so little effort on his part.

"Let's see." He took the leash from her and began to follow the dog.

She glanced toward her sister. Westcliffe reached out and wrapped his hand around Claire's. "They won't get into any mischief."

"How can you be sure?"

"Because they're too busy gazing at each other to notice that we're not directly behind them to ensure they behave."

She scowled at him. "Why do you care so much about what the dog has found?"

He pulled her. "Come along. I'll show you."

They ascended a small rise, and she could have sworn that Westcliffe was leading the dog more than the dog was leading him. They went around the tall brush and the tree.

"So what did he find of such interest?" Claire asked.

Westcliffe grinned, snaked his arm around her, and pulled her flush against him. "A spot away from prying eyes."

Before she could protest, he was kissing her deeply, intimately, as though they were alone in her bedchamber. She should have shoved him back. Instead, she wound her arms around his neck. It seemed that the moment his mouth touched hers, she had no will to do anything except welcome him.

He had such a skillful way of plundering her senses. Everything came alive. He did have the good graces not to touch her hair, for she was certain he'd have created a mess that would have made it impossible to deny what was happening within the shade of the towering tree.

He dragged his mouth to her ear. "We should go home now."

Pressed up against him as she was, she was well aware of his readiness. She was surprised he didn't hike up her skirts here, more surprised that she might not have even objected. She could barely contain her disappointment when he was the first to step back. His gaze roamed over her, and everywhere it lighted, she tingled.

"Yes," she rasped, "we should inform Beth."

Turning, she staggered back with a small screech. Beth was standing there, an amused smile on her face. Lord Greenwood had the good manners to have his back turned, his gaze turned upward as though he were trying to determine how clouds remained in the sky. At that moment, Claire's opinion of the young man soared.

"Well, it seems my sister and her husband are the ones in want of a chaperone," Beth teased.

"The very fact that we are married signifies that we are not in need of a chaperone," Claire said tartly to cover her embarrassment at being discovered.

"But such public displays." She tsked. "I daresay if you weren't married—"

"But we *are* married, so any further discourse is nothing except irritating." She began marching down the incline. "Come along. We've had quite enough of the park."

She was halfway down when Westcliffe caught up with her and offered his arm. She placed her hand on it and slowed her step. "I cannot believe I am setting such a bad example."

"As you said, we are married."

She glanced over at him. He was smiling again. She so loved his smiles. "I think you enjoyed getting caught."

His grin grew wider. "I cannot deny there is a certain added excitement when the risk is there. Perhaps someday we'll do more than kiss someplace where the threat of discovery is great."

She shook her head. "Never."

But he merely looked satisfied, and said, "We shall see."

Good Lord, he was correct. Just the thought that someday . . .

* * *

Sprawled in a chair in Anne's parlor, Westcliffe watched as she paced. He remembered a time when he'd thought her magnificent in her fury, but now she seemed somehow diminished, petty, spoiled.

A half hour earlier he'd received a missive from her: *I must see you. Now.*

So he'd dismissed his investment manager and rushed over here, expecting to find her ill or in some sort of dire emotional distress. Instead, she'd greeted him with nary a word, simply a look that might have sliced a man to ribbons if he were dependent upon her affections.

Her reddish blond hair was piled into an elaborate coiffure, every strand in place. He couldn't recall ever seeing a strand out of place unless she desired it. Nothing escaped her. She was wearing a white dress with a voluminous skirt that she continually grabbed and snapped around so it didn't interfere with her quick steps and sharp turns. Her red lips disappeared and reappeared, depending upon how hard she was pressing them. Her breaths, like her movements, were agitated.

He considered speaking, but he'd once attended a lecture on volcanoes, and he had a feeling that he was on the verge of watching one erupt. The lecturer had described them as beautiful but dangerous. Westcliffe couldn't argue that point.

"I went riding along Rotten Row yesterday," she finally spit out. She neither looked at him nor ceased her pacing, but everything within him stilled. "Imagine my immense surprise when I spied you kissing your wife."

She did stop now to glare at him with all the force of her fury. He slammed his eyes closed. It had never occurred to him that she would see him or that what he'd meant to be a quick buss over Claire's lips would turn into moments of distracting delight. The latter, he should have known. He could not touch her without wanting more.

He opened his eyes to discover that her fury had evaporated, and in its place was devastation. Tears that he suddenly realized appeared with uncharacteristically good timing welled in her eyes.

"Why would you kiss her in public?" she rasped. "Why would you kiss her at all?"

Very slowly, he came to his feet. "Anne—"

"You're going to get a divorce."

He wasn't sure if she was making a statement or asking a question. He shook his head. "The situation has changed. I should have come to see you the moment—"

"How has it changed?"

He had witnessed his father hurting his mother and been determined never to bring harm to a woman. Yet in the span of three years he had hurt two. It did not matter that neither loved him. He was part of their lives, and he had treated them poorly. "A divorce is no longer . . . desirable," he said quietly, the words difficult to say, and yet doing so also brought a sense of relief.

Growing pale, she staggered back and slowly lowered herself into a chair. "You've bedded her?"

She said the words as though he'd admitted to eating dog excrement. For some reason, anger surged through him, not for himself, but for Claire. That Anne would not realize what a treasure his wife was, that any man would be fortunate to have her.

"She is my wife," he said, enunciating each word carefully and putting all the force of his position in society behind them.

"Do you love her then?"

Did he? He cared for Claire. He enjoyed greeting the day with her nestled against him. He certainly relished their lovemaking. Whatever feelings he had for Claire, she should hear them first, before anyone else. It would help if he could identify the need and want that battled inside him. "I'm sorry, Anne, but my feelings for her . . . are not to be shared with you."

"And what of your feelings for me? You have been my lover for six months. You have stayed with me longer than you have with any other— save your wife. And your time with her has been one of separation. Surely she has not won you over in so short a span of time. She has bewitched you with her constancy in your home. But you cannot desire her more than you desire me."

"Anne, I had not planned for my relationship with Claire to take this turn, but now that it has, I can give you no promises."

Looking down at her hands, knotted together,

she breathed deeply. "When my husband died, I made up my mind that I would love my next husband dearly." She lifted her face, her gaze filled with entreaty. "You are the one I wanted. Knowing your marriage had never been consummated, that you and your wife were estranged, gave me hope for happiness such as I've never had."

Swiftly, holding her gaze, he moved to kneel before her and brought her hands to his lips. "Anne, you must understand that I am incapable of love."

"Then you don't love her either. You can petition Parliament for a divorce. I can be happy without your love; I simply cannot be happy without you."

"It would not be fair to Claire. I have set my course. I intend to stay with her. You must accept that."

It pained him to see the tears rolling down her cheeks. Working her hands free of his, she cradled his face. "I shall miss you terribly, but if you believe you will be happy with her"—she brushed her lips, damp and salty with her tears, over his— "then I shall do as you say. I shall accept that you shall never be mine."

Pulling a handkerchief from her pocket, she blotted her tears and gave him a smile of bravado.

Standing, he pressed a kiss to her forehead. "Be happy, Anne."

Straightening, he strode from the room. For the life of him, he couldn't recall why he'd ever wanted to be in her company.

Chapter 19

Claire had decided there was little she appreciated more than seeing her husband dressed in his evening attire—unless it was seeing him not dressed in anything at all. During the past week, she'd learned he was an incredibly attentive and adventuresome lover. He didn't limit lovemaking to the bed. No piece of furniture was spared: a couch, a settee, a chair, a desk, a table. Even the bench in the garden if the hour was late enough and they were not likely to be discovered. She was surprised he'd not yet taken her to the park. Perhaps he would when there was no moon to reveal them.

Standing with him in the library, waiting for Beth to join them, she adjusted his cravat.

"How many more of these blasted balls must we attend?" he grumbled.

"As many as Beth wants," she answered. Tonight's ball was the Countess of Claybourne's—at last. Beth's gown had arrived only that afternoon. "Please don't pay any gentlemen to dance with her this evening."

"I shall be too occupied dancing with you to care who is giving attention to her."

"Well, unfortunately, as her chaperone, I will be paying attention to her."

"Not if I have my way." There was a wicked glint in his eye that caused her breath to catch.

"You're not thinking of doing something naughty while we're there."

"I wasn't until you put the thought in my head."

"We're going to behave."

"We'll see."

"I'm ready," Beth announced, and Claire spun around, hoping her cheeks were not as flushed with desire as she feared.

Beth twirled, showing off her pale blue gown, edged with dark velvet. "What do you think?"

Before Claire could respond, Willoughby strode quietly into the room carrying a silver salver with an envelope resting on it. "I'm sorry, my lord, but a missive has arrived. I was told it is quite urgent."

Claire watched with dread as her husband opened it, read it, and quickly tucked it into his jacket.

"I'm sorry," he said, his voice calm, absent of emotion. "You'll have to attend the ball without me."

"Whatever's wrong?"

"Nothing to worry over. Simply a situation with which I must deal." He put his hands on her arms, drew her in, and kissed her on the forehead. "I'll join you at the ball as soon as I'm able. Save me a dance."

Before she could question him further, he was striding from the room.

"That's a bit of a bother," Beth said. "I wonder what was so urgent."

Claire shook her head, wondering if a time would ever come when her husband trusted her completely, shared everything with her.

Claire would have been impressed with the Claybourne ball—if she hadn't been preoccupied with thoughts of Westcliffe. She didn't want to admit to herself that she feared he'd gone to the rescue of Lady Anne Cavill.

Jealousy was not an emotion she relished, but worrying that something was amiss with him was worse. She'd not wanted to come to the ball. She'd wanted simply to wait for his return, but Beth had told her she could pace at the Claybournes' as easily as she could pace at home.

Only she wasn't pacing. She was talking with people, trying to give the impression that she cared about the weather or which gentleman had taken an interest in which lady. While Beth's dance card had not filled up as quickly as before, she did not want for partners. Claire had even been asked to dance, but she'd politely refused both gentlemen. It wasn't because she feared Westcliffe would get jealous or angry—although he might very well do both. It was simply that she had no wish to dance with anyone other than him.

"Claire?"

She recognized the soft voice so the informality didn't surprise her. Turning, she smiled. "Lord and Lady Lynnford. How good it is to see you."

They'd often been visiting when she visited Ainsley's estate with her father. She'd always considered Lynnford to be one of the most handsome men she'd ever seen. Even as a child she'd recognized that he'd been blessed with perfect features. His hair was the color of wheat, his eyes the blue of the sky that overlooked the grain. It always surprised her that his wife was so unimpressive in comparison, so much shorter than he, with a roundness that reflected the five children she'd given him. But she knew no one who was kinder.

"We heard you were in London," Lady Lynnford said as she took Claire's hand, pulling her down gently as she reached up to kiss her cheek. "You look well."

"I am, thank you. I didn't see you at the first ball."

"We were taking the waters in the south of France."

"Is all well?"

"Oh, yes." She laughed with a hint of self-mocking. "We're simply growing older and more weary."

"To me you always look the same." Although she didn't, now that Claire studied her a little more closely. It did seem she'd aged, and not favorably. Whereas Lynnford did appear unchanged.

"Is Westcliffe about?" he asked.

"No, he had a matter to which he needed to attend."

"I see." She heard the disapproval in his voice.

"It was very urgent," she assured him.

"I'm certain it was."

And she suspected he thought her husband was with another woman. "Things are very good with our marriage."

He seemed surprised, and she realized she'd accurately judged what he was thinking about Westcliffe. "Are they?"

"Yes, we've made amends."

"I'm very glad to hear that."

She didn't know where to take the conversation, so she said, "My sister, Beth, is in London for the Season."

"Is she?" Lady Lynnford asked with true delight. "A pity our sons have no interest in marriage at the moment."

She tried to remember their ages. She thought they were younger than Stephen. "Ainsley feels the same," she said.

"And what of Stephen? Do you hear from him?" Lynnford asked.

"No. His regiment must be keeping him very busy."

"I'm sure it is."

"Well, my dear," Lady Lynnford said, squeezing her hand. "We must go speak with others. Do not be a stranger."

"I won't."

Watching them walk away, she wondered if Lynnford had always been so disapproving of Westcliffe. She wouldn't let his doubts about her husband weigh on her. She would know if he'd been with Lady Anne. She'd know—

"He trusted you to come alone?"

Spinning around, to her immense surprise, she found herself facing Lady Anne Cavill. She was stunningly gorgeous. There were no other words to describe her. And she smelled strongly of lilac. Claire forced herself to smile politely. "I don't believe we've been formally introduced."

"But I know who you are, and I suspect you know who I am." She glanced around. "I've not seen Westcliffe here."

"I'm not surprised. As he's not here, which I assume you knew since you mentioned my coming alone."

Lady Anne smiled, but there was nothing generous or kind in it. "You have not won him, my dear."

Claire's stomach knotted up so tightly that she almost doubled over.

"You may have him for the Season," Lady Anne continued, "but I shall have him for always."

"No," Claire said coolly. "I will not give him up, not to you, not to anyone. There will be no divorce."

"Is that what he told you?" She looked at Claire as though she were a silly child, as though she'd not changed or grown at all since her wedding night. "A man will always change his mind given the right incentive."

"He won't. And neither will I."

"For your sake, I hope you're right. I don't know if you could survive another scandal."

"Do not make the mistake of underestimating me. I will fight to keep him."

She arched a brow. "It seems you're not quite the gullible girl he said you were."

"You, however, seem to be quite the whore he said you were."

Claire saw her hand come up and was raising her own to block the strike when she heard, "Lady Anne, I've been looking everywhere for you."

"Ainsley." She spun around, smiled becomingly, and allowed him to kiss her cheek. "I was just talking with your sister by marriage."

"Really? How fortunate for her. I, however, am in want of a dance. Tell me the next waltz has been reserved for me."

"Of course, dear man."

As he led Lady Anne away, Ainsley winked at Claire. She tried to draw comfort from it, but she was trembling from head to toe. She hated knowing that Westcliffe had spoken about her with that woman. What had he seen in her beyond the beauty?

Beth was suddenly at her side, with Lord Greenwood standing nearby. "Was that Lady Anne Cavill speaking with you? Everyone is talking about the ball she'll be hosting at the end of the month. We've yet to receive an invitation. Is that why she was here? To invite us?"

"I do not think we'll be invited, and even if we are, we'll not be going."

"Why not? I want so desperately—"

"You can't have everything you want, Beth," she snapped. "I *want* my husband to be here. I want my marriage to be more than it is. I want—"

She pressed her hand to her forehead. "Let's get our wraps. It's time to leave."

"But there are more dances. I won't be happy if we leave."

"And I won't be happy if we stay. Tonight, my happiness comes before yours."

"That's not fair."

"You have no idea all I've done to ensure you have this Season. Do not speak to me of fairness when all I ask is that for one night we do what I want instead of what you want. I don't want either of us to make a scene here. You will come with me now, or I shall send our regrets to the hostess of the next ball."

Beth set her face in a mulish expression. "But what if Westcliffe comes here looking for you? He said to save him a dance."

Oh, he had, blast him. If she wasn't here, Lady Anne would certainly dance with him. But she couldn't expect Westcliffe to trust her if she didn't him.

"I'll explain to our hostess to tell him we had to leave early."

"You really do want to leave badly, don't you?" Beth asked.

"I truly do."

Her sister nodded. "Very well then."

Chapter 20

Westcliffe was not in residence when they returned. Claire prepared for bed, then went to his bedchamber, climbed into his bed, and began reading *The Last of the Mohicans*. It made her feel closer to him. While there was much he didn't share with her, at least he'd shared his favorite author.

It was a little past midnight when the door opened. She glanced over, and her breath caught. Her husband wore no jacket. His waistcoat was unbuttoned and his cravat missing. He was disheveled, his clothes torn and covered in dirt and blood. Black smudges marred his face. His right hand was wrapped in a filthy cloth.

"Oh, my God." She scrambled out of bed and rushed over to him. "What happened?"

"What are you doing here? Why are you awake?"

"I was worried about you." He seemed distracted as she led him over to a chair and forced him to sit. She cradled his face. "Westcliffe, what happened?"

"There was a railway accident. I don't know

what happened. The train went off the track. It was . . . awful."

"Why did they send for you?"

"I'm one of the investors. It was my railway. Nine died, Claire. At least forty were injured."

"I'm sorry. I'm so sorry. Why didn't you tell me? I would have gone with you."

"I didn't want you to worry. There was the ball." He shook his head. "You didn't need to see this."

"You didn't need to go alone." She touched his hair, his face. She could see the effect the night had on him in the strain in his face, the weariness in his eyes. Gingerly, she lifted his injured hand, realizing he'd wrapped his neckcloth around it. "What happened here?"

"I tore it, lifting metal. A man was trapped beneath what remained of a car. We got him out, but there was so much blood. I don't know if he'll be all right. His wife was crying, just standing there crying. Her dress was torn. I gave her my jacket."

He was rambling. He never rambled. It frightened her to see him like this. Leaning up, she pressed a kiss to his forehead. "I'm going to have the servants prepare you a warm bath."

"It's too late."

"No, you're trembling. I think a bath will help."

He nodded. "All right then."

"Just wait here until I have everything ready."

Claire had been right. He needed this. His aching, bruised body soaking in the steaming water. The tumbler of whiskey that she'd filled three times already. Her hands slowly, methodically washing the grime from his body.

He knew the horrific scenes would haunt him for as long as he lived. He couldn't imagine that a battlefield could look much worse. When it was all over, when there was nothing left for him to do, when he could finally leave, the only place he'd wanted to be was here—with her.

That terrified him more than anything. That he'd *needed* to be with her. He knew no other woman would console him as she did. No other woman would care for him as she did. No other woman could reach below the surface of him like she could.

Her hands gently massaged the lather through his hair and scalp. It felt wonderful. She didn't pressure him to talk. She didn't ask questions. She was simply there. It was more than enough.

"Close your eyes," she said, and she poured warm water over his head—again and again until the soap was gone. When she was finished, she moved around beside him, took a cloth, and began to tenderly wash his face. Earlier, she cleaned the gash on his hand and wrapped linen around it, with orders to keep it out of the water.

He thought he'd never smile again, but he did when he saw the wet spots on her gown, one in particular that made the shadow of her turgid nipple very visible. He flicked a finger over it. "Your nightgown is getting wet. You should take it off."

Cradling his cheek, she forced him to look at her. "I need more between us than just . . . bedding."

He blinked in confusion. What was she talking about? He felt as though his mind were swimming through thick pudding. His thoughts jumped around, never seemed to be sharp enough to grab onto conversation. Her words made little sense. No woman had ever wanted more from him than a good romp between the sheets. "I thought you enjoyed it."

"I do. It's wonderful." She dipped the cloth in the water and began scrubbing his chest. "But I want so much more. When your dog is dying, I want you to come to me, tell me, let me share the sorrow with you. When you have bad news, I want to know so I can share the worry or can help you find a way to make it all better. You don't have to do everything alone, Westcliffe. It's why I'm here. Not only to be beneath you, but to be beside you."

He cupped her face. "Claire, no woman has ever meant more to me than you. But you ask too much."

"You don't have to do it all tomorrow. Just know that I will never, ever betray you again. Whatever you tell me, whatever you share with me, it will be safe with me. I want to be here for you, Westcliffe."

"You want to give me what I need?" he asked.

"Yes."

He took her hand, carried it beneath the water, and used it to cover his rigid shaft. "This is what I need. Right now. I need you to stop talk—"

She rose, grabbed the hem of her nightgown, and lifted it over her head, revealing her slender, glorious body, inch by marvelous inch. He'd seen her naked before, but tonight it was a reaffirmation of the beauty of the human form—not mutilated or torn or battered. It was perfection.

Standing there, she unbraided her hair, then bent forward and brushed it through with her fingers before tossing it back. He couldn't believe how provocative so simple an action was. He started to get out of the tub, to take her to his bed if he could make it that far. Lifting a leg, she pressed her toes against his chest and pushed him back down.

She slid her foot down to his hip and slipped it into the water. Gracefully, she brought the other foot to rest in the tub. Straddling him, she lowered herself, enveloping him in a cocoon of molten heat. Wrapping his arms around her, burying his face against her breasts, he came fast and hard, with an intensity that nearly caused him to black out. For that brief moment, the horrors he'd seen had ceased to exist.

All that existed were the two of them.

She was stroking his back, combing her fingers through his hair, whispering that all would be all right, that she loved him. He couldn't repeat the words, couldn't allow himself to become that vulnerable to hurt, but he held her close for the longest time.

When the water had gone lukewarm, he rolled her over and washed her while she washed him.

After they dried off, he lifted her into his arms and carried her to the bed.

Claire hadn't meant to tell him she loved him, but the words had slipped out of their own accord. Strange to think that when she'd married him, she'd feared the physical side of their relationship—and to realize now that quite possibly he feared the emotional. He used his body to communicate, much more than words.

As he laid her on the bed, his mouth came down on hers with an urgency, then a gentleness. He massaged her neck, stroked her cheek. There was almost a sweetness to the kiss, as though he were imploring her to accept him, to want him. To be content with what he could give, even as he seemed to be acknowledging that he knew it wasn't enough. He could carry her to incredible heights of pleasure, but he couldn't reveal his heart.

He trailed his lips along her throat, a leisurely sojourn, leaving behind the dampness of his mouth and little tongue tickles. The urgency he'd expressed in the bathtub was gone. He'd needed her for a physical release that would cleanse him as much as the soap and water. She understood that, the importance of it. But how did she convince him that she could be so much more?

Had all the women he'd been with wanted nothing more from him than this? As exquisite as it was, she wanted him to know that he was so much more than this. But it was a task for another time, because he was very skilled at *this*—until all her concerns melted away, until she was lost in sensations.

His tongue circled one breast while his hand kneaded the other. Desire swirled, clamoring for the release he could provide. She threaded her fingers through his hair, as he scooted down, his breath wafting over her stomach. Delicious, intoxicating. He moved lower, parting her thighs.

"Westcliffe?"

"Shh." He looked up at her with heavy-lidded eyes. "It's your turn now."

He buried his mouth in the soft curls, and his tongue swept over her sensitive flesh. She nearly came off the bed, only he held her down, the fingers of one hand splayed over her stomach. They inched upward to cup her breast, and his thumb toyed with her nipple while his tongue continued its wicked doings below.

She skimmed her hands over his shoulders, felt his muscles rippling beneath her touch, just as her own body undulated with each stroke of his tongue. He suckled and nibbled. He thrust and soothed. The pressure built until she was arching against him, crying out, experiencing a cataclysmic release that had her soaring among glittering stars before falling back, breathless and limp.

His low moan echoed around her. He slid up her body, leaving a trail of kisses as he went. When he reached her throat, he eased off her and nestled his face in the curve of her shoulder.

She thought she felt his mouth form a smile before he drifted off to sleep. His arm and leg were draped heavily over her. She couldn't move. But she wouldn't have even if she'd had the ability. She simply wanted to stay curled against him.

Blood and carnage. So many crying out for help. He struggled to reach them—

He awoke with a start, a cry echoing around him. And she was immediately there, caressing his chest, kissing his shoulder.

"It's all right," she murmured softly. "Were you there again, in your dreams? At the railway accident?"

Not dreams, nightmares. He wondered how long before they'd dissipate. "Yes."

"Would you like to talk about it?"

"No."

The lamp on the bedside table was burning low, creating a halo around her. His angel. He combed his fingers through her hair. Why was she so different from the others? Why was being with her so different?

"How was the ball?" he asked.

She shrugged.

"Did you dance?"

"No."

"Did Beth dance?"

"Repeatedly." She tapped her finger on his chest. "What is it?" he asked.

She peered through her lashes at him. "You wish me to talk about what bothers me, but you won't talk about anything that you're feeling."

"Why don't you teach me how to do it by demonstrating?"

Grinning wryly, she shook her head. "After what you went through earlier, my troubles are nothing really."

"Troubles? What troubles?" He threaded his fingers through her hair, anchoring her head so she couldn't prevent him from studying her face. "Did something happen at the ball?"

"Lady Anne spoke to me."

He swore beneath his breath. Anne could be cutting when she wanted—and she very often *wanted*. "That can't have been pleasant."

"She said you told her I was a gullible girl."

"I didn't." He touched her brow, trailing his finger over her scar. "She uses her tongue as a weapon. Ignore her."

She gnawed at her lower lip before saying, "You might want to ignore her as well. I told her you told me she was a whore."

"Oh, God." He didn't know whether to laugh or groan. His wife had turned out to be a feisty wench. He so enjoyed her. He paused in his thinking. He did enjoy her, and not just here, in his bed. It was a startling realization.

"Do you still have feelings for her?" she asked, interrupting his musings.

Holding her gaze, he said, "No." He traced his finger around her face. "We never had our wedding journey."

She lifted a shoulder, shook her head.

"Let's take some time to do it."

She sat up, staring at him as though he'd gone insane. "What?"

"Let's go away for a few days."

"But what of Beth?"

"My mother could serve as her chaperone."

"Your scandalous mother as a chaperone?"

He dragged his finger down the center of her chest, his knuckles grazing the underside of one breast. "Please, Claire. I want to be absolutely, completely alone with you."

A warm and wonderful emotion he didn't recognize but still appreciated washed over her face. "We could be ready to leave by noon."

He owned a small stone residence that overlooked the sea. As Claire stood on the balcony of the master's bedchamber, inhaled the salt air, and watched the white-capped waves kick up, she couldn't help but feel this isolated spot was simply another example regarding what she didn't know about her husband. She wanted to sit him down and demand that he tell her everything about himself. Everything. Yet she also couldn't deny that there was pleasure in each discovery.

The stone cottage was maintained by a small staff. His manservant and her maid had accompanied them. But in the way of servants, they were discreet and noticeably absent. Which Claire acknowledged was the closest they'd come to being absolutely, completely alone.

She heard a noise, glanced back, and saw West-cliffe standing in the doorway, leaning against the doorjamb, his arms crossed over his chest. He'd divested himself of his jacket and waistcoat. The sea breeze ruffled his shirt, his hair. More strands than usual had escaped her own coiffure, and she imagined he would soon approach to begin tucking them back into place.

"What do you think of it?" he asked.

"I like it very much."

He stepped forward to stand beside her and put his arm around her waist, drawing her near, tucking her beneath his arm. "I like to come out here and simply watch the ships sailing in the distance. I imagine where they are going, what adventures those on board might experience."

"You would like to travel the world."

"I would indeed. I very much might when I have an heir who can see to managing my affairs."

Her stomach dipped as though a wave had taken it under. Speaking of an heir gave a permanence to matters.

Turning her slightly, he tucked strands of hair behind her ear—only to have the wind set them loose again. His lips curved up in a self-mocking grin. "You said you didn't wish an end to our marriage, and we have taken matters too far for its end to come about easily or simply. I believe our course is set, and we must make the best of it."

They were not the sweet words of undying devotion, but they were sweet nonetheless. He was not a man who gave easily of his heart. She was beginning to understand that. But he was the man with whom she wished to spend the remainder of her life. She had little doubt that in time he would say the words she longed to hear.

"I will not be able to stand it if you ever take another woman to your bed," she stated honestly.

"Since I discovered you were in London, I've desired no one else."

A burst of joy went through her. Even sweeter words.

"You should also know," he continued, "that I've never shared this place with anyone else. But I wanted to share it with you because you are not like the others." He shook his head. "I can't explain it, but you are simply not like the others."

It was enough. For now, it was enough. In time, she had little doubt, he would give her more. He would give her all of himself. She was partially to blame for his unwillingness to reveal everything within his heart, but she had seen enough of his small kindnesses, his love, his strength, to know that she loved him. She would do what she must to have him love her.

Rising, she wound her arms around his neck and kissed him.

* * *

"Is it here?" he asked.

He drew his tongue along the center of her sole until her toes curled.

"No," she answered, peering down at his dark head, rubbing her hand along his calf. He was stretched out beside her, but in the opposite direction. The windows had been left open, and the breeze fluttered the curtains. She could hear the ocean thrashing at the shore. As darkness had descended, they'd spotted the pale lights of a distant ship. She did find something calming about this place.

"Here," he said, twirling his tongue over her ankle.

"No."

"Can you not at least give me a hint?"

She gave him a seductive smile. "I'd rather you explore."

She couldn't believe her boldness, lying completely bare before him. His smoldering gaze traveled over her, causing her breathing to quicken.

"It must be someplace I've not touched, but I swear I've touched all of you." He studied her intently and she fought not to squirm. He sat up and skimmed his long, talented fingers along her leg, past her knee, along the sensitive flesh of her inner thigh. He teased the juncture between thigh and hip. She jumped but only smiled. His eyes narrowed.

"I've been very thorough," he murmured seductively, "along your front, along your back. Have I neglected your side?"

She shivered as he made his way up her body, like some predatory beast, until his face was directly over hers. "Which side, Claire?"

Shaking her head, she instinctively pressed her left arm closer to her body, and his beautiful, naughty mouth spread into a victorious smile. He released a low chuckle before moving to the side as though to leave her. The second she relaxed, he pounced, grabbing both her wrists, and carrying them over her head, holding them in place with one hand, his leg pinning her hips against the bed.

"Westcliffe—"

His laughter was both dark and teasing, just before his fingers lightly taunted her skin, near the swell of her breast. Beth had tickled her when they were girls, her fingers probing and jabbing—still she'd been powerless not to laugh. But his touch—

"Oh, God, don't!" She tried to buck him off, but he was too large, too strong, too powerful—except for the touch at her side that was more devastating, that made her squirm until a bubble of laughter erupted. "Don't!"

He stopped abruptly. As her laugh died, he cradled her face. "I love your laughter." Then he was kissing her deeply as though he wanted to explore for the sound.

Love. A word she was certain didn't come easily for him. But could he love her laughter without loving more of her? Perhaps eventually all of her?

He released her wrists. The game changed. It was no longer about tickling and making her laugh. It was about touching intimately, making her moan. And she did. She never could have imagined there were so many different ways to touch. Light and hard, soft and firm. A slow stroke, a tantalizing circle. A cool breath stirring the fine hairs on her nape. A warm breath heating her throat. There was nothing he would not do. There was nothing she'd not allow him to try.

She trusted him completely—in her bed and out of it. She believed he trusted her implicitly in his bed. She hoped that he was tentatively beginning to trust her beyond the bed. He'd brought her here, shared with her a place he'd shared with no one. They talked on the balcony about his dreams of travel. He wanted children with her. He wanted a legacy that was not a crumbling estate and a need to marry for coin. He'd even told her how very well-off they were now—he'd never be content with it, would always want more. He knew what it was to be dependent on another's good graces. He didn't want that for his children. He'd work to obtain what he desired, when most nobles wouldn't.

He was a man she respected, admired, and had come to love.

The passion between them flared as it always did. He entered her with one sure thrust, and she received him gladly, welcoming the thickness of him. They moved together in rhythm. Holding his gaze, she watched the contours of his face strain against the escalating pleasure. Beneath her hands, the muscles of his back bunched and undulated. Within her, the sensual sensations rippled and grew—until they could no longer be contained. When they burst through her, he was there with her, his body jerking, his hoarse calling of her name echoing and mingling with her unrestrained cry.

They came down from the pinnacle together, their arms wrapped around each other, their bodies slick and heated. Outside the waves crashed, but within, she knew a contented peace.

Stretched out on the sand, raised up on an elbow, he watched her wading out into the water wearing only a light cotton shift. This was an isolated stretch of coastline. There was little chance that anyone would come across them. He should join her, but the desperation with which he wanted to do so troubled him.

He'd never before felt anything beyond the physical with any woman—but with her he felt far too much. Always, he could hold his own satisfaction at bay, prolong it to draw out the pleasure, but when he made love with her, the emotional satisfaction of watching her climax heightened his pleasure to such a degree that he lost all control. His body shuddered with its intense release as hers did or so very near that he barely had time to draw in a breath.

With other women, he'd always felt something was missing. With Claire, he feared he might have found it. Her. He wanted her as he'd never wanted anyone. He needed her—and he had no desire to need anyone. He enjoyed her company. He appreciated all aspects of her.

He would awaken next to her, and his chest would tighten with such gladness—

He didn't like being dependent on her in this manner. He'd been dependent before. It made a man feel closed in, uncertain, less than a man. He felt none of those things with her, yet he knew she had far too much power. She could hurt him as she had once before.

She knelt in the water, then rose like some sort of nymph and began walking toward him. Devil take her! He laughed at the sight of her shift clinging to her, the stark white revealing the darkened shadows of her body. When she reached him, he grabbed her hand, pulled her down, and tucked her beneath him.

Smiling up at him, she issued her invitation. Bending down, he kissed her deeply, with longing. It had been only a few hours since he'd last taken her, but he intended to have her here while the sun and clouds watched, and the tide lapped at them.

She wanted him to trust her with everything. He wondered when she might recognize that he already did. That against all odds, he trusted her with his heart.

Chapter 21

⟨◦◦⟩

Claire sat on the ground in the garden, pulling a red stick on a string, chuckling as Fen jumped on it and attacked it with such vigor. A week had passed since she and Westcliffe had returned from the seaside. Beth had survived her time with the duchess remarkably well. Leo had begun painting a portrait of her. Another suitor, the third son of an earl, had begun calling on Beth, although she still favored Greenwood above all others.

She glanced up as Beth flounced down beside her. "You seem so remarkably happy," Beth said. "Are you glad you came to London?"

Claire bit her lower lip, then nodded. "I should have come long ago. I should not have accepted exile so docilely."

"What choice did you have? A woman is supposed to obey her husband."

Reaching over, she squeezed Beth's hand. "Which is the reason that it is important for you to consider all suitors. You wanted a choice, and you seem to have very quickly settled on one."

"But he's perfect. Why do you have such a difficult time believing that?"

Claire sighed. "Perhaps because I thought if I'd been given a choice, I'd have chosen another, and now I realize that marrying Westcliffe was the correct thing to do."

"What happened with you isn't going to happen with me."

"But sometimes what we think is right, isn't. I just want you to be cautious."

"I would rather listen to my heart."

Claire rolled her eyes. "Oh, you are quite the romantic."

Beth smiled. "Because I'm being courted by a very romantic man. When we take our daily walks through Hyde Park, he recites poetry. A different poem each day. Does Westcliffe read you poetry?"

Claire laughed softly. "No. Lately, we've been discussing how to ensure that Fenimore learns not to do his business in the house."

Beth groaned. "*That* is not something to be discussed."

"At least he is finally warming up to Fen. I had not considered that he would need time to mourn his loss. It made me like him all the more for it, though."

"At least he finally gave you flowers."

He had. That morning a dozen red roses had arrived for her, with a note. *Simply because.*

Because what? she'd wondered. Because he cared for her? Because things were right between them? She could think of a hundred things—and perhaps they all applied.

"Can you believe how many have arrived for me?" Beth said. "I think if Greenwood does ask for my hand in marriage that I might delay giving him an answer until next Season."

Claire worried that her sister might be becoming infatuated with the wrong things. "You risk losing him altogether. What if he decides you're not worth waiting for?"

"Then he doesn't deserve me."

"Wherever do you get your confidence?"

"I don't know. But I do know that I'm not marrying old Hester."

Claire looked up as the butler approached. Bending down, he presented a card on a silver salver. Everything within her went cold as marble when she saw the name: Lady Anne Cavill.

"Oh, my word!" Beth exclaimed, snatching up the card. "Do you suppose she's come to invite us to her ball?"

Claire was hit with a sense of dread. Nothing good could come of this meeting. Westcliffe wasn't here. He had matters concerning the railway to deal with. He'd been gone since early that morning. Perhaps that was the reason for the flowers— just to let her know he was thinking of her. She turned her attention back to Beth. "I don't know why she's here."

"We must welcome her immediately."

Beth made a move to get to her feet, and Claire

grabbed her arm, stilling her actions. "I shall see her. Alone."

"But, Claire, why? To be accepted by her—"

"Willoughby, on whom is she calling?" Claire asked the butler, hoping to put a swift end to further argument with Beth.

"You, my lady."

Claire handed Beth the string. "Keep Fen occupied, please."

Beth pouted, then shrugged. "Very well."

With the butler's assistance, Claire rose to her feet. She did hope Lady Anne was gone before Westcliffe returned. She couldn't imagine what the woman wanted. Or perhaps she could imagine only too clearly because her stomach was knotting. Ridiculous really.

If Westcliffe held no affection for Claire, surely he'd not continue to come to her bed and to remain there all night so he awoke to her each morning. He wouldn't hold her near. He wouldn't murmur in her ear. He wouldn't make her feel cherished. While he'd never proclaimed undying love, she couldn't help but feel that they were growing closer.

Inside the residence, she removed her bonnet and gloves, tidied her hair, and pinched her cheeks, not that they really needed any more color. She strolled as casually and calmly as she could to the parlor, taking pride in how welcoming it felt. She had truly begun to make the house into a home.

As Claire entered the parlor, Lady Anne Cavill

turned from the window. Her pale green dress was the perfect accent to her red-tinted hair.

"My lady," Claire began, grateful that her voice did not quiver and give away her nerves, "how kind of you to call. I've sent for tea."

"I doubt I'll be here that long." She extended a creamy white envelope. "I'm having a ball, and I wanted to personally extend an invitation."

Claire took the invitation. "Thank you. I'd—I'd not expected such kindness. Particularly after our last encounter."

Lady Anne blushed, her high cheekbones almost scarlet. "I must apologize for my behavior that night. I still had hope that I would be victorious. But it seems, my dear, that Westcliffe has developed an affection for you. He has informed me that there is no hope for anything between us."

Studying her, Claire did not think she could take being turned aside so calmly, not if she truly cared for the man. Now that she knew Westcliffe, she thought she would fight for him tooth and nail. "Will it not be difficult to have us present at your ball? I know it was no secret that you were his lover."

"And now it is no secret that I am not. But I've never been one to seek solace in shadows. I enjoyed his company and am grateful for the time we had together. I have little doubt that he will be reluctant to accept the invitation. As I'm sure you're aware, he has never been one to welcome attention. But it would truly mean the world to me if you would attend my ball. I believe in time we could become friends."

Claire thought that highly unlikely. The woman was too cold. She couldn't see Westcliffe wanting to be with this woman. But neither was she one to run from an uncomfortable situation. Not any longer. "I shall certainly consider it, and I shall talk with West—"

"Oh, Fenimore, come back here!"

Suddenly, Fenimore was scampering into the parlor, with Beth quickly in pursuit. Claire had the sneaking suspicion that it was not by accident that the dog had escaped his leash and run into the parlor to create havoc.

"Oh, please get him away!" Lady Anne exclaimed as Fen threw his small wiggling body against her skirt. "I can't tolerate the creatures."

"I'm so sorry," Claire began, bending down and picking up the excited Fen.

Clearing her throat, Beth nudged Claire's arm, giving Claire cause to remember her manners. "Lady Anne Cavill, allow me to present my sister, Lady Beth."

Claire thought perhaps she'd misread the earlier chill because the smile their guest bestowed upon Beth was warm and sincere. "I've heard quite a bit about you. You are all the talk among the gentlemen."

Beth blushed with pleasure. "Thank you, my lady."

"I daresay Lord Greenwood has set his cap for you. He is quite the catch. I hear he is of good fortune, three thousand a year, and when he inherits, it will be far more than that."

Beth's smile quivered. "It is not his potential wealth that draws me to him."

"But it is his wealth that will keep you warm, fed, and clothed. Do not take offense at what I've told you. When a man is of independent means, then you can be assured that his affections for you are based solely on yourself, which was all I was attempting to convey with my feeble efforts. My husband, may he rest in peace, married me for my dowry. It was a cold, loveless marriage. Sometimes I think he even resented that I was responsible for getting him out of debt. I was not sorry to see him pass, which no doubt makes me appear heartless, but there is nothing worse than knowing a man visits your bed out of obligation rather than desire."

Lady Anne's parting words haunted Claire long after their guest had left.

"We *are* going to go to Lady Anne's ball, aren't we?" Beth asked.

It was early evening, and they were in the parlor sorting through other invitations that had been delivered that day. Glancing up, seeing the keen expectation on Beth's countenance, Claire hated to disappoint her. "You have your suitor. I don't know that it's really that important."

Beth gave a quick pout before smiling. "You are

the one who said that I needed to explore my opportunities. This ball is supposed to be the grandest of the Season."

Claire returned her attention to sorting the invitations. "Each week there is at least one ball that is declared the grandest of the Season."

"Is it because of the attention she gave Westcliffe at the first ball?"

Claire snapped her head up. "You saw them?"

"They were difficult to miss." She furrowed her brow. "I don't know why she was licking her fan. If she was hungry, food was available in one of the other rooms."

But Claire suspected it wasn't hunger for food that she'd craved.

"Anyway," Beth said, "I would really like to attend this ball."

"I'll speak with Westcliffe when he returns home, but do not set your heart on going."

He arrived an hour before dinner. Claire was in her bedchamber having her hair put up after taking a relaxing bath, when he walked in, leaned against the post at the foot of the bed, crossed his arms over his chest, and studied her.

"Did you see to all your business?" she asked.

"The important business, yes."

Seeing that her hair was as tidy as it could be, Claire dismissed Judith. After she was alone in the room with Westcliffe, she turned on the stool to face him. "What was the important business?" she asked.

"The railway."

She was gratified that he didn't hesitate to tell her. "Will it ever run again?"

"I'm certain it will, but we're going to sell it to a bigger railway company."

"Why? Because of what happened? It wasn't your fault."

"The larger companies have bought out many of the smaller ones. Our choice was to work to become a larger company or move on to something else. I thought the larger company that was already established could do a better job of handling the railway, so I voted to move on."

"And you can take the money and invest elsewhere."

He glanced down as though suddenly enamored of his shoes. "We are going to do what we can to distribute the money among those who were injured or suffered the loss of a family member."

She'd wanted him to share with her, and as he lifted his gaze to her, she realized he wasn't a man who cared only for money. He wasn't like Lady Anne's first husband. Their marriage wasn't like hers. "It was your idea."

"I can't make a profit on something like this. We should have sold sooner. The larger companies have more resources. This tragedy might have been avoided."

She could see that he wasn't quite comfortable revealing this much about himself, his thoughts, his character. But this little peek, this little window into his soul was enough. She crossed over to him and placed her arms around him, leaning her head back and looking up into his stern, beloved face. "I love you."

"Claire—"

"It's all right. You don't have to return the words; you don't even have to feel them. It's like Leo said. It's enough for me that I feel them for you."

He touched her face as though she were porcelain, easily breakable. "Pity I saw how much trouble it was for Judith to put up your hair as I've a mind to take it all down."

Stretching up, she nipped his chin. "She can always put it back up."

As his laughter echoed around them, she knew they were going to be tardy to dinner.

Dinner had been an absolutely ghastly affair, Westcliffe reflected as he lay sprawled over the bed. He and Claire had been late. Then he'd discovered that Anne had called earlier in the day to invite them to her ball personally. After a brief discussion, Beth pouted, shouted that her life was ruined, then marched off in a tantrum because he and Claire had agreed they were sending their regrets to Anne. They would not attend her ball.

He didn't understand the girl's behavior. What was one ball among a dozen? Claire had attended none, not a single one, before she was married, and she'd not flounced around in a fit of bad humor. At least not that he'd seen. But he couldn't see her having done so.

Beth's reaction had put him in a foul temper. He'd retired to his library for a brandy. He'd only just finished it off when Claire had joined him.

"Have you a moment? I need you to help me find something."

The something she was searching for, as it turned out, was his ticklish spot.

"I'm telling you that I don't have one," he told her now.

"Shall I stop searching then?" She looked up questioningly from where she'd been running her tongue along his thigh.

He shook his head and grinned. "No, you should probably continue exploring."

She lowered her head to the soft flesh at his hip, and her hair trailed over his arousal. The touch was so light, like a cloud come to earth, that he thought it should have tickled, but all it did was make him harden even more, make his breath hitch, cause his body to feel as though he were suddenly surrounded by flames.

She was such a willing partner in bed, ready to try anything he might suggest, on occasion even suggesting something wicked, like drinking his brandy from her navel. He'd also sipped it from between her breasts, licked it from her nipples. She'd squirmed, protested faintly, and when he was done, she'd had her own brandy on his skin.

She toured his body as though someone had given her a map, but she took her sweet time arriving at her destination.

Slipping her hands beneath his buttocks, she dug her fingernails into his skin. He issued a low growl of satisfaction as her mouth closed over him, her tongue flicked—

Bucking, he threaded his fingers into her hair as his back arched off the bed, and he emitted an animalistic sound that he'd barely recognized as coming from him. Whenever he'd thought of bedding a wife, he'd never considered that she might have an adventuresome streak. He'd sought to pleasure her and experience his own gratification in the process, but he'd never expected that she would take such delight in pleasuring him.

"You're driving me mad," he ground out.

"Laugh for me," she said, before gliding her tongue up, then down.

Laugh? He could barely form coherent words. Every muscle was taut. Every inch of him begged for release. He thought he was skilled in the bedchamber, but she rivaled him with her wickedness. Here at last there was complete honesty between them, trust.

What surprised him the most was how desperately he wanted her. She was not forbidden, she was not illicit, she was not prohibited. The scandalous aspects of relationships he'd had with other women that had excited him before were absent with her.

She was legal. She was his wife. She was duty-bound to warm his bed.

Bedding her should have been dull, unexciting. It should have been predictable.

But inexplicably, each time was more amazing than the time that had come before it. Each passing day he learned more about her, so he enjoyed taking her to bed that much more. Each encounter was a discovery, each had him anticipating the next.

He watched her mouth, watched the swaying of her breasts . . .

God help him, he'd had enough.

Rising, he reached down and grabbed her beneath her arms. She laughed as he tossed her onto her back and pounced on her.

"You shall have to finish your exploring later." Hungrily, greedily, he kissed her, relishing the saltiness of his skin coating her lips.

She drew up her legs, wrapping them around his hips. He could feel her moist entrance and heat pressed against him. She was ready, but it was his turn to torment. He kissed, caressed, taunted, and teased until she was writhing beneath him. Then he rose and plunged into the velvety hot depths of her.

She cried out, her release immediate and swift, the spasms drawing him deeper as he hammered into her. She was no delicate miss, his wife. She was fire and passion.

He roared out as the cataclysm hit him, and he

slammed into her one last time, his seed scalding, his body replete.

Collapsing on top of her, burying his face in the curve of her neck, he fought to catch his breath. Another spasm, another tremor.

He wasn't certain he'd ever experienced a moment as intense. He felt the lethargy rushing in and barely managed to roll off her before sleep claimed him.

He awoke to find her sprawled on her stomach, her face turned away from him. Not the direction he fancied. He'd spent hours watching her dream. It had become one of his favorite things to do. He lightly tickled the now-familiar spot on her side.

With a low laugh, she turned her head to gaze at him. He loved the sleepy look of her, the way her eyes only opened halfway, the way her lips curled up as though she'd had pleasant dreams. And there was something about the scent of sleep on her skin that aroused him.

It was strange that when she was in his bed, he found it difficult to remember any woman who had come before, didn't want to contemplate any other woman.

"I think we should attend Lady Anne's ball," she said.

So much for arousal. He flopped onto his back, turned his head to study the canopy. "Is that what all this extra attention was about tonight? To sway me to your way of thinking?"

Her brow furrowed as she worked her way up to her elbows. "No. Using intimacy to gain favors from you would make me . . . well, not a very nice lady."

"A whore, darling. That's the word."

She scowled. "I don't like that word."

He arched a dark brow, and she amended, "When applied to me."

"And I don't like to be manipulated."

Scooting over, she pressed a kiss to his shoulder. It was going to take much more than that to get him thinking pleasant thoughts again.

"Earlier had nothing to do with my thoughts now," she said. "But if we don't go, then she'll have won."

"Won what?"

She shook her head as though to organize her thoughts. "She wanted you. You wanted her. You told me you wished a divorce. Now you've settled for me—"

"I didn't *settle* for you," he growled, interrupting her. "I'd have never walked into your bedchamber that night if I'd not wanted . . . more between us."

She began swirling her finger around his shoulder. "Are you fond of me?"

Trust her, his heart screamed. *Trust her with all you're feeling.*

But he couldn't open himself up completely. Couldn't tell her how deeply he'd come to care for her, so he *settled* for, "I adore you."

Her eyes lit up. "Then we must make an

appearance. We must leave no doubt that we are content with each other."

"We are more than content."

She began stroking him. "So we shall go?"

He growled a yes, then proceeded to tickle her senseless, to relish her laughter, before making love to her again.

Chapter 22

Claire took extra care preparing for the evening. It was ludicrous to be so concerned with impressions, but she didn't want to be found lacking in any manner by anyone. In some ways, tonight was more important than her wedding. It was an affirmation that her marriage was no longer floundering.

She wanted Westcliffe to stride into the ballroom, pride evident in his stance, contentment in his smile. She wanted him to be glad that she stood at his side. Wanted him to have no regrets.

She knew her efforts had been worthwhile when he wandered into her bedchamber. Appreciation darkened his eyes.

"Perhaps we shouldn't go," he said.

"Why ever not?"

He took a step nearer, raised her gloved hand to his lips. Through the material, she could feel the heat of his breath. "I'd much prefer spending the evening ravishing you."

"I would prefer to spend it being ravished."

"Then why, pray tell, are we going?"

"To make a point—"

"Which I do not believe needs to be made."

"—and for Beth. Whether Lord Greenwood asks for her hand or not, she will only have this Season. By next she will be married. She should enjoy every ball that comes her way, and this one is the talk of the town."

"That's Anne's way. She is not demure."

"I want it to be perfectly clear to her that she will not steal you away from me."

"But I might. She has a rather impressive conservatory. If I get too bored, perhaps I'll have you meet me there."

Her stomach knotted. She'd not considered that he might be intimately familiar with the lady's residence, as intimately familiar as he might be with the lady herself. To distract herself, she tapped him playfully with her fan. "Behave yourself. I'll not have us become the latest scandal or source for gossip."

"I find no pleasure in behaving." He reached for the wrap draped at the end of the bed and settled it over her shoulders. "Let's get this done, shall we?"

As they stepped into the hallway, Beth released a very unladylike squeal. "I did not think you would ever be ready."

Claire crossed over to her and slipped a stray strand of hair back into place. "You look lovely, dear heart."

"Thank you. And thank you for letting me have a new gown." It was white, edged in a royal blue that brought out the shade of Beth's eyes. Claire wondered if Lord Greenwood had stated that blue was his favorite color because he'd known what it would do to her eyes.

"I wanted you to have a magical night," Claire informed her.

"It will be the absolute best of the summer."

"Until next week's ball."

Beth laughed. "Yes, until then. Now, come along. We're going to miss all the fun."

As she started down the stairs, Westcliffe offered Claire his arm. "I believe your sister is anticipating the night enough for all of us."

"She still seems more child than woman."

"I cannot recall your ever being quite so . . . childish."

"I don't think I ever was."

The residence was lavish. Claire could think of no other way to describe it.

So many people were attending that almost every room was swarming with guests. The footman directed them to the parlor, where the ladies left their wraps and the gentlemen divested themselves of their hats and capes. Then they were escorted to the drawing room, where refreshments were served before guests were to enter the ballroom.

"Have you ever seen anything like this?" Beth

asked, clearly in awe of her surroundings.

"No," Claire admitted, wanting to answer quickly before Westcliffe had the opportunity to announce that he had seen it all. Probably many times over. She was already regretting that they'd come. Why had she felt a need to prove that he was now hers in every way? She feared her need to prove it meant it wasn't true. She wasn't nearly as secure about his feelings for her as she'd thought. Strange to suddenly realize that she did need him to say the words.

"Would you care for any refreshments?" Westcliffe asked near her ear, and she inhaled his familiar scent, drawing strength from it.

She had believed, still believed with all her heart, that Lady Anne was trying to make a statement, issuing a challenge by hand-delivering the invitation. Claire was determined to make a statement of her own: *He is mine. You cannot have him.*

"I don't believe I can eat a thing," Claire admitted.

"I would like some champagne," Beth said.

"Will this suffice?" a deep voice asked, and Beth turned in amazement to find Lord Greenwood extending a flute of the golden liquid toward her.

"Lord Greenwood, what a pleasure," she gushed.

"Lord and Lady Westcliffe. Good evening."

Pleasantries were made all the way around, then Lord Greenwood said, "Lady Beth, I've been watching for you. Knowing how quickly your dance card becomes full, I wanted to be certain I reserved my two dances."

"Were there any in particular you wanted?"

"The first and the last."

Beth beamed up at him. "You shall have them."

With a bow, he took his leave.

Beth took a sip of champagne before grinning at Claire. "He is the one, sister."

"The one what?" Westcliffe asked.

Beth rolled her eyes. "The one I shall marry."

Claire squeezed her hand. "He must ask first, dear."

"He will. I've told him Westcliffe speaks for my father."

"Maybe you should have asked your father first," Westcliffe said.

"He doesn't care," Beth insisted. "Come along. It's time to dance."

They wended their way through the crowd until they reached the stairs. As they were announced, and Claire squeezed her hand on her husband's arm, she couldn't help but feel a sense of ownership, of pride. This man was hers until death did them part.

"Good God," Westcliffe muttered, as they were descending the stairs. "Is that my mother?"

Claire looked in the direction he was gazing and saw the duchess talking with Lord and Lady Lynnford. Leo stood solicitously beside her. "Yes, I believe it is. And there's Leo. I suppose we should try to find time to finish the portrait."

"After the Season. We should have more time then—when your sister isn't bouncing from ball to ball."

There it was. Confirmation that they would be together after the Season.

Then they were approaching their hostess. She was stunningly gorgeous in a pale green gown. She took Claire's hands as though they were dear friends. "I'm so glad you could come."

"We're very happy to be here," Claire said. "It's so lovely."

"And you, Westcliffe," Lady Anne said. "You're looking well."

"I have much for which to be grateful."

Claire couldn't prevent a surge of gladness because she knew he was speaking of her.

"You are such a handsome couple," Lady Anne said. "She complements you, Westcliffe. I wish you every happiness."

With that, she turned to the next couple she needed to greet.

As they walked away, Claire said, "That wasn't so awful. I could almost see why you were drawn to her."

"Strange," he responded quietly. "I couldn't."

Now and then, stopping to speak to an acquaintance or two, they made their way to a group of chairs. Just as they did so, the music began, and Greenwood was immediately at Beth's side, whisking her onto the dance floor.

"I don't think she will be condemned to a life with Hester," Claire murmured.

"I would say not. I wonder if anyone has bothered to tell him so he can begin looking for other prospects."

"Perhaps we should wait until everything is official."

"After spending her Season flirting with Greenwood, even if he does not ask for her hand, do you really think she would even consider Hester?"

"It would all depend upon our father's wishes."

They'd been raised that their father's wishes came above their own.

"Now that you have experienced your sister's Season, do you regret that you didn't have one?"

"Not really, no. I don't think I would have found anyone I would have been happier with."

"But you will never know."

She was getting tired of this conversation. "Do you wish you'd been wealthy so you'd have not had to marry me for my dowry?"

"Unfortunately, yes. For your sake."

"You can make it up to me, you know."

"Can I?"

She smiled. "Ask me to dance."

She should have had a Season. It was all Westcliffe could think as he watched her dancing with the Earl of Lynnford. Their own dances had made him want to take her home. Her eyes had glittered more brightly than the chandeliers, and she'd never taken her gaze from him. He supposed he couldn't keep her all to himself when they were at an affair such as this, but he'd certainly wanted to.

He'd been surprised by Anne's warm welcome. Perhaps she had forgiven him. Knowing her, she'd probably already found another lover.

"Ignoring your mother?"

He swallowed his groan. He'd not seen her approach. Leaning down, he placed a kiss on her upturned cheek. "How could anyone ever ignore you? I simply didn't want to intrude when you were entertaining your admirers."

She tapped her closed fan against his arm. "Shame on you—lying to your mother that way. I know good and well when I am being ignored. You don't approve of my being here?"

"I'm *surprised* you're here."

"How could I miss such an event? The papers will be full of it tomorrow. Lady Anne has outdone herself this year. Do you still warm her bed?"

"Do you still warm the painter's?"

"He is an artist, and what I warm of his is none of your business."

"He is young enough to be your son."

"Only if I'd given birth to him when I was a child. Why do you dislike him so?"

"I dislike the gossip that surrounds you."

"I have survived far worse gossip than this. It has made me stronger, and at my age I do not care what others think. You, however . . ." She angled her head and looked him over with a discerning eye. He'd always hated it because she could tell when he was lying. "You're making a go of your marriage. Jolly good for you."

"How do you know?"

"The way you watch her. She is safe in Lynnford's arms. I'm glad for you. I know you've always loved her."

He closed his eyes, clenched his jaw, before glaring at her. "I do believe you are the most irritating mother in the world."

She smiled. "How lucky you are then that I am yours." She rose up and kissed his chin, the highest point on him that she could reach without his bending, and he was annoyed with her not to accommodate her and allow her access to his cheek.

"I shall see you later," she said, turning to go.

"Mother?"

She glanced back at him.

"Do you love him? The artist."

"I would be unwise to do so. He *is* young enough to be my son, and one day he will decide I have one wrinkle too many and off he will go to firmer pastures. But until then, I do intend to enjoy the devil out of his company. Besides, he makes me laugh."

He watched as she strolled through the throng as though she were a queen, granting an audience with one person, then another. He wondered how different she might have been if his father had made her laugh instead of cry.

He was distracted from his musings as a servant discreetly handed him a note.

"One of the guests asked that I deliver this to you, my lord."

Westcliffe waited until the man had walked off, then unfolded the paper.

The conservatory. Now.

No signature, but none was needed. They'd discussed the possibility of meeting there. He glanced around the room and spied Lynnford dancing with his countess, Angela. When had one dance ended and the next begun? He realized the music was different now than what had been playing when Claire was on the floor. How many songs had passed? How many rounds of dance?

He studied the note again. Oh, she was a wicked girl his wife. It was part of the reason he loved her.

The realization nearly doubled him over. His mother had spoken correctly. He had always loved Claire, but it had been a quiet fluttering in his heart, an untried man feeling a need to protect, to harbor. What he felt now was a deep need, an acknowledgment that she had become the center of his world. What he was experiencing terrified him, and yet at the same time it brought him an immense satisfaction and sense of well-being.

She'd wanted, needed, to come here tonight because he'd failed to reveal to her the true extent of his feelings. He attempted to show her with his body, with his gifts, but she needed the words. And those were so terribly difficult for him to give to her.

But she deserved them and so much more.

Tonight, now, in the conservatory was the perfect time for him to offer the last part of himself to her. He would wash away all her doubts, make her understand that the past hurts were completely forgiven and behind them.

Across the room, Anne, speaking with the Duchess of Greystone, caught his gaze, a brief flicker of farewell. No tantrums from her this evening. She'd welcomed them into her home and made them feel at ease. He would send her a gift tomorrow, to wish her happiness. All was over between them. They could each move on.

But for now, this night, this moment, belonged to his wife.

The conservatory was not at all difficult to find. Claire saw it in the corner away from the gaslights that lined the garden path. It was all glass but difficult to see into because of the abundance of plants, leaves, and fronds that filled it.

She wasn't exactly sure where he was going to meet her. The servant had simply said that her husband would be there, waiting. Coming to this ball had been the right thing to do. She and Westcliffe had danced four times, gone for refreshments, smiled, laughed, and conversed about nothing at all. Lady Anne had been warm, generous, and solicitous. And Westcliffe's attentions had been all Claire could have hoped for from a husband, friend, lover.

Their relationship had progressed to the point

that she felt nothing could tear it asunder. They'd grown stronger over the summer, individually and as a couple. They'd shared intimacies and sorrow. They were learning to rebuild.

Glancing quickly around, seeing no sign of anyone, she slipped into the conservatory. It smelled lovely inside. Rich dirt and scented blossoms. She'd like to see it during the day, see all the varieties that were being grown. No doubt the reason the ballroom was overflowing with flowers.

Carefully, she walked through to the back of the building. She was alone it seemed. She'd arrived first.

Small tremors of anticipation rippled through her. She wondered if such assignations happened often, if they were part of the Season. Briefly she wondered if she needed to keep a closer eye on Beth, to ensure that she didn't engage in any of these midnight trysts.

She heard the door open, close softly, and her heart began to gallop. She didn't turn to greet him, instead she looked out through the glass into the night. She could imagine him coming up behind her—

She heard his footsteps. Such large feet. The tread softer than usual, cautious, as though he wasn't exactly certain what he'd find. She imagined him lifting her skirts, envisioned her unbuttoning his trousers. She'd become so comfortable with the intimacy between them.

She barely moved as his arms came around her,

and he pressed his hot mouth to her nape. She tilted her head to the side, granting him easier access to the slope of her neck. He found the sensitive spot behind her right ear and swirled his tongue along it. Hunching a shoulder, she released a small laugh.

"Mmm. I've wanted this for so long."

Her insides froze, and she felt as though ice filled her veins. That voice—

He turned her around and planted his mouth on hers. The taste . . . no . . . it wasn't that of the man she craved. She pushed on his chest but his hold was like a vise, and the best she could manage was to bend her back like a bow to put as much distance between his mouth and hers. Although he was indistinct in the shadows, there was such a familiarity to him—

"Stephen?"

She felt his surprise in the jumping of his muscles. "Claire?"

She didn't know what possessed her to reach up and touch his cheek. She'd been so worried about him, and here he was. However had this come about? Before she could ask anything else of him, another familiar voice reverberated off the glass surrounding them.

"Well, now, isn't this cozy?"

Her husband was furious. Thank the Lord he'd not gotten into fisticuffs with Stephen although she was fairly certain that he desperately wanted to. But Stephen, perhaps knowing his brother's temper, had managed this time to quickly sidestep.

"Morgan, I can explain this," Stephen said.

"Of course you can."

"It wasn't supposed to be her."

Westcliffe merely laughed and grabbed her arm in a punishing hold. "Let's go."

He began dragging her—

"Do not handle her roughly," Stephen ordered, emerging from the darkest shadows.

"She is my wife, and I'll do with her what I bloody well want to!"

"Westcliffe—" she began.

"Don't talk, for God's sake, don't talk."

"Morgan—"

"No, Stephen," she commanded, holding up her free hand. "It'll be all right. He won't hurt me."

But neither would he release his hold as he pulled her from the conservatory. She nearly tripped, but his grip was so strong that he held her up.

"I don't blame you for being angry," she said.

"I wouldn't care if you did. We're going home."

"You're not going through the ballroom in this fit of temper, are you?"

"No, we'll go around to the front."

"What about Beth?"

"Damnation!" He staggered to a stop, waited a heartbeat, then continued on. "I'll deliver you to the carriage and go retrieve her."

"You must let me explain."

"Later."

She knew he was too lost in fury to truly hear what she had to say, so she merely allowed him to escort her to the carriage.

Claire watched as he strode back and forth in her bedchamber, grabbing armfuls of her clothes and stuffing them in the trunk, a duty normally reserved for a servant, but she assumed he thought a servant would take too long and too much care with her things.

"I want you out of this house and on your way back to Lyons Place tonight," he said.

"What about my Season?" Beth asked, standing horrified in the doorway, at the sight of Westcliffe.

"It's over," he declared.

"But a month still remains."

Westcliffe slammed a drawer.

"You are a tyrant!" Beth yelled.

He swung around and faced her. "And you are a spoiled miss who, like your sister, is not content with one man's devotion but must have more!"

Claire stepped in front of him. "Do not dare talk to my sister in that tone of voice."

"Do not push me tonight, Countess."

Claire glanced over her shoulder. "Beth, go pack your belongings."

"But Claire—"

Claire marched over to her and grabbed her arms, her own temper flaring at this abominable situation. "I will find a way to get you back to London for the Season, but for now it is best that you do as you are told."

Releasing a heartfelt sob, Beth ran down the hallway.

Claire pivoted around to face the wrath of her husband, who was closing the trunks. She took two steps toward Westcliffe and came to an abrupt stop when he swung around to face her.

The devastation, the look of betrayal on his face tore into her heart. But that he could believe this of her, after all they'd shared, pushed the knife that much deeper.

"You must listen to me!" she beseeched him. "Lady Anne Cavill arranged the entire meeting in the conservatory."

"You believe her to be that conniving?"

"Why will you think the worst of me and not of her?"

"Because you've betrayed me once, and she hasn't. You were the one who insisted we attend this damned ball!"

"I didn't even know Stephen was in London. You must believe that."

"I saw you in his arms."

"He mistook me for someone else."

"And did you mistake him as well, to allow him such liberties? We have not the same height, the same build, nor the same complexion so explain to me how you mistook him for me."

"I didn't."

"So you were in his arms knowing he was not me."

"Please, you must give me a chance to explain. We must sit down and talk calmly."

"I want you out of my sight tonight."

She took a bold step toward him. "If you persist in judging me without truly listening to what I have to say and send me back to Lyons Place when I wish to remain here, I shall never forgive you."

"Then we share that in common, for I shall never forgive you. Not again."

Chapter 23

I swear to God, when I first took her in my arms, I did not know it was Claire."

Ainsley sat in his library, sipping his nightly brandy, studying his brother who had arrived with an unbelievable tale. "If I'd known there was going to be so much excitement, I'd have gone to the ball, but they've been so dreadfully dull all Season that I could not bear the thought of attending another."

Stephen lifted his gaze from his knotted hands. "You don't believe me."

"Sorry, puppy. You're rather like the boy who cried wolf."

"I was supposed to meet Lady Anne there, but Claire arrived first. Then Westcliffe appeared." He shrugged. "I suppose they were going to have a tryst as well."

"Rather bad timing there, but explain to me why you would want Westcliffe's cast-off?"

"She's beautiful."

Ainsley laughed, then settled back in his chair. "Give him a day or two for his temper to ease."

"I'm worried about Claire."

"He won't strike her. That's not his way."

"But there are other ways to hurt her."

"In all likelihood, he'll do what he did before and send her back to his estate. He has never mastered dealing with unpleasant situations that involve women."

"What man has?"

Ainsley swirled the brandy in his snifter. "You know, running errands for the War Office is not exactly what we had in mind when we purchased your commission."

Stephen shrugged. "I knew Mother wouldn't let me leave England's shores."

"Perhaps you should consider cutting the apron strings, before you become a very unlikable fellow."

"I have a better idea. Let's trade places."

Ainsley knew that Stephen was being facetious on several levels. Stephen was well aware that even if they had shared the same father, they couldn't trade their positions simply because one of them wished to do so. Besides, even in the world of fantasy, something larger was at stake. As much as Ainsley had always loved his brother, he'd also been constantly disappointed that Stephen thought of little except his own pleasures. He found it difficult to admire him.

"You've never understood that possessing a title doesn't mean that one lounges about. As much as your offer appeals to me, and as much as I would love to shed my mantle of responsibilities—unfortunately I cannot leave the fate of all those who depend upon me in your hands. Sad to say, puppy, but you'll simply have to continue to resent me."

"It doesn't help that you call me that."

"Then by all means, waste not a moment more, put away your childish things, and grow up."

Beth was inconsolable, alternating between weeping and railing about Westcliffe, wishing he would rot.

Under normal circumstances, Claire would have been irritated beyond all enduring, but she was barely bothered by Beth's outbursts. She was immersed in her own grief. For Westcliffe to have refused to listen to her side of the story, for him to have jumped to his conclusions and clung to them so tenaciously meant he did not trust her, and without trust, he couldn't possibly love her as she had begun to believe he might.

She'd been physically ill on the journey back to Lyons Place. Several times she'd had to ask the driver to stop so she could empty her stomach on the side of the road. She'd grown so pale and weak by the time they reached their destination that even Beth had finally stopped bemoaning her unfair situation and begun to take notice of Claire's pallor.

In the days that followed, while she did not feel nearly as bad as she had on the journey, she seemed unable to shake off this cloud of nausea. It was always worse first thing in the morning, when she awoke to the realization that Westcliffe was not in bed with her. She'd spent a week staring out the window waiting for his arrival and his forgiveness. If he forgave her, in spite of her harsh words to him, she would forgive him as well.

By the second week, she'd regained her senses. She was not going to wallow in pity. She was going to get on with her life.

If only she didn't wake up every morning feeling so weakened and ill.

The missive delivered to Westcliffe, no fewer than ten minutes ago, by a servant of his estate was succinct.

I am with child. I hope it pleases you.

No signature, no affectionately yours, no nothing. Simply a few words that hit him in the gut as though they had been delivered with a battering ram. The first communication from her in a little over two months. Could she even comprehend how much the news would please him . . . and shame him? Regret for his behavior that night, for sending her off without even allowing her to speak, had been eating at him. Even all the whiskey he'd consumed couldn't drown it.

Sitting behind the desk in his library, Westcliffe peered up at the young man who'd had the honor of delivering the message. He didn't remember hiring him, but then he'd established a household allowance that Claire was to use as she pleased.

Obviously, it pleased her to hire comely young men.

"You're to stay the night here," Westcliffe said, as pointedly as the note. "I shall be sending a reply with you in the morning."

The young man bowed. "Yes, m'lord."

"What was your name again?"

"Blyton, sir. My father is the butler, although I go by Bly to avoid confusion."

"Bly. I see." He cleared his throat. He hated to admit that not a single hour went by that he did not think of her. "How is her ladyship?"

"Very well, I believe, sir. She is quite loved by the staff."

Westcliffe leaned back and rubbed his finger along his chin. "Why?"

Bly looked surprised, as though someone had come up behind him and pinched his bum. "Well, m'lord, she's fair in all matters. Manages the household with a firm but tolerant hand. I daresay, the manor is always more joyful when she's in residence."

So was his home in London. It had returned to its somber bleakness with her departure. She'd even taken the dog with her. Her scent had stayed behind, on her pillow. He'd forbidden the maid to wash it. He stared at it every night, remembering the way she'd looked, lying there, dreaming.

"I shall endeavor to work a visit into my busy schedule," he told the young man now, not certain why he felt a need to tell the man anything.

Bly bowed. "Very good, sir."

"Go see Cook about having a meal prepared for you."

"Thank you, sir."

After the young man left, Westcliffe got up and walked to the window. His heir could very well be on his way. He'd not expected that. He'd always taken such care not to get a woman with child, but then he'd taken none at all where his wife was concerned. But then why should he? After all, it was her responsibility to provide him with an heir.

If a son was born, he could grant Claire complete freedom.

A week after the ball, he'd gone to see Anne. She had been the one to send him the missive about the conservatory. She'd seen Stephen and Claire disappear inside.

"I thought you should know," she'd said.

"Why not tell me in person?"

"Because I knew you'd come to love her, and I could not bear to see the pain in your eyes when you discovered the truth."

Since then they'd attended one opera together, and he'd dined with her once. But he was not pleasant company these days because he could not seem to stop thinking about Claire. And now that she was with child—

He wanted to see her, to hold her, to place his hand against where his child now grew. But they had parted with harsh words and vows of never forgiving. He suspected she'd hold firm to her vows of not forgiving him.

He was having a damned hard time forgiving himself.

The three-inch-wide gold bracelet encrusted with diamonds was the most beautiful Claire had ever seen, the most extravagant gift she'd ever received. Only two words accompanied it: *Thank you*. Scrawled in script as bold as the one who'd held the pen.

Disappointment smashed into her. She'd wanted more. His arrival, his presence.

Standing in the parlor, she flung the gift across the room. It was nothing. It made a mockery of their relationship. Sparkles to hide the truth of their unhappiness. She despised living alone here. Even Beth had abandoned her, returned to London. With the possibility of a betrothal to a titled gentleman not in need of a dowry, she'd been able to convince her father to let her and the aunt who had raised them hire rooms in a hotel.

Claire couldn't be happier for her sister. If only she could find her own happiness. Although for those wondrous weeks in London with Westcliffe, joy had abounded.

She glanced over at Bly, who was standing as erect as when he'd first entered bearing the gift. She gave him a tremulous smile. "Thank you. You're dismissed."

"Yes, m'lady. If there's anything—"

"Nothing."

He turned to go.

"Wait."

He looked back at her, and she could see that he did indeed wish to do something to make this entire horrid situation better. The servants cared for her. Why couldn't her husband? Why couldn't he trust her? Why wouldn't he listen?

"Please have the groomsman ready my horse."

Bly seemed surprised by her request. "Are you certain it's wise—"

"Do not question me."

He bowed. "Yes, m'lady."

After he left, she retrieved the stunning bracelet, called for her maid, and went upstairs to change into her riding habit. Half an hour later, she was cantering over the moors, the wind whipping around her, ushering in the dark clouds in the distance. The groomsman followed along behind her, keeping a respectful distance. She hadn't wanted him to come along, but they all watched out for her since it was obvious her husband would not.

She would go to London. She would confront him. She would make him understand, because the more she thought about that horrid night, the more convinced she was that being caught in the conservatory with Stephen had been Lady Anne's plan all along. Issuing the invitation personally. Being so accommodating, so understanding that Westcliffe loved Claire. So many guests that the likelihood of spotting Stephen—

If he'd even gone into the residence. Perhaps he was only ever to meet her in the conservatory. She needed to speak with Stephen, to ask him why he'd been there. She should have done it before, but she'd thought it would only exacerbate the situation. Now she realized he might have vital information that could help her get Westcliffe back.

She couldn't deny her love for him, and this child was a chance for a new beginning. They did not have to remain estranged. If she could only make him see that they'd all been part of Lady Anne's elaborate scheme to get Westcliffe back.

With a renewed determination to face her husband and set matters to rights, she kicked her horse into a gallop. Was he with Lady Anne now? Was he back in her bed?

She couldn't tolerate the thought. The possibility brought tears to her eyes, blurred the countryside around her. The horse picked up speed, but Claire was paying little attention as the salty droplets rolled down her cheeks.

She was aware of the horse's sleek strides suddenly changing, the muscles bunching—

And then they were in the air, sailing over a hedgerow that Claire had not even noticed. Her hold on the reins was loose, her seating precarious. She'd not prepared for the arching movement. The mare landed hard and ungraceful, screaming as though in pain. Claire lost her balance, lost her seat. The rough, uneven terrain absorbed her impact as she landed in an ungainly sprawl. Blackness hovered, and she was aware of a single raindrop landing on the curve of her cheek, just before the agony ripped through her and dragged her into the darkened abyss.

Chapter 24

⟨⟩

"Where the bloody hell is she?" Westcliffe yelled as he burst through the door of the manor.

"In her bedchamber, my lord," Blyton answered.

Westcliffe couldn't recall ever seeing the butler so drawn and pale. He'd no doubt been up all night awaiting his master's arrival. The missive had arrived the day before in the late afternoon, delivered by Bly, and Westcliffe had been riding like a madman since. But it had still taken him longer than he wanted to get here. It was almost midnight.

Now he was rushing up the stairs, taking them two at a time. The house was so damned quiet. He couldn't recall it ever being so damned quiet.

At the top of the stairs, he saw a young maid coming out of the bedchamber carrying an armload of bloody linens. It was all he could do not to lean against the wall for support.

"How is she?" he barked.

Tears rolled down her cheeks. "She lost the babe, m'lord."

He slammed his eyes closed, the force of the grief hitting him hard. Not only the loss of the babe, but Claire suffering through it alone, when she had always been with him through the worst nights. He should have been here. Opening his eyes, he croaked, "Was it a boy?"

"We couldn't tell, m'lord."

"And my lady? How is she?"

"Fevered, m'lord. Not at all well."

"I must see her." It was a silly thing to say. He was the master. He needed no one's permission, and yet he worried over what he might find or what further ills his presence might cause.

The maid—he couldn't recall her name and at the moment he didn't care what it was—nodded.

Taking a deep breath, he opened the door she'd just closed and strode into the room. The sickly sweet smell of blood, death, and sweat battered him. He dreaded what he might see upon closer inspection, but he forced his legs to move forward.

Claire lay there, appearing so vulnerable, her hair damp, her face sprinkled with the sweat of fever. Another maid was carefully dabbing a cloth along her forehead. Claire looked as though all blood had been drained from her. This was his doing. His pride, his jealousy, his anger. He shouldn't have sent her here. He should have listened. He should have been a better man than he was. She was the only woman who had ever said she loved him—and he'd cast her aside because of his pride.

He reached out to touch her, hesitated, and

finally dared to lay his fingertips over hers, just the barest of touches.

"Stephen?" she croaked through cracked lips, her eyes opening only a fraction before closing again.

"My lord, she's delirious," the maid said quickly. "She knows not what she says."

Ignoring the woman, he bowed his head in anguish, shame, and regret. She'd loved his brother all along. He'd been willing to get a divorce so he could have Anne, a woman he cared for but did not love, but he'd been unwilling to get one so Claire could have Stephen, so Stephen could have her. If they weren't allowed to marry in England, they could always go to America.

The truth slammed into him. He'd not wanted Stephen to have Claire. He'd been jealous of the fact that Stephen had always had the lion's share of their mother's love—and he'd not been able to bring himself to allow his brother to have Claire's as well. No man deserved that much love when Westcliffe had none at all.

What a selfish bastard he was! For a few short weeks he'd learned what it was to love. She'd come to love him, but whatever she felt was nothing compared with what she must feel for Stephen. How could he deny her that?

He stormed into the hallway. The butler stood there as though he knew he would be needed.

"Have a horse readied for me," Westcliffe barked.

"Yes, my lord."

Westcliffe went into his bedchamber and stripped off the clothes he'd been wearing when the missive arrived. They were damp with his sweat and the rain that had beaten down on him as he'd neared the estate. Quickly, he drew on dry britches and a shirt. He grabbed the greatcoat from the wardrobe and swung it onto his shoulders. He snatched up a wide-brimmed hat and hurried back out into the night.

The horse was waiting. He hoisted himself onto the saddle.

"M'lord—" the groomsman began, but Westcliffe didn't wait to hear any warnings or advice. He tore down the cobbled drive as though Claire's very life depended on it. Everything inside him screamed that it did.

He changed horses five times before he arrived at his London residence just past midnight the following night. Soaked to the bone, he barked out orders as he strode toward the library, "See to the horse and have my carriage readied."

In the library, he downed a tumbler of whiskey in an attempt to stop the shivers that had begun rippling through him. Whether from the chill of his wet clothes or exhaustion, he didn't know. He just knew he needed them to stop. A second tumbler followed, before he hurried to his bedchamber and changed into dry clothes. A more formal attire this time, including a waistcoat and jacket.

Once outside he gave directions to his driver and climbed inside the carriage. As the wheels began to whir with the rapid movement of the vehicle, Westcliffe leaned back, rubbed his brow, and prayed he'd not be too late.

Stephen loved experienced women. Jocelyn worked nicely in that regard. A very naughty daughter of a viscount, she had consented to visiting him in his rooms. He knew she hoped to trick some poor sod into marriage, but it wouldn't be him. He took too many precautions. Still he intended to enjoy her and to make damned sure she enjoyed him. As he rode her, and her screams reached a never-before-heard pitch, he couldn't help but swell with pride. Tonight, he'd exceeded his own expectations regarding the pleasure they'd share. Tomorrow, the legend of his prowess would grow to unheralded proportions. What a reputation he was obtaining. He suspected when he finally left England's shores, a thousand women would weep, a thousand—

The door crashed open. He barely had time to turn and acknowledge the intruder before he was being dragged from the bed.

"What the bloody hell!" he yelled. "I'm involved here."

"Get your clothes on," Westcliffe commanded in that irritating I-shall-be-obeyed tone that he had as he began gathering up Stephen's clothes and tossing them at him.

"Not bloody likely," Stephen said, as he let his trousers hit him and land on the floor. "I'm not with your wife, so you'll leave—"

"My wife is dying."

Everything in Stephen stilled. "What the devil are you talking about?"

"She took a tumble from her horse, lost the babe—"

"She was with child?"

"Just get dressed. I'll explain on the way." Stephen had heard of men swallowing their pride, but he'd never actually seen it, not until that very moment when every ounce of arrogance Westcliffe possessed drained out of him. "She's calling for you. Please."

Stephen nodded and quickly drew on his clothes, not bothering to button every button or ensure that all was straight. He'd have time for that later.

He returned to the bed and gave Jocelyn a hard kiss on the mouth. "Sorry, love. I owe you."

"Damned right you do. Get back to me as soon as you can."

He gave her a cocky grin before turning to his brother. "Lead the way."

Finding Stephen had taken Westcliffe two stops. He'd gone to Ainsley first. He wasn't sure how the whelp managed it, but he knew everything that happened in the darker corners of London as well as in the brightest salons. His knowledge was uncanny. Ainsley had known where to find Stephen.

Only now, with his goal of finding Stephen achieved, did Westcliffe give himself leave to wonder what their future might hold. If only he hadn't taken Claire, if only he'd allowed his marriage to remain unconsummated, but she'd glided effortlessly into his heart. Then she'd begun her flirtations, her taunting, her teasing until he'd thought he'd go mad with the wanting.

He cursed his soul to perdition. What price would she now pay for his lack of control, his inability to trust, to love?

With dawn easing through the windows, Stephen awoke, stiff and sore, lounging on the bench of the coach. His brother remained exactly as he'd been when Stephen had finally closed his eyes: staring out the window.

"It wasn't my babe, you know," Stephen said quietly.

He thought he detected his brother's grimacing. "I know."

"Don't suppose you thought to bring any liquor."

"We'll be stopping soon to change horses. If you're quick about it, you should have time to get something to eat and drink."

Stephen didn't want to think that they might arrive too late. He might not be so concerned if Westcliffe didn't look as though he'd ridden through hell. "About your wedding—"

"I know what you did and why you did it, but it was still idiotic. I'm not going to relieve you of any guilt you might be feeling, so save the words."

"Rot in hell."

"Do you not think I'm already there?"

Stephen turned his attention to the dreary countryside. For the first time, he wished his mother hadn't managed to keep him in England. He thought facing hordes of Britain's enemies would be preferable to facing what awaited them at Lyons Place.

"It was supposed to be Anne," he said quietly.

"What?"

"In the conservatory." He looked at his brother. "I was supposed to meet Anne there. Claire was the last person I expected to see. Her back was to me. In the shadows I could tell little of her hair, little about her. I thought I was kissing Anne. She'd approached me—"

"She approached you?"

"Yes. In Chelsea. How she found me, I don't know. But she wanted us to have a tryst in her conservatory while there was a ball being held in her residence. She thought it would be wicked, fun."

"That sounds like Anne."

It worried him that his brother's voice was so flat and emotionless. He leaned forward. "I'm wondering, though, do you think her plan all along was to have you find me with Claire? If she knew your temper—"

"She knew my temper."

Stephen heard his brother's harsh curse. "She can't have been that conniving."

"If she wanted you badly enough," Stephen cautioned.

Westcliffe cursed again. "I shall never forgive myself if I am the cause for this."

"Perhaps if Claire recovers, and we know how she came to be there, it will all make sense," Stephen offered.

"Perhaps."

The rain had stopped, but the mud made for slow going.

"Are you sober enough to sit a horse?" Westcliffe suddenly asked.

"I can. Can you?"

"We'll transfer to saddles at the next stop."

They'd chopped off her hair. Westcliffe knew it was a silly thing to mourn: the loss of the glorious golden strands, but mourn them he did. The short tufts gave her the appearance of a baby chick.

"The physician said her hair was holding the fever in her brain," the maid said.

Westcliffe had never heard of such a thing, but then what did he know about the healing arts? He wished he'd had the wherewithal to think to bring a physician from London with him. Surely a doctor in the city knew more than a doctor in the country.

"Has she awoken?" he asked.

"A couple of times, m'lord, but she is so weak—"

She was still blabbering her dire predictions

when he went to the sitting area, selected a chair, and shoved it over to the bed, nearest the side where Claire lay. "Sit," he ordered Stephen.

"What?" Stephen stood at the foot of the bed, his attention on Claire, his face almost as pale as hers.

"The next time she awakens, I want to make damned sure she knows you're here. You're going to hold her hand, you're going to speak to her, you're going—"

"I don't see how it'll make any difference."

Westcliffe grabbed Stephen by the lapel of his jacket and swung him around, depositing him in the chair. "It might not, but it might. Take her hand. Talk to her."

"But you're her husband."

"You're the one she's calling for."

With a nod, Stephen did as he was told. Westcliffe backed away, dropped into a chair in the sitting area that gave him a view of Claire and Stephen. He was not a religious man, but he began to pray.

He remembered her as a young girl, traipsing after Stephen, often looking after Ainsley. She'd played with his brothers, climbing trees, chasing butterflies. Westcliffe had always considered their antics too childish, beneath him. He was so much older, the man of the family after his father had died. Even when his mother had married the eighth Duke of Ainsley, Westcliffe had been reluctant to relinquish his place as the one in charge.

He'd never approached life with the frivolity

that Claire had. It was one of the reasons he'd anticipated marrying her. While he'd recognized that he was ridiculously somber, he'd expected her to balance out his life.

He supposed, in retrospect, he should have told her the qualities he admired in her. He should have courted her. He shouldn't have assumed she'd be delighted to marry him. What did he offer? Nothing of any significance, yet she took it all and made it better than it was.

Perhaps he should have risked scandal and let her go when he realized he was not the brother she wished to marry. Pride had forced him to keep her. Now the price she might pay for his transgressions was too high to contemplate.

Dawn was easing in through the part in the draperies when Stephen rose from his chair with a wide yawn. "I'm going to bed. Wake me when she stirs."

"Sit down." His voice sounded as though a frog had taken up residence within it. It was dry and scratchy, and his body was alternately chilled and hot.

"Westcliffe—"

"Sit. You will be there when she awakens."

With a groan, Stephen dropped back into the chair. His head fell back as he stared at the ceiling. "Nothing is to be gained by forcing me to endure these discomforts."

"God help me, you do not deserve her love."

"And you do?"

Westcliffe placed his elbow on the arm of the chair and began to rub his throbbing head. "No."

"You have a care for her, though."

Westcliffe held his tongue.

Stephen sat up straighter. "By God, you love her. Why are you not sitting here?"

"Because she called for you." Every bone and muscle ached as he rose from the chair, crossed the room, pulled back the curtains, and opened the windows. Sunlight and fresh air. Perhaps they would help. The cool morning breeze had barely wafted into the room when he heard Claire's faint voice.

"Stephen?"

"Hello, sweeting. You gave us quite a fright."

Westcliffe glanced toward the bed. She was giving Stephen a soft smile while he toyed with the tufts of her hair. A fine sheen of perspiration coated her face and throat. He wondered if her fever had broken.

He was halfway across the room to fetch a maid to see to her needs when he heard her quiet voice. "Westcliffe?"

Staggering to a stop, he glanced back. She was holding out a hand to him. He didn't know what she wanted of him, but he crossed back over to the bed. She looked so much thinner. Had she lost weight while they were separated? Or was it simply that she was diminished after surviving her ordeal?

They seemed to stare into each other's eyes

forever. Hers were as blue as he recalled, but the brightness had left them. Finally, she whispered, "The baby?"

Slowly, he shook his head. "I'm sorry."

She started to weep. Without thinking, he crawled onto the bed and folded her into his arms as sobs shook her body. He'd never known such pain, to see her shattering like this. His usually bold and determined wife, her heart breaking. He covered the back of her head with his hand, held her close, murmured reassurances. He was barely aware of Stephen slipping from the room.

He almost called him back, almost told him that it was Stephen she needed—but she'd called to him, had held out her hand to him. He could no more let her go now than he could cease to breathe.

Eventually, she fell asleep in his arms, exhaustion and weakness from her ordeal claiming her. He was awash in regret as he found a maid to see to his wife's needs and sent another servant to fetch the physician.

Once he was assured that his wife would recover, he collapsed on his bed.

It had been two days since Claire had wept in Westcliffe's arms. Since then, he came into her bedchamber every morning to ask after her health, but other than that, she hadn't seen him. They were back to being strangers, and she was once again exiled from his heart.

Now sitting at a small table enjoying the light

breeze of the afternoon, Claire sipped her tea. It seemed she had another ticklish spot. Her scalp, as the wind fluttered the short strands. She touched them self-consciously. She would need some new hats.

She was thinking of such silly things so she didn't have to contemplate the loss of the baby. She'd already come to love him, already missed him.

She glanced up and smiled as Stephen sat beside her.

"I think Westcliffe has recovered sufficiently that we can begin our journey back to London today," he said.

"Westcliffe—recovered? From what?" she repeated.

"I don't think he slept from the moment he received the missive that you'd taken a tumble. Made himself ill."

"I didn't know. I didn't think he cared any longer."

Stephen twisted in his chair and took her hand. "Sweetheart, why do you think I'm here? He forced me to come. In your delirium, you were calling for me, and he feared only my presence would save you."

"I don't remember. I remember thinking . . . before I fell from the horse . . . that I needed to speak with you. Why were you in the conservatory that night at Lady Anne's?"

"She'd come to see me a few days before and issued an invitation for a *private* party in her

conservatory. Said she thought it would be fun
to have an intimate party with me while another
party was going on in her residence."

"I think she arranged for you to meet with me
instead. I'd been dancing with Lord Lynnford.
When the dance ended, before we could leave the
floor, a servant said he had a message for me. So I
followed him. He told me Lord Westcliffe had bid
me to meet him in the conservatory."

"Did you tell Westcliffe?"

"No, I didn't think he'd believe me. I had no
proof. I'm fairly certain she arranged everything
to ruin things for us."

"She succeeded."

She nodded. "I don't know where we'll go from
here." She glanced back at the house.

"He loves you, Claire."

She laughed bitterly, trying not to think about
the tenderness with which he'd held her while
she cried after learning she'd lost the child. "No,
I think not."

"He rode to London to find me—in the storm.
He looked like bloody hell. When we got here, he
wouldn't let me leave that chair. He didn't see to
his own needs until he was certain you were all
right. He does care for you, Claire."

"He doesn't trust me. He wouldn't even listen
that night at Lady Anne's."

"God, Claire, what was he to think? He found
us together on his wedding night. And then to see
us together again? I can't blame him for what he

thought." He took a deep breath. "I can't believe what we did on your wedding night. I knew your reputation would be safe because his pride would prevent him from telling anyone, but I hadn't anticipated that he'd fill his nights with other women. That was incredibly unfair to you."

She was torn between laughing and crying. "Perhaps deserved. We were so stupid."

"You trusted me, and I—"

She gave him a wry smile. "Your plan worked."

"A little too well I think."

Reaching out, she held his hand. "I've missed you. Why didn't you let me know you were in London?"

"I messed things up for you, Claire. The best thing I could do was stay away." He touched her cheek. "I'm going to go even farther away."

She stared at him uncomprehending.

"I'm going to be leaving England, Claire." He bestowed on her the devilish grin she'd always loved, but there was a touch of self-mockery in it. "I've been told that I'm a man without character. I've finally come to believe it. My brothers bought me a commission, and like everything else in my life, I've not made the most of it. They've both wagered that in battle the enemy will see only my back. Can't have them win that wager, now can I?"

"But you could get hurt or worse."

His smile was familiar, cocky, daring. "Not to worry. I have the luck of the devil."

* * *

Claire found her husband in the library, behind his desk, scrawling some letter, some bit of business. He immediately rose to his feet as she neared his desk and came to a stop.

"How are you feeling?" he asked.

She was acutely aware of his gaze roaming over her. She touched the cropped strands of her hair. "Light-headed."

He flashed her a quick smile. "It'll grow back."

"I should hope so. I understand you were ill."

"Exhausted, I think." He shifted his stance. "I'm sorry . . . for a good many things regarding you. I . . . you deserve better." Looking down, he touched the paper on his desk. "I've been working on wording a petition to go to Parliament for our divorce."

Her heart very nearly stopped in her chest. "You told me that you didn't love Lady Anne Cavill, that she doesn't love you. You deserve someone who loves you."

The disbelief, mingled with the sadness in his eyes, told her that he thought she was simply giving him trite declarations—to avoid scandal perhaps, to evade the shame of an unsuccessful marriage.

"Claire—" he began.

And she cut him off, taking a step nearer, desperate to make him understand. "If I called out for Stephen in my delirium, it was only because before I fell I was thinking that I needed to speak with him about our meeting in the conservatory. I was there because a servant had told me *you* were waiting for me. Stephen was there because Lady Anne had told him that she'd be waiting for him."

"Yes, so Stephen told me. She wanted to separate us, and it worked. Some good can come of this. It made me realize that you love Stephen. We can find a way—"

"No!" She stepped forward. "Yes, I do love him, but it is the love of a friend or even a sister for a brother. It is not that of a wife for a husband."

Taking another step, she staggered, grabbed the back of a chair. Westcliffe was immediately out from behind his desk, his arm about her steadying her. Releasing her hold on the chair, she wrapped her arm around his neck and lifted her gaze to his. "You own my heart," she whispered, as tears welled. "I can't tell you the exact moment you took possession of it. I only know that I long to hear your laughter, that I constantly listen for the tread of your boots because even if you are not in the room with me, knowing you are near eases my loneliness.

"I am willing to withstand any public ridicule or scandal so that you might find happiness. If indeed you do love her and cannot love me—"

"Claire," he rasped, his large hand cradling the back of her head, holding her tightly. "How can I not love you?"

Her heart swelled.

"You are all that is good and sweet and

innocent," he continued. "To consider that you could truly love me—"

"Do not consider it, Westcliffe. Be certain of it."

He knelt, but held her hands tightly, giving her the strength to remain standing. "I never asked you to marry me, and for that I apologize. But I will ask you this: Will you honor me by remaining my wife?"

"Oh, you silly man, the honor is mine."

She thought she would forever remember the adulation in his eyes at that moment as the walls he'd built to protect his heart crumbled. How could he have lived his life with only one assurance: that he had the love of a collie?

He was so strong, so good, so noble. She wasn't certain her heart could contain all the love she felt for him. How could she have ever doubted that he was the perfect husband for her?

He swept her into his arms and carried her from the room. On the terrace, where her tea was growing cold, Stephen was waiting to say good-bye, but she didn't care. He would have to wait. The man in whose arms she was now cradled would always come first from this moment on. She'd never give him reason to doubt her affections.

In his bedchamber, they curled together on the bed. She was still recovering, too weak to do anything but lie in his arms, but it was enough, to be held by him.

"If I had it to do over, I would have granted you

a Season," he said, as he trailed his finger along the curve of her cheek.

Cupping his face, she leaned up and kissed him. "But what would it have mattered? At the end of it, I still would have been yours."

"How can you be so sure?"

"Because I think I've been yours all along. I was just too silly to recognize it."

Chapter 25

~~~

Lady Anne Cavill was slipping beneath the sheets when the door to her bedchamber burst open and crashed against the wall. With her hand to her heart, she spun around and nearly swooned at the specter of death charging through the doorway. Terror gripped her—

Then she relaxed as she recognized the intruder. "Oh, my God, it's you. You look like hell."

Relief swamped her because he was once again in her bedchamber. "You don't know how glad I am to see you."

She'd barely laid her hand against his chest, before he closed his fingers around her wrist in a viselike grip, stilling her actions. With her other hand, she tried to pry his fingers loose. "You're hurting me."

"You hurt Claire. She lost the babe."

Her heart stammered. "Don't be ridiculous. I haven't set eyes on her in months."

"I know what you did, Anne. You knew what had transpired on my wedding night. You were the only one I was foolish enough to tell, and you used the information to destroy what Claire and I were building."

He persisted. "You wanted me to find her with another man. From the beginning, the ball you arranged was an elaborate ruse designed to provide an opportunity for me to find Claire with another man. But not just any man. It had to be Stephen. Otherwise, I might have given her a chance to explain. But not if I found her with Stephen. You knew my rage with him would blind me to all else."

She thought she knew this man, but she'd never seen such fury. She jerked her arm back. "Let me go!"

But he held firm. She yanked back again, and he did as she asked. Off-balance, she fell backward and landed on the floor. He took a menacing step forward, towering over her. "I love her, Anne. I will do anything to see that she is happy. Stay clear of me and mine, or I swear before God, that I will destroy your reputation."

She pushed herself up. "You don't understand. I love you!"

He shook his head. "I don't believe you know what love is. God knows until recently I didn't. Stay away from Claire. She owns my heart. She always will."

He turned on his heel and began to walk away.

"No!" she cried after him. "Westcliffe, you can't leave me. You're mine."

He stopped in the doorway. "It's over between us."

He disappeared into the doorway. Uncontrollably weeping tears that for the first time in years did not appear on command, she collapsed on the floor.

He didn't understand how very much she loved him. She loved him far more than *Claire* ever could. Anne would do anything. Absolutely anything for him.

"I adore your hair," Beth said.

Claire laughed. It had been a little over a month since her fever had broken, and she still wasn't accustomed to not having long tresses.

She was sitting on a chaise in the garden. Beth was in a chair beside her, holding her hand as though she thought if she let it go, Claire would disappear.

She and Westcliffe were having a small family gathering at the country estate. They all knew what had happened and wanted to visit. She was feeling stronger. She'd even had a couple of days when she hadn't thought about the child she'd lost. Westcliffe had yet to make love to her. He held her every night as though she were the delicate shell of an egg. She wanted so much more. She supposed it was time to let him know.

After their company left perhaps. His mother and both brothers were here. There was not the easy camaraderie between the brothers that she would have liked to see, but nor was there the strain that had characterized their relationships until recently. She thought that, with a bit more time, they might all become the best of friends.

Leo was also in attendance. He'd decided that the portrait should be completed here. He'd found a salon he thought had the perfect lighting. Since things had improved between her and West-cliffe, Leo no longer thought that a bedchamber was necessary to accomplish his goal of playing matchmaker.

Westcliffe walked over and knelt beside her. Beth, exhibiting a bit more maturity, excused her-self to give them a moment alone.

"You don't want to overdo it with the company," Westcliffe said.

"I was thinking of withdrawing in order to take a short nap. I don't suppose you'd care to join me?"

She saw the doubts in his eyes as he kissed her hand.

"I'm fully recovered. The doctor said so."

"I can't believe I'm going to say this—I'd like to spend a bit more time visiting with Stephen. He'll be leaving England as soon as he gets his orders. He's warned Mother not to interfere. Maybe after your rest, he could walk you about the garden."

"Just the two of us?"

"Just the two of you."

Leaning over, she kissed him. He trusted her at long last, he trusted her completely. "Thank you. Tell him I'll meet him at the pond in twenty minutes."

He helped her to stand, and she felt his gaze on her as she made her way into the manor.

In her bedchamber, she saw the black skirt of one of the maids peeking out from behind the open door of the wardrobe. She was no doubt putting away some things.

"Please see to those matters later," she said. "I'm going to lie down for a rest now."

She walked toward her bed so she could yank on the bellpull. Suddenly, a cloth was covering her mouth—

And the world went black.

When she awoke, she was lying spread-eagled on the bed, her arms and feet secured to the posts. She was gagged, and, to her horror, Lady Anne Cavill was standing over her.

"You're wondering what I'm doing here," Lady Anne said, smiling benignly. "It's simple really. I love Westcliffe. He doesn't understand how much. I would do absolutely anything for him. Presently, you are in the way. So, you are distraught over the loss of the child and are going to kill yourself."

Claire's stomach roiled. Dear God, the woman was mad.

"Hemlock," she said softly, lifting a vial. "It will be relatively quick. Unlike what my husband went through. I used arsenic with him. Took forever because I wanted people to think it was an illness."

Claire shook her head.

"Yes," Lady Anne said. "I had no choice. Westcliffe had standards of a sort. He'd not take as his lover a woman who was married. Which was your fault of course. He knew what it was to find his wife in another man's arms. So I had to eliminate my husband. Then you came to London. Rather convenient, really, because I knew sooner or later that you'd have to go as well. Pity he moved in front of you at Cremorne. The gent I hired was not as good a shot as he claimed."

Good Lord! I was the target.

"Then Westcliffe fell in love with you. I didn't want him mourning your death, and so I needed him to be angry with you again. That was where Stephen and the ball came in. But you figured it out. So here he is, once again at your side and upset with me. So I need you to kill yourself. He can mourn, then I shall be there for him."

Struggling against the bonds, Claire fought to think of some way to get out of this situation. She tried to scream, but the gag made her feel as though she were choking.

"Now, the sticky part," Lady Anne continued as though they were discussing a new flavor of tea, "is that when I remove the gag to give you the poison, you're going to want to scream. Please don't. Ready?"

Claire stared at the vial. The woman was going to force its contents down her throat.

"And don't worry," Lady Anne whispered. "I shall arrange you very nicely."

She reached for the cloth.

The door opened. "I've had as much of Stephen—"

Claire tried to scream through the gag as West-cliffe came to a sudden halt. "My God. What the hell? Anne?"

Suddenly, a small pistol was in Lady Anne's hand. "This is not what I wanted. But if I cannot have you in life, I shall have you in eternity."

She fired.

Westcliffe had never in his life hit a woman. But he darted to the right, the bullet went past him, and his fist caught Anne beneath the chin, snapping her head back. She went down like a sack of potatoes, unconscious.

After snatching up the gun, he removed the gag from Claire's mouth and began untying the rest of the bindings.

"She killed her husband," Claire began, and the story began spilling out of her.

Stephen was the first through the door. "What the bloody hell?"

Ainsley and Leo quickly followed. And, of course, his mother wouldn't be deterred by danger. Even Beth peered around the doorjamb.

"Tie Anne up," Westcliffe ordered as he re-moved the last of the bindings, sat on the bed, and pulled Claire into his arms. He didn't know who was trembling more: she or he.

"I heard a gunshot," Stephen said. "Was she trying to shoot you?"

"Apparently, yes, but she'd come for Claire."

Beth released a small squeal, darted across the room, and sat on the bed, taking her sister's hand.

"It's all right," Claire said. "I'm all right."

"What are we to do with her?" Ainsley asked.

"Take her to London, turn her in to that chap at Scotland Yard," Westcliffe said. "She murdered her husband."

"What do you think will become of her?" Claire asked.

It was late afternoon, and they were lying together in bed in London. Sir James Swindler had officially arrested Anne when they'd delivered her to Scotland Yard.

"How did I miss that she was insane?" Westcliffe had asked.

"Because she was good at hiding what she was," Sir James had said. Then he'd given Westcliffe a hearty pat on the shoulder. "Don't take it to heart, my lord. You're not the first to be fooled by a pretty face."

And Westcliffe wondered if he spoke from experience.

"I suspect Sir James will see that she goes to prison," Westcliffe said now.

"She wanted you badly enough to kill her husband."

"Apparently. And to kill you."

"I never liked her."

He rubbed Claire's arm. "You don't have to

worry about her anymore. Or any other woman for that matter. You have my undying devotion."

She rolled over onto him, straddling his hips. She gave him a saucy smile. "Prove it."

And he did.

Epilogue

Lyons Place
Christmas Eve, 1854

Westcliffe had long yearned to hear the halls of his estate manor filled to overflowing with laughter, tittering, and music.

It was the first time his family had spent Christmas at Lyons Place since his father had died. He could barely countenance the joy he felt as he stood in the large parlor and listened while Beth played the pianoforte, with Lord Greenwood looking on. They had married in June.

The tree in the corner was magnificently decorated, with an abundance of presents waiting below it. Westcliffe was particularly pleased with his gift for Claire. He did hope she would like it. He had found the cradle in the attic and refurbished it himself: sanding and painting and imagining all the Lyonses who had lain within it—just as he and Stephen had.

His mother was sitting on the settee, her hand on Leo's thigh. He wondered how much longer she would keep the young artist in her life. She'd certainly held on to him longer than any of the lovers who'd come before him.

Lynnford had brought his family. His three daughters were singing carols while his two sons sat idly by and listened. He was particularly solicitous of his wife as she lounged in a corner, two shawls draped over her narrow shoulders.

Holding a snifter of brandy, Ainsley ambled over and nodded toward the Countess of Lynnford. "I don't think she's well."

"I thought she looked rather diminished."

"Mother is planning to take her for the mineral waters after the holidays. They share such a close bond of friendship that I'm not sure what Mother will do if she loses her."

"Lynnford either. He's been a good example of how a man should treat his wife." If only he'd reflected sooner on what their guardian had taught them.

"Your wife certainly seems to be blossoming," Ainsley murmured.

Westcliffe couldn't prevent the pride and joy from bubbling up within him. "She's with child."

And this time, nothing on God's earth would take the babe from them.

Ainsley clinked his glass against Westcliffe's. "Jolly good for you. Mother will be beside herself with happiness."

"Yes, I think the news will be good for her."

Ainsley shifted his stance. "I received confirmation from the War Office. Stephen is in the thick of things in the Crimea. Mother doesn't say anything, but I think she knows."

"I'm certain she does. She has an amazing circle of influence."

"This war in the Crimea, I'm not certain I like having it served to me at breakfast every morning. The reporters telegraphing their news each day— as I understand it we've never had this immediacy of reporting before. Brings the war closer to home, doesn't it?"

"Which is where it should be, if you ask me. Our lads are off fighting for Queen and country. They should not be forgotten."

"We picked a bloody bad time to purchase him a commission."

Westcliffe nodded in agreement. "Knowing Stephen, he'll use the opportunity to experience Russian women."

"But dear God, I hear it's cold over there."

"Then he'll definitely be in some woman's bed, for warmth if nothing else."

"I bloody well hope so."

Wearing a mischievous smile, Claire strolled over, Fen trotting along at her hem. "What are you two talking about so solemnly?"

Not wishing to spoil the joy of the occasion, Westcliffe said, "That it's time for Ainsley to begin looking for a wife."

"The hell you say," Ainsley muttered, and stalked off.

With a laugh, Claire slipped beneath Westcliffe's arm, and whispered, "I know exactly whom you were talking about. Will it upset you to know that I miss him?"

There was a time when it would have but no longer. He was confident in her loyalty to him. "I do as well," he said quietly.

The song Beth was playing came to an end. She banged two deep keys to gain attention. "May we unwrap the gifts now?"

The gathering gave their enthusiastic support for the notion and turned to their host and hostess.

"By all means," Claire said.

Before she could move away, Westcliffe tightened his hold on her and lifted his glass. "I wish to make a toast first."

A hush fell over the room as other glasses were lifted.

"I shall start by saying that no matter what gifts await me beneath the tree, Claire has already given me the best of all: her love." Leaning over, seeing the tears in her eyes, he gave her a quick kiss and the promise for a lengthier one later.

"Hear! Hear!" those surrounding them cheered.

Westcliffe nodded and raised his glass again. "I also want to thank you all for coming. I have long wanted this manor to echo the sounds of joy and family. This night it does, and I cannot express my gratitude."

He lifted his glass higher. "And last, a toast to Stephen. May God be with our brother and may he return home by next Christmas."

The *hear, hear* was a bit more somber. But he'd known Claire would take the matter in hand to return the gaiety. "Beth, as you're so anxious to receive gifts, why don't you hand out yours first?"

"I shall be delighted." She got up from the bench and fairly skipped over to the tree.

Claire snuggled against Westcliffe. "I do love you."

And as he'd said in his toast, that was the greatest gift of all.

They are masters of seduction,
London's greatest lovers.
Living for pleasure, they will give
their hearts to no one . . .
until love takes them by surprise.

You don't have to wait long to read
Stephen's story . . .
PLEASURES OF
A NOTORIOUS GENTLEMAN,
the second book in the
London's Greatest Lovers series
will hit stores in December 2010!

Pleasures of a Notorious Gentleman

By *New York Times* and *USA Today* bestselling author Lorraine Heath

Stephen Lyons may be the black sheep of his family, but on the battlefield, he proved himself courageous . . . until an injury stole his memory of the last two years. But how could even he—a notorious rogue—forget his child or the angelic beauty at his doorstep, babe in her arms? Mercy Dawson, a nurse who met the dashing soldier on the battlefield, will do anything to protect the infant in her care—even if it means her own ruin. Taken in by the baby's grandmother, the Duchess of Ainsley, Mercy never expected to force Stephen's hand in marriage. But as duty turns to trust and then to love, Mercy knows their tenuous happiness could be destroyed with just one word if her husband ever learns the scandalous truth.

Northamptonshire
November 1855

Mercy Dawson thought she'd prepared herself for the shame she'd endure at this precise moment.

She'd been wrong.

It hit her with a force so strong that she almost

regretted her decision to return to England. She'd often heard that love was blind and fully capable of transforming even the wise into fools. Apparently, she was no exception. Love—so deep and profound that it had the power to overwhelm and bring her to tears at the most unexpected moments—had driven her here. Well, love and her father's carriage.

In spite of her conviction to the path she traveled upon, she was quite surprised that she was finding it so blasted difficult to hold her head high and meet the gaze of the Duke of Ainsley. With his black hair and sharp features, he looked nothing at all like his half-brother, Stephen Lyons. While Ainsley was the youngest of the three brothers, he wore the mantle of responsibility on his shoulders and wore it well, as though it were a second skin. He understood the influence of his title and gave the impression he wasn't one with whom a person should trifle. Within his dazzling green eyes, she saw evidence of a calculating mind while he studied her as though he'd just pinned her to a board for bugs and, after careful scrutiny, determined her to be little more than a maggot.

Obviously, he doubted the veracity of the incredible tale upon which her father had just expounded.

She was the first to look away, in the pretense of admiring her surroundings. They were in the front parlor of Ainsley's country estate, Grantwood Manor. The room, almost as large as her father's house, had more than one sitting area. White, yellow, and orange dominated the fabrics, giving the room a cheerfulness that would have welcomed her and made her smile if she were here under different circumstances. She imagined on the coldest day of winter one could find warmth within these walls. She was presently sitting on a sofa nearest the massive fireplace. Still, the heat from the writhing flames failed to ease the chill in her bones that had settled in while she and her father had traveled here. A chill that had intensified as Ainsley raked his gaze over her.

"Well?" her father bellowed, standing behind her as though he could no longer stomach the sight of her face. She jumped, but Ainsley's steady gaze never left her or faltered. She suspected he'd have been as courageous on the battlefield as his brother. Stephen Lyons had arrived in the Crimea as a captain, but his daring exploits during battle had seen him rise with surprising swiftness to the rank of major. "Your boy got my girl with babe. You'd damned well better do right by her."

The aforementioned babe was presently having his cheek stroked by Ainsley's mother. The duchess looked up at her son. "He very much reminds me of Stephen at this age."

"All babies look the same, Mother."

"Not to a mother." The duchess's formidable gaze came to bear on Mercy, and Mercy fought not to wither beneath it. She couldn't imagine possessing the confidence these people had. She'd been forced to shore up her own courage for this encounter. She'd known it wouldn't be pleasant, but she also knew her only hope for happiness resided here. So she would stand her ground until the final bastion had fallen.

"Or to a grandmother, I suppose," the duchess added.

Mercy's original plan had been to simply leave the child here, within his relatives' safekeeping, but in the end, she'd not been able to give him up. It was astonishing how much she'd come to love the babe in the three months since his birth. She would do anything at all to protect him, to remain with him. Sell what remained of her soul to the devil if need be.

"What did you name him?" the duchess asked.

"John."

"A strong name."

She nodded. These were good people. She shouldn't have brought her father into the matter. She should have come here first, only she hadn't known where to begin to find this family, and she couldn't very well live on the streets while she'd made inquiries. After all she'd seen and suffered during her months serving as a nurse, she'd thought her father would be as grateful to have her home as she was to have arrived. She'd known him well enough, though, to suspect he'd not look upon a new life as something to be cherished, regardless of how it had come about. Her father had not watched as hundreds of men died. He was landed gentry, and by arriving on his doorstep with a babe in her arms, she'd brought shame to him and his household.

But she didn't regret what she'd done. She couldn't. She wouldn't.

"Your father mentioned that you met Stephen during the time he served in the Crimea," the duchess said, but her voice also held a question. The East was far away, not a place to which a gentle lady should travel.

"Yes, Your Grace. I was serving as a nurse in Scutari." She'd discovered that few people truly understood the geography of the area, although the duchess may have been an exception. In a corner of the room stood a globe, the portion of the world that had caused so much turmoil and heartache clearly in view. Mercy wondered if the duchess had pressed her hand there in an attempt to feel closer to her son, to somehow bridge the endless miles that separated them. "Many of the soldiers were brought there to be tended."

"Admirable. Then you were one of Miss Night-ingale's ladies?"

Miss Nightingale. To the nurses, the doctors, and the patients, she had simply been Miss N. "Yes, ma'am."

"The newspapers paint a rather gruesome por-trait of the war. I do not know how anyone could . . . remain there with the deprivations, the cold, and illness. They say more men die of disease than battle."

Mercy nodded, forcing a tremulous smile. "John is the only good thing to come out of the war as far as I'm concerned."

The duchess's brown eyes softened. Stephen had not inherited his eyes from his mother. His were a rich, dark blue. She remembered the concern she'd seen reflected in them just before he'd taken her into his arms. So tenderly. After what she'd endured at the hands of three ruffians, she'd thought she'd be unable to suffer the touch of a man, but he had proved her wrong. How she longed for those powerful arms at this moment. But she would never again know their strength, would never again feel the firm muscles beneath her fingers. He'd been killed in September. Because of the wonder of the telegraph, the names of the fallen were known quickly and reported in the newspapers. She was surprised the duchess wasn't wearing mourning clothes, but instead wore a dress of deep purple.

"Well?" her father bellowed again. "I want to know what you're going to do for my girl."

"I suppose you're looking for some sort of monetary restitution," Ainsley said.

"That would be a start. But she's ruined. No decent man will have her now. She went to do good works and he took advantage."

"Father—"

"Shut up, girl. The last thing I expected was for you to come home with some bastard."

"Don't call John that." She would fight to the

death to protect John. How could her father not see beyond the child's illegitimacy to what he meant to Mercy? In a world devoid of joy, he was the only bright spot. "Please, Your Grace, I want only to stay with John. I could serve as his nurse, his nanny. I would require very little."

"That will not do at all," her father said. "The shame that has been brought to my household . . . I demand this be made right. You, sir, Your Grace, you should step in where your brother didn't."

Ainsley's mouth twitched, and he looked as though he might burst into laughter. It was the first sign he'd given that he might not be as blasted serious as she'd assumed. "Are you suggesting I marry your daughter, sir?"

"I am indeed."

"Father, no!"

"She needs a husband," he continued as though she hadn't objected. "I'm washing my hands of her."

Madness was surrounding her. She didn't know how to stop it. "Your Grace, this is not why I brought John to you. You are his family. I expect nothing."

"Miss Dawson, do you swear that the child to whom you gave birth is my brother's son?" Ainsley asked, a kindness in his voice that had been lacking before, as though he was beginning to understand that regardless of the unconscionable position in which she found herself, she placed the child first and her father only added to the difficulties of her situation. She was grateful the print of his hand was no longer visible on her face. He'd slapped her for her foolishness, then slapped her for her sins.

"I swear to you, Your Grace, by all that is holy, John is Stephen's son."

"I do not doubt it," the duchess said succinctly, her opinion obviously carrying a great deal of weight with the duke.

Ainsley nodded slowly, then in long strides he crossed the room and opened the door. "Find Major Lyons and inform him that I need to have a word."

Mercy was on her feet before Ainsley had finishing shutting the door. Dizziness assailed her. Her heart pounded with such force that she was certain they all could hear it. Her throat knotted up and it was all she could do to force out the words. "He's here? He can't be. He's dead."

Ainsley seemed quite surprised by her outburst, as was she. She wasn't prone to histrionics, but this turn of events was not at all expected. Relief danced with fear. This changed everything. *Everything.* Her legs weakened, but she forced herself to remain standing. Better to face the devil on her feet.

"Yes, the initial reports were that he'd died," Ainsley said, studying her. Did he have to continually examine every blasted inch of her? What the devil was he searching for, what did he hope to find? Evidence of her deception? "Considering what I've since learned of the carnage that was

Sevastopol, I'm not surprised mistakes were made. He *was* gravely wounded and not expected to survive. But those who doubted his will don't know my brother. He is as stubborn as the day is long. He arrived home only a month ago. He's not quite up to snuff, still recovering."

Gladness at the news almost replaced every ounce of her common sense. Once Major Lyons strode through that door, everything would change. He would laugh at her claims, if he even remembered her. Chaos reigned on the battlefields and in the hospitals. Like thieves in the night, soldiers, doctors, nurses had stolen moments of happiness wherever, whenever, they could. Hoarded the memories away for the exhausting, dreary days when there was nothing except the blight of suffering.

Her time with Major Lyons had been brief, all too brief. But her feelings for him had still managed to blossom into an emotion she didn't understand but that frightened her with its intensity.

She jerked her gaze to John, held securely in the duchess's arms. John. Her son. Her joy. She wished she'd never handed him over. She should dart across to where he gurgled, snatch him up, and dash from the room. Only he belonged here. She couldn't whisk him away from where he belonged. He was her one opportunity for redemption, but the thought of losing him was like a knife twisting through her heart. She'd never expected he would become her salvation.

Good Lord, everything would come to light now. Everything. When Major Lyons saw her—

What if his first words revolved around her shame and suffering. But he'd promised, promised to never tell a soul. While he held her—

The door opened, the *click* echoing through the room like a rifle report. Imminent disaster loomed, but still she hungrily took in every beloved facet of him. Only he was a far cry from the man she'd come to admire, the man with whom she'd become ridiculously infatuated.

Shock reverberated through the very core of her being. He limped in, using a walking stick to steady his stride, which was not nearly as long or as confident as it had once been. He was not wearing the scarlet uniform that had made him such a dashing figure. Instead, he was dressed in a white shirt and cravat, black waistcoat and jacket, and black trousers, as though he were in mourning.

Perhaps he was. How many of his comrades had he watched fall? How many had he held while they died on the field?

He was so thin that he barely resembled the robust young man who had exhibited such enviable self-assurance when he'd been discharged from the hospital that first month after she'd arrived with Miss Nightingale. Then he still spoke of routing out the enemy, sending them to perdition. He urged those not yet well enough to be released to recover quickly, to get the job done so they could all go home. They were not yet defeated.

She overheard him delivering rousing words to so many that he strengthened her own resolve, made her determined to see them all recover.

But he no longer looked to be a man who believed the declarations he'd once articulated with such conviction.

A ragged, unsightly red scar trailed from just below his temple to his chin, yet it did not diminish his rugged handsomeness. But his eyes—his beautiful blue eyes—had changed the most. They held such an incredible bleakness when he looked at her that she almost wept. His wounds went much deeper than his flesh; they had penetrated his soul.

The only thing about him that remained unchanged was the shade of his hair, a golden brown with streaks of blond woven through it. She'd often wondered how it might look with the sunlight bouncing off it. But she'd met him in winter amidst gray skies. Little sun chased back the dreariness of the hospital.

She wanted to race across the room, take him in her arms, and confess everything before he had a chance to denounce her for the fraud that she was. She should be trying to determine how best to save face, but all she could do was wonder about him. What had transpired during the months since she'd last seen him? Had he even noticed that she'd left Scutari? If he'd had occasion to visit the hospital, had he asked after her? He had been so terribly important to her, but he'd never made any declarations of affection. It wasn't his way, she'd been told, but the knowledge had not stopped her from dreaming he saw in her something special, something he saw in no other woman.

"Stephen," Ainsley began, a gentleness, a caution in his voice, a tone that one might use when confronting a wild and unpredictable beast, "surely you remember Miss Mercy Dawson. She was a nurse at a military hospital in Scutari, tending to the soldiers who fought in the Crimea."

She wondered why he'd felt the need to categorize her, to label her as though so many Mercy Dawsons filled his brother's life that he would be unable to identify which one she was precisely. She knew of his reputation with the ladies, knew that he sought pleasure with wild abandon, but surely he was gentleman enough to recall every woman with whom he'd experienced carnal knowledge.

Tension rippled through the room, like they were all connected by the wires on a pianoforte, each of them waiting for a chord to be plucked.

Major Lyons studied her for a heartbeat, then another, but she saw no recognition in his deep blue eyes. None at all. She was but one of many nurses who had garnered his attention. The mortification of this moment, of being relegated to nothingness, of being completely unmemorable in spite of all they'd shared . . . it was almost more than she could bear. She didn't know how she would survive it, but for John's sake she would.

A dilemma reared its ugly head. Should she

fight for John's right to be here, to convince them that Major Lyons was his father, or should she take her son and be done with them, find a way to survive as best she could? She knew her father would not return her to his residence. He was done with her. He was here now only because he thought to gain from the situation, if not a pocketful of coins, then a powerful son-in-law. She wondered what his impressions were, but she dared not look back at him. It took little to earn his wrath these days.

"Of course, I remember her."

She blinked in surprise. Relief and dread beat within her breast. Conflicting desires, conflicting troubles. Everything had seemed much simpler when she thought he was dead. Now the truth picked at the lock, and she didn't know if its release would serve her good or ill.

Major Lyons bowed slightly. "Miss Dawson."

"Major, I'm so grateful you're not dead." In spite of the troubles his resurrection might cause her, the words were heartfelt. Grief had nearly done her in when she'd seen his name on the list of casualties. She owed him more than she could ever express, more than she could ever repay.

"No more so than I am, I assure you."

The rough timbre of his voice sent a quiver of longing through her. *What a silly chit you are, Mercy. He speaks that way to every lady. You are not so special after all.* But there had been times when she'd thought, hoped, dared to dream that he gave her attention because he considered her distinctive, because he could distinguish her from the other nurses. After only one telling, he remembered her name. She learned later that she'd given too much significance to that small triumph. He knew every nurse by name. He could even differentiate the twin nuns—Mary and Margaret—from each other when no one else could.

"And her father, Mr. Daws—"

"You ruined my girl," her father bellowed, interrupting Ainsley before the introductions were properly finished.

Mortification swamped her. *Oh, what a tangled web we weave . . .*

Major Lyons's eyes widened slightly at that, and his gaze swung back to her. His brow furrowed and she could see him concentrating, trying to remember what had passed between them. How could he forget? Had he not seen her clearly in the darkness? Had she only imagined that he'd recognized who she was? She didn't know if it would be better if he did identify her as the lady he'd rescued that horrid night. Perhaps there was mercy in his confusion. She should simply confess everything now and save herself further embarrassment.

But where to begin? How much to reveal? How much to keep hidden? How much would he deduce by whatever she told him? She had sworn an oath. No matter the price, she intended to keep it until she drew her last breath.

"Stephen, darling, do come here," the duchess said, ushering him over to her side.

He walked slowly, as if even in this great room that was surely familiar to him, he was lost, searching for his bearings. She'd seen far too many men with the same haunted quality, the same emptiness of soul in their expression, as though they'd left their essence out on the battlefield and only their bodies had returned. The price of war went far beyond the stores of munitions, food, uniforms, and medical supplies.

"This is John," the duchess said softly when he reached her. "Miss Dawson claims he is your son. I can see a resemblance."

"I don't. For one thing I'm considerably taller."

The duchess released a small laugh and tears welled in her eyes, as though she'd caught a glimpse of the teasing young man her son had once been. Reaching out, she squeezed his hand. "Is it possible do you think? That he's yours?"

He moved around to acquire a better look at John. With his large hand, he cradled the boy's head, the pale, wispy curls settling softly against his long, slender fingers. Mercy's heart lurched, swelling with joy and breaking at the same time. How often she had dreamed of him holding his son, but none of her fanciful imaginings had prepared her for the moment of reality, of seeing him touching this precious child. He would recognize himself in the boy. Surely he would. He would claim John as his, even if he would not offer Mercy the same consideration. For John she could hold no greater joy than that he be accepted by his father.

For herself she knew it held the potential to have John ripped from her. A bastard child was the responsibility of his mother, but this powerful family could circumvent laws. With the proper amount of blunt slipped into her father's palm, Mercy would be relegated to a pauper, with the one thing she treasured beyond her reach.

"Considering my well-earned reputation with the ladies, of course it's possible," he murmured. He lifted his eyes to hers, and she felt the full force of their impact as he studied her again. What did he see when he looked at her? Did he see her as she was the night he'd come to her rescue? Or did he see her as she was now, determined to save the child when she'd been unable to save so many?

"You must do right by the girl," his mother said softly. "If indeed, you have no doubt that she has given birth to your son."

He would tell them now, would laugh at the ludicrousness of her claim. That a man such as he would ever desire a woman such as her—

"Of course, I should do right by her."

Mercy's knees shook and turned into jam. She sank into the chair. Had he just agreed to marry her? Surely not. She'd misheard. The Honorable Stephen Lyons, known rake and seducer of women. Major Stephen Lyons, admired soldier who had managed to make every nurse swoon. He couldn't possibly be seriously considering marrying her with as much ease as he might snap his fingers.

"Miss Dawson, will you take a turn about the garden with me?"

"You can't possibly think I'm going to leave her alone in your company," her father barked.

"Walk along behind us if you like," Major Lyons said, before glancing back down at John. "Although I daresay there is little I could do at this point that would ruin her reputation any more than it's already been." Once again, his gaze leaped across the distance separating them to land on her as powerfully as a touch. "Miss Dawson?"

She rose on unsteady legs. "Yes, Major. I would very much like to take a stroll with you."

It was a lie, of course. She dreaded it with every fiber of her being.

Pleasures of a Notorious Gentleman
Available December 2010
from Avon Books

Next month, don't miss these exciting new love stories only from
Avon Books

Pleasures of a Notorious Gentleman by Lorraine Heath
A once unrepentant rogue, Stephen Lyons gained a notorious reputation that forced him to leave for the army. Upon his return he is given the opportunity to redeem himself, and Mercy Dawson will risk everything to protect the dashing soldier from the truth that threatens to destroy their growing love.

Wicked Nights With A Lover by Sophie Jordan
When Marguerite Laurent learns that she is to die before year's end, she desires but one thing—passion. But as she sets out to experience the romance of her dreams, Ash Courtland— the wrong man—threatens to give her a taste of the once-in-a- lifetime ardor she so desperately craves.

A Most Scandalous Engagement by Gayle Callen
When a scandalous escapade threatens to ruin Lady Elizabeth Cabot, she must pretend to fall in love with Peter Derby, a childhood friend. She never imagined the pretense would feel so real or that the man she's shared her past with could suddenly, irreversibly claim her future…and her heart.

Taken by Desire by Lavinia Kent
Anna Steele is not normally impulsive and Alexander Struthers is not one to seek true love. But when scandal forces these two into marriage, fighting the burning attraction that threatens to consume them proves more difficult than both of them could've imagined.

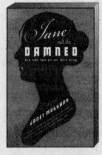